"Let me do my job."

Maria kept her expression flat in the face of Ryan's angry glare. "I can't. Not until I feel confident that you're recovered from the stress of your wife's death." She pulled her calendar toward her. "I have this same time open next Thursday." She held out an appointment card to him, her hand in the air a full ten seconds before he took the offering.

Rising to his feet, Ryan clenched his fist around the card without looking at it. "You're making a big mistake."

Even though he was giving her a hard time, his gaze was so full of pain and grief, a wave of sympathy hit her.

"I'm sorry you see it that way. I believe if we work together, I can help you."

"And if I don't want your help?"

"I'm afraid you don't have a choice, Lieutenant."

He gave her a look that would have made a lesser woman quail. Maria simply stared back. A second later, he stalked out. As he reached the hallway, she heard the sound of paper ripping. The scraps of her card fluttered gently to the carpet.

Dear Reader,

The Listener is the last book in the SWAT team trilogy that I wrote for Harlequin Superromance. It follows *The Negotiator* and *The Commander*. Each story has presented a different view of a SWAT team. It's dangerous, emotional and draining work, the likes of which few "civilians" witness or understand.

This last book tells the story of Maria Worley, a psychotherapist, and Ryan Lukas, the sniper for the SWAT team.

When I started this series I knew I wanted to delve into the emotional life of a sniper. What could be more fascinating than the motivations and conflicts of a man who must take one life to protect another? Then I started to think.... What if that sniper had just suffered a tremendous personal loss? And what if the therapist who was supposed to treat him discovered she was more attracted to him than she should be? How could these people handle that kind of stress? How could they deal with all the possibilities? Just to make the story a little more interesting, I decided Maria should be a single parent, too.

I hope you enjoy reading *The Listener*, and I hope you find it a satisfying conclusion to THE GUARDIANS series. If you'd like to contact me, please visit my Web site, kaydavid.com, or write to me at kaydavid@kaydavid.com.

One last thing...don't forget that May is Get Caught Reading month. Obviously, if you're reading this, you love to read, so why not share your passion? When you finish *The Listener*, pass it on to a friend or a relative...or even a stranger! Reading is one of the greatest pleasures we can give ourselves, and encouraging others to "get caught reading" is a gift to them, as well.

Sincerely,

Kay David

The Listener
Kay David

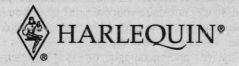

HARLEQUIN®

TORONTO • NEW YORK • LONDON
AMSTERDAM • PARIS • SYDNEY • HAMBURG
STOCKHOLM • ATHENS • TOKYO • MILAN • MADRID
PRAGUE • WARSAW • BUDAPEST • AUCKLAND

ISBN 0-373-70985-4

THE LISTENER

Visit us at www.eHarlequin.com

Printed in U.S.A.

This book is dedicated to all the wonderful listeners
I've had the great pleasure of knowing through the years.
While some have been professional,
like Dr. Amelia Kornfeld or Max LeBlanc,
others have listened because that's what they do best:
my mother, Pauline Cameron; my best friend,
Marilyn Amann; my husband, Pieter Luan.
We all need people to listen to us—
there's nothing more important—
so my thanks and my love go to the people
who always have time to listen.

CHAPTER ONE

"Do you enjoy ruining people's lives or is it just me you have it in for?"

As he towered over her desk, Ryan Lukas's wrath was so intense, so powerful, it filled Maria Worley's office with an almost physical presence. She was accustomed to handling angry men, but *his* fury was different. Above a clenched jaw and beneath an angry frown, the black ice of his eyes revealed a storm just waiting to be unleashed.

At her.

She spoke quietly, calmly. "Is that what you think I'm doing?"

At her question, his expression turned fractionally darker and his mouth, already a violent slash, narrowed into a line of disbelief. He was so tightly wound the changes were subtle, but Maria was an expert at reading faces. It was her job. For the past three years she'd been the chief psychologist for the Emerald Coast SWAT team. Mainly men, the cops who were her clients were officers on the edge, trapped between their own realities and the rest of the world. They were men who didn't know what to do with themselves or the disasters they'd become. Men who didn't know where to turn.

Men like Ryan Lukas.

"If you put me on some kind of bogus leave, that's exactly what you'll be doing!" He glared at her. "I want to work and I *should* be working. The team needs me. Besides, there's nothing wrong with me."

"If that's really the case, then you can return to active duty in record time. Until then, because of the tests I conducted during your routine assessment last week and the talks we've had so far, I feel the need for further evaluation of your situation. As soon as I'm comfortable with your progress, I'll release you."

"And Lena agrees with this bullsh—"

"Lieutenant McKinney and I have discussed the matter, yes." Lena McKinney was Ryan Lukas's boss and commander of the SWAT team. Maria didn't envy her the job. "Lieutenant McKinney believes, as I do, that you need some time off. That's why she moved up your yearly evaluation. She was concerned about you and wanted me to assess you before things got out of hand. Taking everything into consideration, Lieutenant Lukas, surely you can understand the conclusion—"

"I understand one thing," he said icily. "I understand that you're screwing with me...and I'm going to pay the price. One way or another."

Maria looked out her window and tried to gather

her thoughts. The office faced the Gulf of Mexico, and in the distance, the sparkling water glinted. Generally she didn't argue with her patients, but Ryan Lukas wasn't like most of her clients. She turned back to him.

"Lieutenant Lukas, anyone who went through what you have would need to talk about it. Anyone. If you don't believe me, look at the problems you've experienced lately. Emotions escape any way they can, even if it means more trouble for us. Don't you think you should deal with these feelings in a more productive fashion?"

"I *am* dealing with them." His eyes locked on hers. "My way."

She waited for him to elaborate but he wasn't going to—it was his way of taking control. During his initial visit, he'd sat without saying a word for more than half the session. It was the first time she'd had to break a client's silence. She'd never been outwaited before.

"Well, your way isn't working. Ignoring your problem is not a good solution." She paused a moment. "And don't try to convince me you have no feelings about what happened. That's impossible."

At his sides, his hands clamped into fists. She wondered if he was conscious of the movement.

"I never said I had no feelings about what happened." He stopped for a second, then seemed to gather himself. "I do. But I don't intend to share them with you or anyone else."

"Even if it means your job?"

"My wife's…situation had nothing to do with my job."

She noted the word he used; he couldn't even say *death*. It was time to be blunt.

"That's a lie, Lieutenant, and you know that as well as I. You're one of the most important members of the SWAT team. You have to be sharp, on your toes. What happens at home impacts your ability to think and to make decisions. Everyone understands that. Surely you do, too."

His eyes glittered, two black sapphires, dark and hard. "Do you perform marriage counseling?"

The unexpected question took her by surprise and she answered without thinking. "Of course. That is a primary focus of my practice."

"Are you married?"

She saw the trap too late. There was nothing to do but answer him. "No," she admitted reluctantly. "I'm divorced. But my personal situation isn't pertinent—"

"And neither is mine. I can do my job, just like you can."

"That's not a fair comparison. I don't shoot people for a living."

He waited a moment to reply, but somehow it felt longer to Maria. When he finally did speak, his voice was deliberate, each word distinct. "And do you have a problem with what I do?"

"You're a valued member of the team and your

job is necessary. How I feel about that is not important. What matters is how *you* feel about it.''

"You didn't answer my question.''

"It's not relevant.''

"It is to me.''

"And why is that?''

"I need your approval. You've already told Lena I can't do my job right now. If you have some kind of hang-up with what I do—''

She interrupted him, something else she rarely did with patients, her exasperation getting the upper hand over her professionalism. ''Lieutenant Lukas, I assure you my evaluation of your situation will not be influenced by your position on the team. I'm paid to look at you as an individual and that's exactly what I do. What I think about your career choice simply isn't germane to this.''

"Then let me do my job.''

"I can't.'' She made her expression flat, her voice unequivocal. ''Not until we've talked more and I feel confident you've recovered from the stress of your wife's death.'' She pulled her calendar toward her and ran a pen down the edge of one side. ''I have this same time open on Thursday next week. I'd like to meet with you then, but if that's not convenient, you can check with my receptionist on the way out for a different time. One way or the other, I want to see you in here this coming week.'' She put down her pen then picked up one of her appointment cards and held it out to him, her hand in the air a full ten seconds before he finally took the offering.

Rising to his feet, he clenched the card without looking at it. "You're making a big mistake."

Even though he was giving her a hard time, behind his rage, his gaze was so full of pain and grief a wave of sympathy hit her. He was hurting.

"I'm sorry you see it that way," she said quietly. "But I believe if we work together, I can help you." She stood and held out her hand. "I really can."

He ignored her outstretched fingers. "And if I don't want your help?"

She dropped her hand. "I'm afraid you don't have a choice, Lieutenant."

He gave her a look that would have quailed another woman's resolve. Maria simply stared back. A second later, he pivoted sharply and stalked out. As he reached the outer hallway, she heard the sound of paper ripping. The scraps of her card fluttered gently to the carpet and then he was gone.

MARIA EDGED her five-year-old Toyota into the traffic on Highway 98 and headed west. It was the first week of May, the beginning of tourist season in Destin, and the town was already packed. Families in minivans, college kids in Beetles, retired folks in Cadillacs—everyone was on the road and trying to get somewhere else. Up until the seventies, Destin had been a sleepy little fishing village; then its clear waters and beautiful white beach had been discovered. Now high-rises lined the shore and restaurants and shops took up the space that was left. Maria appreciated the growth, but every summer she longed for the town she'd come to fifteen years before as a wide-eyed newlywed. It'd been a lot different.

Then again, so had she.

She'd had a simple life with no child to worry about and no career to juggle. It'd been her and Reed and a rosy future…or so she'd thought. Once she'd gotten her degree and started her career, things had changed drastically. Reed didn't care that she'd worked for years for her Ph.D. He still wanted a wife who made him the focus of her life. She'd started her practice, a practice that took time and energy away from him, and he'd left her. The only good part of their union was Christopher, their fourteen-year-old son. She loved him so much it hurt. But she worried constantly about him and whether or not she was balancing her job and motherhood successfully.

The thought brought her full circle to her newest client. Ryan Lukas. When Lena had first called Maria and set up Ryan's initial meeting, the other woman had told Maria how he'd changed since his wife's death. Gregarious and friendly, he'd been one of the most popular members of the team before that. The first one to arrive, Lena had said, and the last one to leave, no matter how hard the call. Now he was a loner. He did his job then disappeared.

Even without the description of his changes—
even without meeting him—Maria had expected
Ryan Lukas would be a difficult client. Despite her
earlier denial, she did have some feelings about his
position on the team. Anyone who killed people for
a living—even bad people—had to be a complicated
individual with complex motivations and tangled
emotions. The interior life of a countersniper *had* to
be a labyrinth few could understand.

Even taking that into consideration, something
about Lukas was still very different from what she'd
anticipated. A lot of her male clients hid their real
emotions behind the single feeling they felt safe
with—anger—but he'd gone a step further. Unable
to put her finger on the exact disparity at the moment, Maria knew it'd come to her. She had an in-
nate intuition about people and their emotions. Even
as a child, she'd been supersensitive to the imbro-
glios that had floated through her parents' home.
Lord knew there had been plenty of feelings in the
mix. Good and bad.

In the meantime, she had to figure out how to
help Ryan Lukas, and she wasn't looking forward
to the job. Uncooperative clients were always a
challenge. She'd have to approach him just the right
way or they'd never make any progress.

She considered the problem all the way home, but
twenty minutes later thoughts of the troubled sniper
fled when Maria turned into her driveway. Christopher had—once again—left his expensive bicycle,

which his father had purchased, smack in the middle of the approach. She couldn't even pull into the garage. How many times had she asked Christopher to put his bike away when he got home?

She parked the car in the street, then grabbed her briefcase and started up the sidewalk to the front door. Before the divorce, Christopher had been the perfect kid, but the minute Reed had left, Chris had turned into someone different. His grades had plummeted and the boys he wanted to hang around with weren't helping matters at all. He was distant and uncommunicative. Maria understood his conflict; he felt abandoned and left behind, and he wanted acceptance somewhere—so he'd looked to those kids. All her efforts to help him, however, had only made matters worse. Trips to the zoo, quiet time just talking, rock concerts he'd selected—she'd done every thing she could think of to reconnect with him and nothing had worked. She was running out of ideas—and patience.

She unlocked the door and started yelling, something she'd never done in the past. "Christopher! Are you in here? Come down right this minute...."

Nothing but silence greeted her, the house echoing in an empty way that told her he wasn't just hiding. She threw her briefcase on the entry table and shook off her high heels as she went into the living room. His backpack was in the middle of the rug, his jacket on the couch, an open bag of chips on the floor by the recliner.

Just like his father, she thought wearily. Reed couldn't have picked up after himself if his life had depended on it. When he'd come home two years ago and announced he was leaving, she'd almost been relieved...but Christopher had been shattered, and Maria knew then she'd never forgive Reed for the way he'd treated their son.

A father shouldn't do that to his kid.

She snatched up the sack of chips and then the backpack, but the nylon bag weighed a ton. For one brief second, she juggled both, then lost her grip on the backpack, a confusion of books, papers and CD cases flying from the unzipped compartments, then plummeting to the floor.

Cursing softly, Maria set the bag of chips aside and began to pick up the mess. She retrieved a library book and a battered blue notepad then reached over to get a second book. As she did so, the notebook flipped, the pages fluttering open to dislodge a folded piece of paper. Her fingers stilled when she saw what it was.

Christopher's progress report.

From two weeks before.

It was covered with the kind of pen and pencil drawings Christopher constantly produced—a fantasy birdlike figure—but her eyes looked past them and went directly to the grades. They were lower than they'd been the last time! And the comments...she could hardly believe them.

"...didn't turn in homework. Grade: 0..."

"...not paying attention in class. Grade: 74."
"...sloppy work and bad attitude. Grade: 60."

But that wasn't even the worst part. When she read the signature at the bottom of the card, she gasped out loud. *Dr. Maria Worley.* Her name had been scribbled poorly—in fact, it was barely legible—but apparently that was all that was needed. Every one of his teachers had checked the boxes at the bottom of the report indicating they'd seen and accepted the fake signature.

Maria rocked back on her heels, a hodgepodge of anger, shock and disappointment wiping out any other emotions. He must have intercepted the mail and pulled out the report before she'd gotten home. What on earth did he think he was doing? Had her son really believed she'd never find this out?

As soon as she had the thought, her anger turned inward. Of course, he'd assumed he could do it and get away with it. She did everything she could to stay on top of Christopher's life, but it'd been crazy at work lately, and she'd been too involved with her own problems. She should have known it was time for his progress report and been on the lookout for it. She should have been keeping better track of the time.

She considered calling Reed then dismissed the idea immediately. He wouldn't help. He couldn't even admit he was part of the problem. She stood up slowly and was replacing the rest of the items in the backpack when the front door flew open and slammed into the opposite wall. Christopher's startled eyes met hers before they dropped to the bag she still held.

"What are you doing with my stuff?" he demanded rudely.

She resisted the urge to correct his tone and tried instead to focus on staying calm. "I'm picking it up—something you should have done when you got home instead of leaving it here."

Kicking the front door shut, he walked into the entry with the kind of bravado only a guilty kid could affect. "I was in a hurry. The guys called right after I got home and I left. I'm sorry," he added in an offhand manner.

"I'm sure you are." She paused. "And you're going to be even more sorry when I ask you about this." She held out his report.

For just a second, his brown eyes flickered with uncertainty and he was a little kid, a scared little kid. "Wh-what's that?"

"It's your progress report. From two weeks ago. It has a signature on it that's supposed to be mine, but it isn't. What do you know about this?"

It took him only a moment. "You were busy," he said defensively. "I thought I'd help—"

"Don't even try that, Christopher," she said abruptly. "You should have given this to me and you know it. I can't believe you forged my signature. What were you thinking?"

He stared at her defiantly and said nothing.

"Why did you do this? Did you think I wouldn't find out?"

"You're never at home," he snapped without warning. "You're always working so I just did it. If you hadn't been snooping through my bag—"

"I wasn't snooping. I was picking up and even if I had been snooping, that's my right. I'm your mother, Christopher, and I have the responsibility to know what's going on with you."

"You didn't even know it was time for the cards. You don't care what happens to me!"

"That's not true! I love you and you know that! If I didn't, why would I care what kind of grades you make?"

He mumbled something she couldn't understand—except for a single phrase. "If Daddy was here…"

She stood stock-still. "Do you think your father would approve of this?"

He scuffed the carpet with one dirty sneaker, then looked up. "It wouldn't have happened if he was here! He always checked my cards…and my homework, too."

She actually opened her mouth to contradict him—Reed had never shown the slightest interest in Chris's homework—she'd always been the one who helped him. Every night, until last year, she'd sat down with him right after dinner and gone over all of his work. When he'd announced he was too old for that, she'd hesitated, then acquiesced.

She snapped her mouth shut instead of pointing all that out. She'd made a vow when Reed left that no matter what happened, she wouldn't criticize him in front of Christopher. She'd seen too many kids in her office, confused and upset, to visit the same grief on her son. When one parent disparaged the other, it sent a single message. *"Your father is a bad person. Therefore you are, too...."*

She counted to three silently and forced herself to calm down. "Well, then...checking your homework is something we'll start doing again, you and I. Every night. All of it. Just like we did before."

He mumbled another answer she couldn't understand, then he tried to grab the bag from her hands. She held on to it and for just a moment, they were connected by the nylon straps. It made her think of all the ways they'd been joined before. In the womb, by holding hands, by the hugs he *used* to give her. Now this—a link of anger and lies.

The realization made her feel awful and her pique fled, like air suddenly released from a balloon. If she wanted to be upset with someone, it shouldn't be Chris, it should be herself and Reed. This was all their fault. When he'd left his son behind like a old pair of shoes he no longer wanted, she should have taken up the slack. Checking out his friends, keeping track of where he went, watching over him as closely as she could...it wasn't enough. Christopher was hurting inside and handling it like any normal fourteen-year-old boy would. With anger.

The weight of responsibility she constantly carried on her shoulders got a little heavier.

She relinquished the bag with a sigh. "Christopher, this is important, okay? I understand that things aren't the way you want them to be right now, but you can't come up with solutions like this. It's not acceptable."

He opened his mouth to argue but she held up her hand and stopped him. "Tomorrow we'll sit down and discuss this some more and I'll decide how I'm going to handle it. I'm going to visit with your teachers, too. At the very least, you're grounded until further notice."

He was protesting before she even finished speaking. "That's so not right—"

"No!" She spoke louder than she intended and he fell silent. She shook the report in her hand. "Forging my signature like this is what's not right, and you're going to suffer the consequences. Now go to your room and start your homework."

His backpack bouncing behind him, he ran out of the living room and pounded up the stairs. Maria dropped to the couch and covered her face with her hands.

THE PHONE RANG shortly after eight. Maria pulled off her reading glasses and reached across her desk to answer it. She'd been going over Ryan Lukas's report one more time, but she wasn't sure why. She wasn't really paying attention; she was thinking instead about Christopher and wondering where she'd gone so wrong. What kind of psychologist was she if she couldn't even control her own kid?

"Maria? Did I catch you at a bad time?"

Lena McKinney's voice reached through the fog of Maria's thoughts and brought her back to the present. Their relationship had started out as a professional one, but it had slowly evolved into a more personal connection and Maria was glad. She admired Lena tremendously; anyone who could manage the kind of men she did possessed more psychological skills than Maria.

"No, no. I was just thinking, that's all."

Lena chuckled. "That sounds dangerous."

"It can be, then again, who knows?" She rubbed her eyes wearily and spoke. "What's up?"

"Well, two things, actually. I'll give you the easy one first."

"That doesn't sound good."

"I think you can handle it. I wanted to remind you about the open house next week. You're still coming, aren't you? To Angel's Attic?"

Maria drew a blank, then Lena's words registered. She and Lena both volunteered at the local women's shelter. Always short on funds, the home for abused women and children ran a secondhand store called Angel's Attic but it never had enough money. To supplement the budget, a buffet dinner and auction had been planned. "Oh my gosh, the benefit! That's next week?"

"Monday night. It'll be at the shelter. Starts at six and everyone's included. You can bring Chris."

"Thanks for reminding me. Things have been so nutty around here, I had completely forgotten."

"No problem...now for the second reason I called." Lena paused for a moment as if gathering herself. "I wanted to know how it went with Ryan today. I've been worried."

Maria remembered his angry eyes. "Well, he wasn't happy. He thinks the leave is going to ruin his career."

"That's ridiculous. It'll ruin his career if he keeps going like he has been."

"I tried to explain that, but he wasn't buying. He's in complete denial about everything." Maria twirled her glasses thoughtfully. "When you called and set up his initial appointment you mentioned something about the way he approached his job. I can't remember exactly what you said then, but I have a feeling it was important. Can you tell me again?"

"You probably don't remember because I didn't know how to explain it. It might not have even made sense," Lena answered. "The only thing I can say is that he does his job with perfection. Too *much* perfection."

"He's too perfect?"

"He's like a robot. He hits the target every time."

"And that's a problem?"

"Yeah," Lena said softly. "It is. A good sniper

depends on more than perfect aim. And until Ginny died, Ryan had it all—compassion, intelligence, insight—*and* excellent shooting. Now all he's got is his steady hand. That bothers me.''

''He's in a lot of pain.''

''I understand that, I really do. I knew Ginny, and I saw them together…but he's too important to the team for me to let this pass. The decisions he makes are significant. People's lives hang in the balance.'' Lena's voice lost the sympathy it'd held and hardened into resolve. ''You've got a challenge in front of you, Maria, and it's not one I envy. But something's got to be done about him and you're our only hope. I have to have a thinking, feeling man behind that gun, not just a machine.''

CHAPTER TWO

THE SAND was rock hard. It scoured his bare feet as
he ran blindly down the beach in the midnight darkness. Anyone else would have needed more than the
water's phosphorescence to guide him, but Ryan
Lukas had made this trip once a day—sometimes
twice when things were really bad—for the past
eighteen months; he had the route memorized. He
required nothing but time. He pounded down the
shore in silence, his breath contained, like everything else, in the tight rhythm he allowed himself.
Forty-five minutes later, the final pier loomed, a
blacker shadow. He made a wide turn and headed
back, his toes sinking into the softer, wetter area that
marked the edge of the surf.

Usually when he ran, his mind emptied. He ran
for that very reason. Only when his body was in
movement was he able to find a certain kind of
peace. It wasn't the ordinary calmness he'd known
and taken for granted before but it was as close as
he could get to the feeling and still be awake. For
the most part, he lived outside his body. He went to
work, came home, cooked his dinner…did all the
things he had to without any of them registering.

Only when he ran did he feel as he once had. Tonight, even that eluded him and he cursed in the
darkness.

But he went on just the same.

His heart thundering, he reached the lights that
marked the deck of the house he rented, right behind
the dunes. He didn't think of it as home. It wasn't.
It couldn't be. It was simply the place where he slept
and ate when he wasn't at work. His gaze slid sideways toward the patio and he cursed.

As always, the dog was waiting. A full-grown
German shepherd, he had the patience of a stone
statue and the eyes of a sad saint. He tracked Ryan's
progress, but his stare was the only part of him that
moved. He didn't have a name because Ryan hadn't
given him one. When he got up every morning, the
dog would be in the same spot in the kitchen. By
the back door. Ryan would let him out and ten
minutes later, he'd always return.

Ryan hated the animal. Each day, he vowed that
day would be the last. He'd take the dog to the
pound and forget about him. It never seemed to happen, though. Instead, Ryan would fling some kibble
into the bowl in the corner then wash and fill a
second one with fresh water. With quiet dignity, the
animal would accept the offerings then reposition
himself by the door for the rest of the day. On the
rare occasions when Ryan was in the house for any
length of time, the shepherd was his shadow, a si-

lent, black presence that glided through the emptiness, always near but never touching.

Ginny had given the dog to Ryan for his birthday. The day before she'd died.

Slowing down, he jogged past the lights another hundred yards until he was finally walking instead of running. At that point he turned and splashed into the surf, his sweat-drenched body seeking the cool relief of the water.

He swam parallel to the beach, his strokes sure and steady. In the beginning, he'd always headed out, the lights of the beachfront homes shrinking as he put as much distance between himself and them as he could. Then he'd realized the danger in that. The temptation to keep going—until he couldn't— was more than he could handle. Something deep inside him had made him stop and now he swam this way. Along the edge of the surf but not in it. Near the beach, but not too close. Out as far as he could...but not too far.

His strong broad strokes brought him quickly to the point where the lights twinkled. He stayed still and treaded the water, reluctant to get out, his mind going back to the woman he'd talked to today. Maria Worley. She obviously had no idea what she was doing to him. His anger sharpened as he thought about the leave. If he didn't work, he wasn't sure what would happen to him, but he knew one thing: It wouldn't be good.

He emerged from the surf, salty rivulets running

down his chest as his feet found purchase in the sand. He was halfway to the deck and the waiting dog when he paused and looked back over his shoulder. The Gulf waters called to him. He listened for a bit, then he continued to the deck, dismissing the temptation.

For now.

MARIA PULLED the Toyota up to the curb and shut off the engine, her gaze cutting across the seat to the other side of the car. Christopher was slouched down as far as he could possibly get, his earphones crammed so tightly into his ears, it looked painful. Despite that fact, the music still leaked out. Nine Inch Nails. "The Day the World Went Away," his favorite. He probably wished it was "The Day His Mother Went Away."

"We're here," she announced in a fake cheerful voice. "Let's go."

Pretending he couldn't hear, he ignored her, his ploy so obvious it was might have been amusing under different circumstance. He was punishing her for the decrees she'd issued. Friday Maria had rescheduled all of her patients, spending the time instead at his school, talking to each of his teachers as they'd become available. She'd spoken to his counselor as well. Caring and thoughtful, they'd all tried to be helpful, but no one had a magic answer. As usual, Maria was on her own. Finally, after thinking about it long and hard, she'd forbidden him to go anywhere after school for the rest of the month. She'd also reinstated a rule she'd relaxed last year. He had to call her the minute he got home. He was supposed to do that before, but she'd eased up on that. No more.

He'd been so desperate to get out of the house, he'd actually agreed to come with her to Angel's Attic. Now that they were here, Maria found herself second-guessing her decision. He was being so obnoxious she almost wished he'd stayed home. At least then she'd be able to have a good time.

She shook her head at her thoughts—what kind of mother was she?—then reached over and patted his arm. He turned to look at her and she nodded toward the house. "We're here."

He opened his car door without speaking and climbed outside.

With a sigh, Maria followed and they headed up a sidewalk already growing crowded. Someone had strung a line of Japanese lanterns along the railing of the front porch and in the warm spring evening, their lights twinkled brightly. They were miles from the expensive beachfront subdivisions but the air held a sea breeze all the same. Maria's eyes went over the guests. They ranged from previous tenants of the shelter to cops to a group of teachers who helped run the home for battered women.

As Christopher headed for a side yard where a pickup game of basketball was taking place, Maria made her way to the dozen or so tables that held thc auction items. Displayed were a variety of things that would be sold to raise money for the shelter, including a fishing excursion, dinner for two at the Marina Café and a hundred dollars worth of groceries from Delchamps, the local grocery store. It would be a silent auction; people had already filled out slips and left them in baskets by the items. The winning bids would be announced after dinner. Maria walked slowly down the line trying to decide. A full day at the new spa for her or two-hour Jet Ski lesson for Christopher? Maria reached for the slip in front of the Jet Ski offering just as Lena walked up.

"Hey! I didn't know you liked to ride those things!" Lena smiled and nodded toward the photo of the purple-and-yellow Jet Ski on the table. "I've got one. I'll teach you how to use it anytime you want."

Maria returned Lena's smile then acknowledged Andres, her husband, who waited patiently beside her. They'd had a few problems before their marriage last year, but they seemed so happy and contented now, Maria felt a sudden touch of envy. She and Reed had never stood that way, their arms wrapped around each other's waists, their eyes meeting frequently with silent messages that told everyone how much they really loved each other.

"This is for Chris," Maria said, holding up the ticket. "But if I win, things would have to change before he could even think about redeeming it."

Lena smiled sympathetically as Andres made a clucking sound. "What's the problem, *chica?*"

Andres was Cuban, and the Spanish term of endearment rolled off his tongue with ease.

Maria shook her head. "Let's just say if he continues as is, he's going to show up on the Most Wanted list for forgery."

"Uh-oh…that sounds bad."

Maria nodded her agreement to Lena's pronouncement just as someone across the room called to Andres. He excused himself and headed off and the two women turned back to each other.

"You know why Chris is doing all this, don't you?" Lena asked.

"Of course, I do. He's mad because his father left him," Maria said. "I know *why*—I just don't know what to do about it." She made a noise that was half frustration, half resignation. "I feel so helpless sometimes. All this training, all my degrees…and I'm an utter klutz when it comes to my own kid."

Lena squeezed her arm softly. "Haven't you heard that old saying about the cobbler's kids going without shoes?"

"Maybe that is the case. All I know is that I love him, but I don't know how to handle him." She gave Lena the details of the forged signature and the punishment she'd leveled. "I couldn't believe it," she said, shaking her head. "He's never done anything like that before. Never."

Lena looked thoughtful for a moment. "The kids he's hanging out with—do you know who they are?"

"I've met some of them. They're not really the kind of friends I'd like him to have."

"Give me their names," Lena said. "The juvie guys know all the troublemakers and I'd be happy to ask. Let's see if they're on the list of bad boys or just regular, annoying kids."

"That would be terrific," Maria said gratefully. "I've talked to as many of the parents of his friends as I can, but it seems like there's never enough time. I still haven't met some of them. I'd love to know more."

"No problem," Lena said. "It shouldn't take any time at all."

They finished going down the line of auction items after that, Maria feeling somewhat more hopeful. It wasn't until after dinner and they were all ready to leave that Lena pulled her aside.

"I just wanted you to know I talked with Ryan this morning. We went over the terms of his leave. I've given him office duty for six weeks. If he's made some progress at that point, then I'll reconsider the situation and put him back on active status."

"Six weeks?" Maria frowned. "I thought I suggested a month."

"You did," Lena replied. "But I think he needs

more time than that. I'd rather err on this side than on the other, if you know what I mean.''

"He must not have liked that...." And she'd hear about it Thursday, too. He'd come in primed, she was sure, if he even kept his appointment. "What did he say?''

"Not much. I could see he was boiling on the inside, but he's got too much discipline to let it out."

"And that's part of the problem." Maria felt sorry for him before she could stop herself. Her reaction was unexpected; usually she detached herself from the problems of her patients. She had to—helping them required that she see their situations objectively. Psychologists who didn't frequently ended up in another career or went nuts themselves. Why she felt differently about Ryan Lukas, she couldn't say.

"He's keeping all his emotions bottled and trying to deny them," she explained. "The end result isn't good. It'll lead to a meltdown."

Lena nodded, her worried gaze holding Maria's. "Do you think you can help him?"

Maria answered "I hope so," and Lena nodded, walking off a second later with her arm linked inside Andres's. As Maria watched them leave, though, she wondered if she had told Lena the truth. Some of the cops who came through her office were past helping. They'd seen too much, done too much...lost too much. She hoped Ryan Lukas wasn't one of them.

But she suspected he might be.

HE'D HAD ENOUGH.

After two full shifts of office duty, Ryan knew he'd never make it six weeks. No way. Every day was torture, every hour an endurance test. How did people do it, he asked himself, his eyes blurring as he studied the report in front of him. How could they just sit like this, at a desk, in an office, hour after hour, day after day…year after year?

When the crawling hands of the clock reached 4:00 p.m., he couldn't stand it another minute. He grabbed his jacket, mumbled an excuse to the sergeant at the front desk, and charged out of the building to drive home. Which was an even bigger mistake.

The dog met him at the door, the house as silent as a tomb.

Ryan pushed past the animal and dropped his coat on the kitchen table. At the refrigerator, he pulled out a can of cold beer, popped the tab and managed one swallow before a beeping sound broke the quiet. His pager. He stared at it, frustration rolling over him in a wave as he realized what had happened. A call for the team. And he wouldn't be there. He cursed and the dog whined softly, answering him.

Ryan ripped the pager from his belt and tossed it to the tiled counter where it slid upside down until it hit the toaster at the other end. He then strode into the bedroom, peeling his clothes off as he went. In a matter of minutes, he was outside on the deck, stretching his calves and trying not to think. The dog padded past him to sit at the top of the stairs.

The running did no good. In the days since he'd seen the good Dr. Worley, the physical activity had come to help him less and less. Halfway down, he simply gave up and returned to the house. Collapsing on the deck, he found himself eye to eye with the dog.

A confusion of thoughts swirled through his mind as he stared into the German shepherd's black eyes.

"To hell with it..." Ryan finally said. "What are they gonna do? Put me on leave?"

He got up and stomped into the house, the screen door banging behind him as he made his way to his bedroom. Nabbing a fresh T-shirt from the chest, he peeled off the sweaty one he'd been running in and thrust his arms into the clean one. Another minute and he was in his truck heading back to town. It took a while for him to find the address still flashing on his beeper, but when he got close, the red and blue lights led him the rest of the way.

He slowed his truck and turned into a side street, catching a glimpse of the War Wagon down another. Along with the surveillance gear it contained, the enormous customized Winnebago was equipped with every high-tech communication device known to man. The team used the equipment to stay in touch with each other and to reach the station during a call-out. More than a single bullet hole on the side explained how it'd been used for cover once or twice as well.

Three black and whites—the arriving officers probably—had the nearest routes barricaded. Ryan eased his truck to the curb just outside their line of sight. Despite his pronouncement to the dog, there was no need to deliberately aggravate anyone.

He looked around as he climbed out of the truck. The area wasn't one that generated a lot of calls. An industrial park made up mostly of warehouses and loading docks, the complex was located on the outskirts of town. He couldn't remember having ever received a call from here, and now he understood why. The place was empty. There were no tenants in any of the buildings. An air of desertion hung over the entire area.

A sudden movement near one of the black and whites caught his eye. An older man wearing the uniform of a security guard bent over as he talked to the officers inside the car. He'd probably been the one to call in. But what in the hell was going on? Ryan realized too late he should have taken the time to listen to his radio before jumping in the truck and driving over here. The awareness of what he'd done—acting so impulsively—suddenly registered. Where had his deliberateness gone? His careful thinking? He never did anything without much consideration, but the boredom and agony of sitting all day had brought him to this.

Thanks, Dr. Worley, he thought bitterly. *If it weren't for you, I'd know what the hell had happened and I wouldn't be standing here like some ignorant kid, gawking instead of helping.*

The thought barely had time to register when a shot rang out.

Ryan fell to the pavement automatically, the truck his only protection. A second report registered almost immediately, the sound coming from somewhere inside the complex. Ryan chanced another look toward the clump of buildings. He couldn't see any team members, but he didn't expect to. If they were doing their job right, they were already in place, as silent and invisible as ghosts. He lifted his gaze to the roofs of the nearest buildings. There were no easy holes, he thought. No place Lena could have put a shooter without someone seeing him take his place. He looked a little closer, though, and then...there!...right by the fourth building on the left. He caught a glint of metal, the hint of the slightest movement. No one else but Ryan would have seen it, and his gut tightened as he realized what it meant. It had to be Chase Mitchell, the countersniper for Team Alpha.

Ryan spoke Maria's name like a curse. He should have been up on that hot, humid roof. It should have been him doing the job, not Chase.

When the third shot sounded, Ryan was prepared.

Listening closely, he cataloged the popping noise, relaxing as he did so. He wouldn't have bet his life on it, but he was ninety-nine percent sure he'd just heard an air rifle go off and nothing more. Peeking around the edge of his tire, he caught sight of the security guard and two uniformed officers. The excited gestures of the older man led Ryan to the obvious conclusion. This is what had brought out the team. The old guy had heard something or seen something, then the uniforms had shown up and shots had been fired.

As soon as Ryan had figured it out, the situation appeared to be over. The front door of the nearest building banged open. Sliding cautiously up from his spot behind the vehicle, Ryan looked over at the building. Three men wearing black came out. He squinted in the dying sunlight and made out their faces—Peter Douglas and John Fletcher, two of the rear-entry men, and J. L. LeBlanc, a front entry officer. In between their cordon was a figure in jeans and a T-shirt.

From his long distance vantage point, Ryan couldn't tell much more, but their body language confirmed his initial assessment. No one looked too nervous, and in fact, when Peter said something into the headset microphone the team members wore, he grinned as he spoke. He wouldn't have done that if there had been a serious gun involved. The three officers walked the suspect to the black and white and a few minutes later, the uniforms took off with their shooter in the back seat. Ryan caught a quick glimpse as the car sped by. The only thing visible was a blond head hanging down—a young kid headed in the wrong direction, in more ways than one.

Ryan stuck around for another half hour, but there wasn't anything else to see. What he did witness—the team gathering around the War Wagon for their debriefing—only made him wish more that Maria Worley would take a flying leap off the top of her office building and land in the Gulf. Ryan thought briefly of storming up to the Winnebago in defiance, but it wouldn't be worth it. Lena would kick his ass all the way back to the office and he'd look like a fool.

Finally, after a bit more useless watching, he trudged back to his truck and climbed inside, the summer sun fading, as it could sometimes do, seemingly within an instant. In that moment—in that quick second between light and total darkness—he happened to look west, directly into the glare, and a movement caught his attention. He blinked, then blinked again, holding his hand up to shade his eyes against the blinding rays.

He saw nothing but the orange ball of the sun against a glowing sky and finally decided he had imagined the motion. Then he saw it again. A small figure behind one of the warehouses, a black baseball cap on his head, a blue backpack hanging off one shoulder. Ryan's breath stopped in response, the adrenaline flowing before he assessed the situation. It was just a kid, he realized, a kid watching the action just as Ryan had been doing. As Ryan watched, the youngster turned around and loped away. A few minutes after that, Ryan left the scene as well, the bitter taste of exclusion his primary sensation.

He was sitting on the deck after midnight when the question finally hit him.

How had a kid gotten to a deserted warehouse so far out on the edge of town?

He reached for his cell phone he'd brought to the deck out of habit, but before he could finish dialing the number, he stopped, his fingers growing still. If he told Lena what he'd seen, she'd be pissed because he was there. She might even add more time to his "sentence." Chances were, the kid's appearance meant nothing anyway. Ryan had passed a trailer park a mile or so before the complex. The boy had probably walked over from there to see what all the excitement was about. He ought to be home studying instead, Ryan mused. Why did he even care?

Why did Ryan?

Dropping the phone, Ryan answered himself. He was off active duty now. It didn't matter what he thought about the case. He was out of the picture. Leaning his head back into the recliner, he stared at the endless black sky above him. He could see

Ginny's face in the stars and for one crazy minute he even thought he smelled her perfume. Cursing to himself, Ryan closed his eyes. Beside him, the dog sighed softly, then settled in to wait.

CHAPTER THREE

MARIA ADJUSTED the fresh tulips and freesias that sat on the corner of her desk—for the third time that morning. The fussing was pointless, but she had to do something and she didn't want to look at her watch again. If she did, she'd only get more angry than she was already. After a second, she gave up and looked anyway. It was twenty-five past the hour.

She stood suddenly and crossed to the window. A summer storm was threatening to move in, with billowing clouds hovering over the water, turning the green sea into a metallic gray. She watched a line of sailboats head for the marina and thought about Ryan Lukas. She'd been pretty sure he wasn't going to show up for his appointment, but the inconsiderateness still irked her. She could have used the time to meet with Chris's counselor again. She'd wanted to have a follow-up meeting this week, but because of her schedule had been unable to do so. How much trouble would it have been for Ryan to pick up the phone and call her?

She was kidding herself, of course. Ryan Lukas wasn't going to acknowledge her in any way; to do so would mean facing his problem, admittedly in a minor fashion, but even *that* was more than he could handle. Full and complete denial was his only mode of operation at this point.

Her aggravation fled as the observation registered. Ryan needed help and needed it now. He was aching inside and didn't know how to ease the hurt.

She turned away from the glass and buzzed the receptionist. "Sher, I'm going to make a call. If my 3:00 p.m. comes in, would you beep me on the other line?"

"Sure thing." Sherlyn Eliot was a cheerful motherly type who handled all the calls for the five therapists who shared Maria's suite. "He's the hunky one, right? Lieutenant Lukas. I remember him."

"Uh…right. Lieutenant Lukas."

Maria put the receiver down, the woman's words ringing in her mind. She never saw her patients as anything other than patients. Ethics demanded this, and in addition, Maria had simply stopped looking at men after she'd married. She'd considered herself out of the race, and for all the reasons every single woman understood, she hadn't bothered to start looking again.

She wasn't about to change that, either. With Christopher's problems and her stressful workload, a man was the last complication Maria needed. Especially someone with an emotional life as tangled as Ryan Lukas's. Even if he *wasn't* a client, he'd never be the kind of person she'd date. The one man she'd seen since her divorce had proved to be such a disaster she need only remember him for encouragement—he'd wanted free therapy, not a real relationship.

Having been there for Maria then, she could imagine what Jackson would think about Lukas. He'd roll over and die, she was sure.

With that thought, she lifted the phone again and speed dialed his number. Jackson Maxwell had been her therapist and consultant on various cases for the past ten years. Now they were best friends. He always listened with a neutral ear and guided her toward the right decisions without actually telling her what to do. It was a skill not too many people had, but Jackson had perfected the art. And Maria loved him for it.

"Powell's Antiques." Richard Powell, Jackson's partner, answered the phone on the first ring. He and Jackson had been together for twenty-five years and when Jackson had retired from his practice, Richard had immediately recruited him into his business. Claiming forced labor, Jackson had complained, but Maria knew deep down he'd actually been scared. Leaving the profession he'd loved and having spare hours to fill could be a frightening prospect. She wasn't sure how well the arrangement was going, but personally, she couldn't imagine having all the time in the world to do whatever caught her fancy. She'd always had more work, at the office *and* at home, than she could handle.

"Richard, this is Maria. Is Jackson around by any chance?"

"Maria! He's supposed to be here somewhere, but I swear he's hiding. I told him to dust the crystal vases in the back room and he disappeared."

Maria laughed. "I'd disappear, too, if you told me that. Last time I was in there you pointed to one and said 'Twenty thousand.' That'd scare off anyone!"

"Well, we'll be drowning in crystal if someone doesn't get back there and clean it up so I can sell it. Just a minute, though, I'll see if I can unearth him...."

She heard him drop the phone and yell Jackson's name. A few seconds later, an extension clicked on, Jackson's voice coming out in a whisper. "Come save me, Maria! I swear to God, he's driving me crazy.... Is this really what he does all day?"

Maria laughed again. "You wanted a new life," she warned. "This is what you got."

"I'm ready to go back to the crazy people, then. Do you want a partner?"

"Maybe we could work out a deal.... What do you think about switching with me? You take my whole life and I'll take yours."

"Is Christopher part of the package?" Jackson and her child had always been close; Christopher was the son Jackson didn't have. "I might consider a switch if he comes with the deal."

"I don't think you'll feel that way after you hear why I'm calling."

With as little fanfare as possible, she told Jackson what had happened. "I don't understand what's going on with him," she concluded.

"He misses his daddy."

"I know that."

"And he feels abandoned."

"I know that."

"Then what's the problem? Cut the little guy some slack, for God's sake!"

"You don't understand." Sighing heavily, she realized her mistake; Jackson would defend Chris as staunchly as he could. "You haven't seen him for a few months, Jackson. It's not just the grades—he's changed. He won't talk to me at all and when he does, his attitude is surly. And the music he listens to...you wouldn't believe it."

"Do you think he's doing drugs?"

"No." If there was one thing she *was* sure of, it was this. "We've had a lot of discussions about drugs and he's always talking about the 'stupid' kids he knows who do that."

"Things can change."

"Of course," she agreed, "but not that. I'm sure."

"Have you tried talking to him?"

"I've talked until I'm blue in the face. But he doesn't talk back."

"Then you're going to have to find another route.

You've got to get the lines of communication open, Maria. That's the key."

Frustration filled her voice...and her heart. "I know," she said. "But what I don't know is how."

"Bring him out here. He and I have always seen eye to eye. Maybe he'll talk a bit to me and that's all it'd take."

The suggestion immediately sounded like a good one, but Maria hesitated. "Are you sure? He's not exactly fun to be around...."

"Neither am I right now," Jackson snorted. "We'll get along just fine. Bring him out."

They talked about the situation a few more minutes and Maria ended up promising Jackson that she and Chris would visit soon. Just before they finished, almost as if by afterthought, she spoke casually. "By the way, I've got a new client who seems interesting...or at least I *should* have a new client. He's the countersniper for the SWAT team. He didn't show up for his appointment today."

"The countersniper? That should be a fascinating brain to examine. Wait just a minute...." She heard the sound of a paper rustling. "I see him," Jackson said over the noise. "The team's photo is in the *Log* today. Something about a rally they're holding."

Maria walked from behind her desk to a table by the window, cradling the phone between her shoulder and ear. She'd brought the local newspaper, the *Destin Log,* with her this morning and stuffed it into her briefcase, hoping to scan it at lunch. Lena had already told Maria about the event—and was holding tickets for her at the station. Maria reached into the case and brought out the paper.

"Page five," he said.

She quickly flipped to the proper page. The photo was front and center, and Ryan Lukas's face immediately jumped out at her. Except for Beck Winters, a blond giant who was the team's former negotiator, Ryan was the tallest person in the photograph. Dressed in the black uniform of the team, his hair ruffled in the wind, he wore a stony expression.

Maria realized without warning that Sher's description had been accurate. Ryan Lukas *was* a hunk. Dark hair, compelling eyes, a body ready for anything.

Jackson's words jarred her. "He does look the part, doesn't he?"

"What do you mean?"

"He's got a thousand-yard stare, for one thing. But for another…"

"But for another…what?"

"Just something about him, that's all. He looks like trouble."

"That's what he's been so far. He's certainly not been too cooperative in session."

"How'd he get in therapy?"

Maria gave him a brief case description, including the death of Ryan's wife. She and Jackson consulted on so many of her cases they almost had a special language of their own to describe clients.

"I guess that explains everything," Jackson said after she finished. His voice changed slightly. "You sound as if you're worried. Don't you think you can handle him?"

Not surprised by his perception, Maria started to answer then stopped. She *was* more worried about Ryan Lukas than she should have been. She spoke slowly. "I think he's in a lot of pain but he's made it clear he doesn't want my help. I guess I just hate to see anyone suffer like that."

"It's nothing else?"

"Why do you ask?"

A slight silence built. Jackson finally broke it. "You aren't thinking of mounting a rescue attempt, are you?" He chuckled then. "So to speak..."

It took her a minute to understand. "No, God... Jackson, it's nothing like that. I'm not attracted to him, in any way."

"He's a handsome man."

"He's a client," she protested at once. "And that's all he is. And all he *will* be, I assure you."

Jackson took a second too long to answer and she realized her mistake. She was being too defensive. Jackson might be retired but his clinical radar was still intact. He'd think she was covering something up. He started to come back at her, but she said goodbye and hung up quickly. She didn't have the time to explain, she told herself later. Her evasiveness had nothing to do with Lieutenant Lukas being so attractive. Nothing at all.

RYAN SPENT the weekend doing household chores and trying to read the latest David Lindsey novel. By the time Monday rolled around he was actually glad to see it even though it meant another torturous day at the desk. Heading into the station that morning, he thought again about the kid he'd seen at the call-out last week. He hadn't said anything to Lena and still didn't intend to, yet something about the incident continued to bug him.

His mind was focused on a blue backpack and a black baseball cap when he rounded the corner to see Maria Worley in the corridor.

She was standing next to Lena and she had on a dark-gray suit with some kind of silky blouse beneath the jacket. Ryan knew little about women's clothing, but the way it flattered her figure meant the outfit had to be expensive. Snuggled against one hip, she held a black leather notebook. As he watched the two women talk, Maria lifted her right hand and absentmindedly tucked a strand of her dark hair behind one ear. The movement was graceful and fluid, full of the kind of femininity he had once appreciated seeing in a woman. *Once.*

He wasn't conscious of it, but he must have made some kind of noise. Both of them looked up. He met Maria's eyes and ignored Lena. As she recognized him, the doctor's gaze went from startled to wary.

"Hello, Lieutenant," she said in a neutral voice. "How are you this morning?"

He ignored her question. "What are you doing here? Haven't you done enough damage already?"

Lena held up a warning hand. "Ryan, don't start—"

Maria cut her off. "It's all right, Lena. Let him talk."

Her support, even as insignificant as it was, made Ryan angrier, although he would have been at a total loss if asked to explain why.

"Well?" he continued rudely before she could say more. "What *are* you doing here? Ruining someone else's career or just bad-mouthing me?"

"Actually I came by to pick up my tickets for the rally this weekend. I also stopped to tell Lieutenant McKinney that you failed to make your appointment last week." She looked at him coolly. "Which concerns me greatly."

"These sessions are mandatory, Ryan." Lena spoke sternly. "If you don't intend to keep them, then we need to talk—"

"My appointment?" Ignoring Lena, he stared at Maria and drew a complete blank.

"I gave you a card the day you were in my office. It had the date and time of our next scheduled conference, which happened to be last Thursday but you never showed up." She raised one perfectly arched eyebrow. "I'm assuming something important must have kept you?"

For one long second, all he did was stare at her. She had brown eyes, he saw now, and they were deep and dark. She would never believe him if he told her he had completely forgotten about the appointment, but he had. A glimmer of remorse, which he immediately ignored, shot through him.

"I was busy," he said abruptly. "I couldn't make it."

"I charge for missed appointments."

"So send me a bill."

Lena sighed loudly. "The department will take care of it, Ryan, but in the future—"

He shot her a warning look. "I understand."

"Good. I'll expect to see proof of that shortly." She turned without another word and disappeared into the office behind them. The door clicked firmly as she shut it. Too firmly. That wasn't a good sign, but Ryan didn't care.

Maria made no effort to move. He wondered what she was waiting for, then she spoke and he wished he'd made his escape when he'd had the chance.

"When can you come in?" Her voice was crisp as she opened her notebook. "I have the Thursday after the rally open again. Is that convenient?"

"No." He had no intention of letting this woman probe his brain. "It's not."

"Then when?"

"I'll let you know after I look at my schedule."

He started to walk off, then he felt a hand, light as a bird's wing, brush his arm before dropping. Surprised, he turned back.

"Lieutenant Lukas..." Two lines had formed across her forehead. It gave her an air of concern he didn't believe for a minute. "You're facing an emotional crisis and you need help. Forgetting these appointments—"

"I didn't forget it," he said. "I was busy."

Conceding the point even though both of them knew better, she nodded slowly. "Well, then not making time for these sessions is a symptom of how strong your denial really is. You can't continue in this fashion."

"I can do anything I damn well please."

"Not and keep your job."

"Are you threatening me?"

Her expression stayed calm and even in the midst of his anger, Ryan marveled that she could be so cool. He was doing everything he could to annoy her, but it wasn't working. Her collected demeanor almost made him envious. He'd been that way once.

"I'm not threatening you at all," she said quietly. Her expression shifted and this time he couldn't deny the apparent genuineness of her attitude. Either she really cared, or she was the best damn actress this side of Hollywood.

"You're a grown man and you can screw up your life any way you want to. But you need help and I can provide it. It's what I do and I do it well." She surprised him by smiling slightly. "Lieutenant Lukas, neither of us has a choice here. If you want to keep your job, you have to come talk to me. And if I want to keep mine, I need to listen. It's really that simple."

Just as quickly as it'd come, her smile disappeared. From the side pocket of her notebook she pulled out another card, carefully wrote something on it and handed it to him. "That's an appointment for next week," she said, businesslike. "I suggest you work your schedule around it, instead of the other way around."

She turned and walked quickly down the hall— so quickly he could say nothing more. She was persistent, that was for sure.

He looked down at the card she'd given him. She'd printed out the date and time, her handwriting as neat and streamlined as she was, the letters extending above the printed line exactly where they were supposed to be.

Thursday. 3:00 p.m. On the side, she'd scribbled something else. He had to turn the card sideways to read the words.

No excuses.

RYAN TRIED to concentrate the rest of the day but Maria Worley's image kept interrupting. He fought the dark hair and brown eyes each time they disrupted his train of thought. He didn't want to think about her. For some crazy reason, it made him feel as if he were being unfaithful to Ginny. Leaning back in his chair, he put his hands behind his head and stared out into the parking lot. The sun was hot and strong, beating into the asphalt and sending shimmers of waves along the blackened surface. He followed their path until they disappeared in the distance.

But could she be right?

Was he heading for disaster?

He immediately dismissed the questions, telling himself he was letting Maria's sympathetic manner and warm smile get to him. He was fine. He'd been at the range the day before and never missed once. The heart of his paper target had been shredded in seconds, the one-inch circle gone in a puff of smoke. Yet somehow Maria Worley, and her questions, wouldn't leave him alone.

Everything else aside, he couldn't deny the logic of her argument. Lena could keep him behind this damned desk until eternity if she wanted to…and she wouldn't have any qualms about doing so, either. Despite how her obstinacy affected him, he had to admit it was one of the qualities about his boss he appreciated. She was a stand-up person who believed in right and wrong, no matter how tough the situation. He'd watched her face off with men twice her size and mean as hell. Every time, she'd won.

Something told him Maria Worley might be just as stubborn.

But they were both wrong, dammit! He was fine,

and furthermore, he didn't need to talk to anybody about what had happened. Ginny was gone, he was alone, and nothing he could do would bring her back. His throat tightened and burned. That was it. End of story.

With an angry, muttered curse, he turned to the file before him, his front chair legs hitting the floor with a screech. The report was on last week's situation. The one he'd spied on.

Flipping past the paperwork that meant nothing but was always required, he found the on-site notes Lena had taken during the actual confrontation. He skimmed them quickly and saw that his immediate impression had been right on target.

Hearing shots and voices coming from inside the abandoned buildings, the security guard had phoned the local police department. The arriving officers had investigated as much as they could, then had requested support. They couldn't penetrate the interior of the buildings without being seen. Lena had issued the call, her notes indicating she'd initially ordered a skeleton crew only. That told him a lot; she hadn't been too concerned but had not wanted to blow it off, either.

He skipped over the minute-by-minute account and found the sheet on the perp. He was only fifteen, and the gun had been the air rifle that Ryan had thought it was. The case was headed for juvie court.

Then something else caught his eye.

Peter Douglas had gone into the building after it

had been secured and cleared. Sweeping for evidence, he'd found nothing but half a dozen empty CO_2 cartridges, five cigarette butts and two crushed beer cans. He also listed some ''miscellaneous drawings,'' at the end of the report. It had all been checked into evidence.

Ryan tapped his pencil on top of the desk and reread the last line. ''Miscellaneous drawings.'' What the hell did that mean? It was probably nothing, but the description bothered him and for no reason other than that, Ryan headed down the hall to the evidence room.

Ten minutes later, he had the box in his hand. Pushing aside the various plastic bags, he came to a larger one with several sheets of crumpled paper inside. He snapped on a pair of rubber gloves then opened it up, removing the sheets and smoothing them so he could get a better look.

They were covered with pencil sketches, the same image depicted over and over. It took him a minute to recognize the stylized birdlike shape and another five to puzzle out where he'd first seen the form. When he did recall, he whistled softly to himself, not understanding fully, but understanding enough.

The drawings were identical to one Maria Worley had framed and hung behind her desk.

CHAPTER FOUR

SATURDAY MORNING Maria got up early and cleaned the house. She hadn't been able to afford help when she and Reed had first married and now, although she could hire a service or even a house-keeper, she did the chores herself. She liked the rhythm of sweeping and dusting and mopping. It gave her time to think.

Today she didn't have even that luxury, though. She and Christopher had to be at the police training facility off Highway 30-A by 10:00 a.m. for the rally. She'd promised to meet Lena at the chili dog stand so they could set everything up and be ready by lunchtime. Each hot dog they sold meant more money for Angel's Attic.

The event had originally been planned to raise community awareness about the local police force and the Emerald Coast SWAT team, but Lena had persuaded her guys—in no uncertain terms—that the gathering also presented the perfect venue to help the shelter. They hadn't argued.

Maria put away the vacuum cleaner and called up the stairs, one more time, for Christopher. "We're going to be late if we don't leave in five minutes. Come on down, honey!''

She disappeared into her bedroom to run a brush through her hair and change into a sundress, then she came back out, purse in hand. Christopher was waiting by the stairs, a churlish frown on his face, which Maria ignored. "Ready to roll?"

"I don't wanna go to this dumb thing." Under the backward brim of his black baseball cap, his brown eyes were full of sullen anger. Not that many years ago, he'd stared at her in adoration. She found herself wishing he was four again, instead of fourteen.

"Then why don't you stay home?" Maria spoke calmly as she walked toward the front door. "I told you last night you didn't have to go." She turned as she reached the entry. "But if you stay here, you cannot have friends over and you cannot use the phone."

"I don't wanna stay here if I can't talk to anybody."

She waited by the door and looked at him. "Well, I'm sorry, but those are the rules. You decide."

Instead of answering her, he glared a bit more, then he crossed the room and pushed past her to walk through the door. With a sigh, Maria followed.

Twenty minutes later they arrived at the camp. Located just outside of town, the setting provided the local police force and, more importantly, the SWAT team with everything they needed to keep in shape, including a work-out facility, a running track and a mock setting where they practiced hard tactic entries. In the rear, there was also a well-equipped shooting range. Lena had brought Maria out once and given her a tour. As she pulled into the gate and began to look for a parking spot, Maria could see they'd added several more buildings since she'd been there. Two enormous white tents had been set up as well, obviously for the rally.

Angling the car under the shade of a nearby oak tree, Maria stepped out of the Toyota and opened the trunk. She'd brought boxes of buns and paper plates along with several cases of chili that she'd purchased the night before. Christopher's door slammed just as she bent down to lift out the first carton. She called out to him. "Would you come back here and get one of these, please! You can wander off as soon as I get this stuff out."

He didn't answer, and yelling his name again, louder than was necessary, Maria leaned over the side of the car. "Christopher! Come back here and—"

Her demand broke off in midsentence. Christopher was nowhere to be seen, but the towering shape of Ryan Lukas stood beside the fender of her car. He was dressed in his SWAT uniform—a tight black T-shirt and black pants—and he looked every inch the intimidating man that he was. Tall, powerful...scary.

"Lieutenant Lukas!" Maria straightened and met

his eyes, feeling her face go warm as she did so. Had he heard her yelling for her son? He'd probably grab the opportunity to ask if she did counseling for children. "I'm sorry," she said stiffly. "I didn't see you standing there—"

"Lena sent me out here to look for you," he said. "She said you had some boxes to carry over to the booth. I can get them."

It wasn't a very gracious offer, but under the circumstances, Maria understood. "Yes," she said, "I do. This is all the food for the hot dog concession..."

He didn't wait for her to finish but reached into the trunk. Lifting out the largest and the heaviest of the cartons, he tucked it under one arm then reached in and got a second. "I'll be back for the rest."

Standing by the car, Maria watched him walk away. Like some kind of dark ghost, he moved without making a sound then disappeared into the sparse crowd. It was uncanny. One minute he was there and the next he was simply gone.

Deciding she'd just as soon carry the rest by herself, Maria pulled out the remaining paper plates and napkins then closed the trunk. Juggling the bags, she started toward the back of the area, one eye looking for Christopher and the other searching for the booth. She found the latter first.

Ryan was talking to Lena as Maria walked up.

"I told you I'd come get those."

Her gaze met his over the awkward bundles. "It wasn't a problem," she answered. "I didn't want to put you out."

Ryan's eyes sparked, then he turned abruptly to stalk away from the booth. The two women watched him blend into the crowd.

"Does he always do that?"

"Act obnoxious?" Lena shook her head. "No, actually, he's a very nice guy. Or at least he used to be before—"

"That's not what I meant." Maria tilted her head in the direction he'd taken. "I mean how he disappears like that. I see him walk away then all at once, he's gone.... Poof!"

Lena laughed, then raised one eyebrow. "It's a SWAT trick," she said. "We have special ploys, you know."

Maria added her own laughter to Lena's and they began to set up the booth. As she worked, Maria thought about Lena's words. In a lot of ways, the SWAT team *was* special. The stress they faced every day would have killed some men, but time and time again, as Maria had counseled various members, she'd come to realize they actually thrived on the intensity. They were a breed apart. As the sniper of the team, Ryan Lukas was at the top of that chain. He *had* to be. No other kind of man could have done what he did and survive.

The question was...*would* he survive?

RYAN STRODE to the other side of the facility, past the training building and through the crowd. He was in charge of a lecture about weapons later on and he had to make sure everything was ready. His mind wasn't on the guns or targets, though. It was back in the hot dog booth with Maria. When Lena had told him she was coming and asked if he'd go help her, he'd wanted to scream, "Hell, no!"

But he hadn't, of course. Lena was his boss and she was already very unhappy with him. She'd made it a point to come by his desk the afternoon following Maria's appearance at the station to tell him so.

He took the well-worn path toward the range and the unexpected image of Maria Worley's shoulders came to him. She'd been wearing a sundress, a white, backless thing that tied around her neck, leaving her shoulders exposed. Without even knowing why, he thought of Ginny. Maria Worley was dark and petite with deep-brown eyes. Ginny had been a blonde, blue-eyed, and plump—she'd always battled her weight, bemoaning every inch. But he'd loved her curves and softness.

Without any warning, a searing pain shot through his chest. It wasn't physical, he knew at once, but it was real all the same. He gasped and stopped abruptly, reaching out blindly toward the nearest tree. It was a pine, and the rough sticky bark bit into the skin of his palms. He could see Ginny perfectly. Every inch of her, every little detail, even the mole she'd had in the center of her left calf. He tried to shut off the memory but the harder he tried, the more real it became.

Finally, he did the only thing he could—he relaxed and concentrated on the image instead of fighting it. Like a wisp of smoke, it disappeared. He took a deep breath and then another, lifting his head once more.

A kid stood on the path in front of him.

About thirteen, maybe fourteen, he had on a black T-shirt, baggy jeans and a baseball cap. His hands were stuffed into his pockets as he stared at Ryan with a scared expression. "Hey, man, you okay?"

The youngster seemed familiar, but Ryan couldn't place him. Did he belong to one of the team members? Ryan tried to concentrate but couldn't. "I'm all right," he said slowly. "It's nothing...."

"You want me to go get somebody?"

"No, no. I'll be fine." Ryan straightened slowly. "I feel better already."

The boy nodded. He'd heard adults lie before, the motion said, and he knew better than to challenge them. Without another word, he edged around Ryan and headed back to the crowd. Ryan turned and strode in the opposite direction, toward the range, the kid already forgotten.

Damn Maria Worley. What in the hell was she doing to him?

"I'LL HAVE three dogs, two with chili, one without. And lots of onions. Oh, and we want three lemonades, too. No...make that one lemonade and two iced teas...."

With a frazzled nod, Maria took the older man's order and began to prepare it. Business had been nonstop all morning and she was ready to collapse. Lena had promised to help but once the organized activities had begun, she'd disappeared, her presence needed elsewhere. Just as Maria was about to scream, her relief appeared. A teacher from the elementary school, Cindy took one look at Maria and waved her off. "I'll handle this now," she said with practiced aplomb. "You go on..."

With a grateful nod, Maria removed her apron and stepped outside the booth. She wanted to find the nearest picnic table and collapse but she'd only been able to check on Christopher once since they'd arrived. She needed to find him first, then she could relax.

Wading into the crowd, she searched for him. The task seemed impossible. A lot of people had shown up in the past few hours and there were even more arrivals pouring into the gates as she walked about. Just as she was thinking of giving up, Christopher materialized at her elbow.

"Hey, Mom..." He seemed in a much better mood, his earlier surliness a distant memory.

"Hey, yourself," she answered with a smile and a secret sigh of relief. "Are you having any fun or is this as terminally boring as you thought it would be?''

''It's kinda interesting,'' he said, surprising her once more. ''I've seen where the cops work and where they train and stuff....'' He turned slightly and pointed over his shoulder. ''Back there, they even have a shooting range. In a few minutes they're gonna show off some of the weapons they use. Wanna go?''

''Weapons? You mean with guns?''

Christopher rolled his eyes. ''Yesss, Mom, guns! Whaddaya think they use to get the bad guys? Bows and arrows?''

She'd asked the question to gain some time—she barely heard her son's smart-aleck reply. There was only one person who would be running *that* operation, and she wasn't really sure she wanted to see him in action. Ryan Lukas was scary enough just standing still and saying nothing. What would he look like with a gun in his hand?

''C'mon, Mom,'' Christopher urged. ''I wanna see, but they aren't lettin' kids in by themselves. Come with me...please?''

She looked down and into Chris's excited eyes. It was the first time in weeks she'd actually seen him interested in something other than giving her a hard time. She couldn't refuse. ''Okay,'' she said, throwing up her hands. ''You lead the way, I'll follow.''

He took off so fast she had trouble keeping up

with him. In just a few short minutes they were at the rear of the facility. People were being funneled into a cordoned area, passing by a uniformed officer first, a man Maria didn't recognize. He smiled at them both in a friendly way and waved them through. Christopher pushed into the throng to head for the front, Maria apologizing for him as she dogged his steps. They came to the edge of the roped-in crowd where Ryan Lukas was already speaking.

His voice was low and steady. Maria might have had to strain to hear him except everyone around her was completely quiet. They were focused on the sniper, she realized at once, and when she followed their stares, she understood why.

He was mesmerizing. His commanding presence made it impossible to look elsewhere. Tall and muscular, Ryan Lukas appeared as if he were ready for anything. But only part of his magnetism was physical; the rest came from the unspoken sense of purpose that seemed to radiate from an internal source of energy.

Even Christopher fell under Ryan's spell. Usually fidgeting, easily bored, her son leaned over the yellow ribbon and stared at the sniper with fascinated concentration.

"We didn't always have SWAT teams," Ryan was explaining as Maria began to listen. "The first one came into existence after an incident in Austin, Texas, in August of 1966. Does anyone here know what I'm talking about?"

The people around the rope shook their head. Maria had no idea herself. She'd been born that year.

"A man named Charles Joseph Whitman, an honor student at the University of Texas in Austin, climbed into the elevator of what was known as the Texas Tower. At that time, it was the tallest building in Austin—308 feet high. Whitman was twenty-five and he was wheeling a dolly that contained a footlocker. Inside the footlocker was a sawed-off shotgun, two handguns and three rifles. He also had hundreds of rounds of ammo, a container of gasoline, a gallon of water and his lunch."

Christopher hadn't moved an inch, and neither had Maria. She felt herself tense as Ryan began to speak once more.

"No one knew at the time, of course, but Whitman had already murdered three people—his mother, his wife and a receptionist inside the tower. When he reached the thirty-second floor of the building, he shot three more people, a woman and her two children who happened to be looking over the campus. He then set up his equipment. For an hour and a half he fired. He killed more than a dozen people and wounded over thirty."

The group of people standing around Maria and Christopher murmured quietly. She felt her stomach roll over at Ryan's calm description, but underneath his outer shell, she sensed a deep disquiet. He'd obviously told this story more than once, yet the details continued to disturb him.

"Officers from every law enforcement agency in the area responded—the Texas Highway Patrol, the Austin Police force, the Capitol Grounds Police Force, even the campus police—but they were helpless. They even tried to fire on him from a plane above. Nothing worked. The cops and medical people couldn't even rescue the wounded or dying. Finally, two officers from the Austin police department gained entry by using a tunnel located underneath the tower. Once inside they climbed up. Whitman spotted them when they came out to the observation deck and shot at them. They returned fire and wounded him. He continued to shoot until they killed him." He paused and took a breath. "Some people believe this was when the need for a SWAT team—Special Weapons and Tactics—was born."

Maria blinked then glanced down at Christopher. He was completely enthralled, and she felt uneasiness brush over her.

"The tools of the SWAT team are just one of the things that set them apart, allowing them to disable people like Charles Whitman," Ryan continued. "Today I'm going to show you a few of the guns. We won't be firing them, of course, but you can see what they look like and how they work...."

As he brought out a variety of wicked-looking weapons Maria suddenly wanted to pull her son away from the gleaming barrels and turn and run. Just as quickly, though, she realized she was being silly. Guns didn't create violence on their own. Maybe it was good for Chris to realize how carefully they needed to be handled. Ryan's large hands wrapped around the grips comfortably, she saw, but still he was treating them with a great deal of respect.

In the end, she stayed where she was and let Christopher listen to it all. When Ryan finished and the crowd began to disperse, she moved away as well, but Christopher tugged her back.

"Mom, I saw him earlier, but I didn't know who he was then." He tilted his head toward Ryan and spoke in a low, almost confidential voice. "He was on the path out back. He seemed sick, but he looks okay now, doesn't he?"

Maria's attention focused at once. "You saw Lieutenant Lukas? And he looked sick?"

Christopher nodded importantly. "He was standing on the path all by himself. I thought he wanted to puke or something but when I asked him if he was okay, he said he was."

Maria started to reply but Ryan had already crossed the patch of ground between where he'd been lecturing and the roped-off area where she and Chris stood. She fell silent. Christopher's eyes grew huge as he took in the tall man who now addressed his mother.

"Are you interested in weapons, Dr. Worley?"

Maria's pulse surged unexpectedly. She wasn't too sure why she had the strange reaction, but she *was* sure she didn't like it. "Not really," she replied coolly, "but my son wanted to see." She turned to Christopher and reluctantly made the introductions. He immediately put on an air of indifference and shook Ryan's hand with conscientious disregard.

Ryan didn't return the casual attitude. He studied Christopher carefully. "I think we saw each other earlier, didn't we?"

Christopher shrugged.

"Did you enjoy the demonstration?"

"It was okay."

"There's a lot of information about the team on our Web site if you want to know more. I'm in charge of maintaining it. I've posted some photos and other material about our weapons and the War Wagon, too. You might want to check it out sometime."

From the pocket of his black T-shirt, Ryan took out a small notebook and scribbled something on it. From her upside down advantage all Maria could read was "www..." Ryan ripped off the page and handed it to Christopher who stuffed the paper into his pocket and mumbled a quick thanks.

Before Maria could add her own thank-you, someone called out Christopher's name. He raised his head and she followed his glance. A group of his school buddies stood by the other end of the fence, snickering and trying to act cool. Pretending he hadn't been caught talking to some adults, Christopher sent them a nonchalant wave, then he glanced askance at Marla, his brown eyes begging her not to embarrass him.

"Go ahead," she said. "But meet me back at the stand in fifteen minutes, no longer."

He took off without a backward glance.

"How old is he?"

Ryan's question took her by surprise. She wouldn't have thought him interested in children, but she didn't know why. She decided not to say anything about Christopher's revelation and see where the conversation went.

"Christopher's fourteen." She gave Ryan a wry smile. "It's a difficult age."

"Does his dad live around here?"

She started to ask how he knew she was divorced, then she remembered. During their first session he'd brought up that topic, asking her if she did marriage counseling. "He lives in Pensacola. They don't see much of one another, I'm afraid. When he left me, he left Christopher, too."

Ryan turned his dark gaze on her. She could feel the intensity of it as he stared at her. "So you're on your own with him then?"

His voice held a hint of something. She glanced up to see if she could figure out what by looking at him. She couldn't.

"Yes. I'm on my own. Reed isn't interested in helping raise his son."

"Well, you *are* the expert, right?"

They'd been having an almost normal conversation; Maria wasn't prepared for the sharply spoken question. "I'm a therapist, Lieutenant, not a miracle worker. I can't give a boy his father no matter how badly he might need him. I can only be his mother."

"And that isn't enough." The words were spoken flatly.

Again, she heard an echo of the past. After a second's thought, she risked a question. "You grew up without a dad?"

"My father was a cop. He was killed during a robbery when I was ten years old. My mom raised me and three sisters on the salary of a secretary."

"That must have been hard," she said softly.

"He was my hero." His profile was granitelike, almost as hard as his voice. "I worshiped him and then he was gone."

The simple words told her everything she needed to know. How hard it must have been for him to fall in love with his wife. How much he must have suffered when he'd lost his heart the second time. The shell he'd erected to protect himself was almost impenetrable—it had to be, she saw now.

"I'm sorry."

Her reply seemed to jar him. He shook his head slightly and seemed to step back into the present. "There's nothing to be sorry about. When you've got a cop in the family, it comes with the deal. Death is part of the package."

"Not for a ten-year-old."

Their eyes met for half a heartbeat, then he

glanced away once more. When he faced her again, a moment later, his gaze was so distant she felt a chill ripple down her spine.

"The week before last, on Tuesday afternoon, what was your son doing?"

It took Maria a second to understand. "Tuesday? I—I don't know. Why do you ask?"

"You don't know where he was in the afternoon? After he got out of school?"

"He was at home. He's supposed to call me when he gets there, and I'm sure he actually did that day. He was…well, he was grounded a couple of weeks ago, for something he'd done at school. For the time being, he's not allowed to go anywhere but straight home." Her voice came out more defensively than she meant it to, but the way he asked the question made her react automatically. "I had a meeting after work and got home about five. Why do you ask?" she repeated.

"I saw him—" he paused for a second then finished "—somewhere he shouldn't have been."

Maria felt a jolt all mothers dread. "Where?"

"At a SWAT situation on the outskirts of town. The team was called out to an industrial park where there had been a shooting. A teenager was arrested for taking potshots at a security guard with an air pistol."

"Oh, no…was anyone hurt?"

"No."

Her mouth went dry. "The kid—what was his name?"

"I can't tell you that."

His answer made her angry even though she understood. "Well, what on earth makes you think you saw Christopher there?"

"I saw a kid with a blue backpack and a black baseball cap hanging around the building. He was just about Christopher's size."

She felt her heart ease, her pulse begin to slow. "There are a hundred kids in Destin with blue backpacks and black caps. How on earth could you be sure you saw him?"

"I'm not sure." He reached into his back pocket and removed a folded piece of paper. Smoothing it out, he turned it so she could see. "But this was found at the crime scene. Does it look familiar?"

Maria stared at the drawing, disbelief rendering her silent. Slowly she reached up for the paper. It was a copy, she saw, the original obviously locked up as evidence.

He released the sketch as her fingers took hold. She brought it closer even though she didn't need to—she'd seen the design a thousand times. Had a particular rendition framed and matted, hanging behind her desk. That was why he recognized it, she realized abruptly. He'd seen the pen-and-ink version when he'd been in her office.

"Did your son draw that?"

She wanted to lie, but she couldn't. Anything was

possible with Chris, and to deny what might be the truth would make her look like one of the struggling parents she saw all the time in her own office, denial their only coping technique.

"It looks like one of his," she admitted. "I—I'm not sure."

"Well, you better get sure," he said bluntly. "A Destin cop is going to find your son next week and ask him the same question. And he won't leave until he gets an answer."

CHAPTER FIVE

MARIA WORLEY'S brown eyes took on a different hue as he spoke. A glimmer of green entered their depths then quickly disappeared.

"I'll give him the same answer I'm giving you. Christopher would not be involved with something like that. He—he just wouldn't."

"Then how do you explain the drawing?"

"I'm sure there's a perfectly acceptable reason it was there that doesn't involve his presence." She looked down at the stylized bird as if she wished it could answer Ryan's question. "Maybe Chris gave it to the other kid and that kid dropped it."

Despite her words, her expression turned worried, and Ryan felt an unexpected flash of sympathy. She was less sure than she sounded. How many times had he put that same look on his own mother's face when he'd been a kid? He blinked the thought away.

"Well, I hope you're right," he replied, "because if he was there, he's hanging out with the wrong crowd."

"I'll discuss this with him," she said grimly. "Thank you for your help."

She walked away, her back straight and her

shoulders—those white, bare shoulders—stiff with an emotion Ryan could only wonder about. He'd debated with himself for days whether or not to say anything to her. He had no business sticking his nose into her life, but meeting the boy had made up his mind. The youngster's eyes had held the same confusion Ryan had felt at that age. He'd *had* to do something.

He watched until the crowd swallowed Maria, then he turned and went the opposite way. Earlier in the day he'd asked himself what in hell Maria Worley was doing to him. Now he knew he'd asked the wrong question.... He should have wondered just what in the hell was he doing himself?

MARIA HELD herself in check until the end of the afternoon. It wasn't easy, but she managed because she didn't want to create a scene anywhere near Ryan Lukas. She wasn't sure if that was because her ego was involved—or because she halfway thought he might want to set Christopher straight himself. For whatever reason, she kept quiet until she pulled into the driveway, then she couldn't stand it another minute. She turned to Christopher as he started to climb out of the car.

"Just a minute." She reached out and put her hand on his arm. "I want to talk to you about something."

He immediately put on what she thought of as his cornered-animal look.

"What?" he asked suspiciously.

"I heard something this afternoon that really has me worried." As she spoke she reached into her pocket and removed the drawing Ryan had given her. Unfolding it just as he had, she held it up for her son to see. "Is this yours?"

His face cleared. "Yeah, it's mine. Nobody draws that but me. You know that, Mom...."

"Then I want to know why this was found at the industrial park out on the edge of town. The park where a SWAT incident took place."

As she spoke, she watched him closely. Analyzing your own flesh and blood was not always a good idea, but she *was* the expert, right?

His expression ran the gamut from scared to defiant to confused. He didn't say a word, but he didn't have to. Her heart sank, but she continued. "A kid was arrested for shooting at someone with an air pistol. I want to know why this picture was there."

"I don't know," he said finally. "It musta blown out there from school or something—"

"Blown out there? Christopher, that park is nowhere near your school. Paper does not 'blow' like that, trust me."

"Well, I don't know!" His voice edged into anger. "Maybe the trash truck went out there and it got caught in the blade thingie and then it—"

"Stop it." She glared at him and he fell silent. "Lieutenant Lukas saw a kid with a blue backpack and a black cap out there. Was it you, Christopher? Tell me the truth. Right now.''

''No.'' He glared back. ''I wasn't there, okay? I don't know who in the hell he saw but it wasn't me—'' He stopped suddenly, the curse word filling the empty air between them. Maria stared at him and felt something twist inside her. They'd had their arguments before but he'd never used that kind of language while talking to her. She knew he probably talked like that with his friends, but he hadn't with her. All at once he looked as if he hadn't wanted to cross the line, either.

''I—I wasn't there, okay?'' He swung his head around to look out the window on his side of the car. ''I wasn't there.''

In the quiet stillness of the early evening, Maria looked at the back of her son's head and wondered how they'd reached this point. She was fairly certain he was lying, but what could she do about it?

''Was it Jason?'' She named the boy before she could stop herself. A few years older than Christopher, the kid was trouble. Maria had overheard the two of them talking one day and decided she didn't want Chris being friends with him. He had some serious problems. Just to make sure, she'd gotten his phone number and talked to his mother before telling Christopher how she felt. Unfortunately, the mother had confirmed Maria's first opinion. There was no supervision in the home; the woman wasn't interested in anything but herself and her son was suffering because of it.

"Lieutenant Lukas couldn't tell me the name of the boy that was arrested. Did you give this to Jason? Did he leave it out there?"

Chris spoke to the window. "I don't know."

"Well, you'd better think about it some more because I may not be the only one asking you questions about this, Chris."

He turned and glared. "What do you mean?"

"Lieutenant Lukas is the one who found this drawing. He said an officer is probably going to want to talk to you about it."

He didn't react at all to her pronouncement, and Maria knew she'd hit a brick wall. "Can I go now?" he finally asked.

She nodded wearily and Christopher shot out of the car. As she watched him round the corner of the house, she shook her head in disgust.

Maybe the trash truck went out there and it got caught in the blade thingie....

Did he really think she was that big of an idiot?

With a quiet curse, she leaned over and rested her head against the padded steering wheel. The fake leather was hot and she stuck to it. Her father and mother, now both retired, had been doctors. Her father, a neurologist, her mother a pediatrician. Maria had known better as a kid than to try to con them. Until she was almost eighteen, she'd really thought they had ESP. Controlling and overprotective, they'd driven her nuts. Somehow they'd always seemed to know when she was lying, always known when she'd done something she shouldn't have. Her mother had told her that more than once. *"I know when you're lying to me, Maria, so don't you even try...."*

But Christopher knew she was human. He'd heard Reed point that fact out so often there was no way now she could convince him otherwise. He knew her flaws.

She wished there weren't so many.

MARIA THOUGHT about Ryan Lukas's revelation all day Sunday and by Monday she had gone through fifteen different scenarios. Only one conclusion remained clear; Ryan had gone out on a limb to tell her what he suspected about Chris. When she stopped to think about his actions, she couldn't come up with a reason for them, though. Ryan had made it more than clear he resented her. Why help her out like this?

She didn't have an answer. Finally, after her first session and before her second one, she picked up the phone and called Lena.

They talked a bit about the rally as Maria tried to decide how to ask Lena about the situation with Chris—and not really ask—when Lena spoke up first.

"So...what's up? I get the feeling this isn't just a friendly little call."

"You're right," Maria answered in what she hoped was a casual voice. "I was wondering if you'd ever asked the juvenile guys about those friends of Chris's I mentioned." She twisted the telephone cord nervously. "You said you'd ask them when we talked about Christopher at Angel's Attic."

"Oh, man, I completely forgot to tell you. I'm sorry, Maria. I did ask the juvie squad and they hadn't heard of any of the kids whose names you gave me, I guess they're just your ordinary obnoxious kids and not juvenile delinquents! I should have told you on Saturday."

"I was worried about the boy who was arrested for taking potshots out at the industrial complex...."

"His name wasn't on the list."

Maria let out a huge sigh but before she could feel too relieved, Lena continued, "Ryan showed me the drawing, though. Do you think it's possible Chris was at that scene? Could he be friends with that boy and you not know it?"

"I quizzed him about it Saturday evening, Lena. He swears he wasn't there, but..."

"But you aren't sure you believe him."

Caught between telling the truth and defending her son, Maria picked what she hoped was safe ground. "I'm sure he couldn't have had anything to do with this shooting, Lena, but I guess it's possible. Guns and Christopher, though... I just can't see him having anything to do with that sort of trouble. I really can't.''

''I understand. I'll pass that on to the investigating officer, but he may give you a call about it.''

''Give me his name,'' Maria responded. ''I want to make sure we talk, regardless.''

They chatted a bit more then said goodbye. As Maria hung up the phone, all she could remember was Christopher's face as he'd watched Ryan give his lecture that weekend. Her son *had* been fascinated by the weapons in the tall man's hands.

With fingers that trembled, she punched out the police department's number and asked for the officer Lena had just mentioned. The conversation was quick and pointless. The man couldn't really tell her any more than Lena and Ryan had. No one could say—for sure—whether or not Christopher had been present, but they all suspected he had been. The officer wanted to come out and talk to Chris, one way or the other, and Maria agreed, setting a time. If nothing else, maybe it'd scare some sense into her son.

She ended the call, a sudden overwhelming weariness hitting her hard. No matter what she did or how hard she tried, it seemed like she wasn't doing enough. She wrapped her arms around her chest and stared out her office window.

IT WAS SMOKY and crowded in A.J.'s for a Wednesday evening. Ryan made his way through the confused tourists who'd wandered into the tavern by mistake and went to the back, where the cops hung out. The place was little more than a shack, hanging on to the edge of the docks with a precarious grip, the peeling paint and falling-down deck untouched for years. The last hurricane had taken the southern wall and half the roof. A.J. had left most of the damage untouched and told everyone he was now the owner of an al fresco establishment. Heading to the bar, Ryan ordered a beer then turned to see who was in the crowd.

All the usual suspects, he noted, including Diane St. Cloud. He ducked his head but he wasn't fast enough. The vice cop saw him. She made her way through the throng to where he stood.

"Hey there, Lukas." She had a Cuba Libre in her hand and it probably wasn't her first. Before he and Ginny had gotten engaged, he'd dated Diane a bit, the relationship a rocky one. He wasn't too sure why, but they hadn't clicked and they'd each been too stubborn to quit first. Since Ginny's death, though, Diane had been kind to Ryan every time their paths had crossed.

"Hello, Diane," he said. "How's it going?"

"I can't complain." She stared at him. Her dark-green eyes seemed to glow in the low lights of the bar and he remembered how they'd looked at him from the other side of his bed. "How are you?"

People asked him that question all the time, but with Diane he knew she really wanted to know. She actually cared…and that knowledge made him even more uncomfortable.

"I'm fine," he lied. "Just fine. Couldn't be better."

"That's not what I understand." She had a cigarette in her other hand and she took a deep drag, staring at him through the smoke. "I heard you're seeing the doc."

Ryan turned sharply and stared at the woman. "Who told you that?"

"Nobody told me." She tapped the tip of the cigarette against the bar and spoke quietly. "I saw you coming out of her building the other day. I happened to be headed there myself."

The admission stopped Ryan cold. He and Diane hadn't been the perfect match but she was one of the steadiest cops he knew; an officer he'd want to back him up any day of the week. "I didn't know you were seeing Dr. Worley," he said carefully.

She looked him straight in the eye. "I've been having some problems. You heard about it, I'm sure.…"

He nodded but said nothing. The year before, Diane's partner had been killed. She'd shot the man who'd done it.

"Maria Worley's good, isn't she?"

"I wouldn't know," Ryan replied.

She looked at him in surprise. "But aren't you—"

"I had an appointment, that's all."

They stared at each other for a second; Diane looked away first. She wrapped her hands around her drink and spoke quietly. "You should talk to her, Ryan. She could help you."

"I don't need any."

"I didn't think I did, either," she said. "But I was wrong, and so are you."

His voice went tight with warning. "I'm fine."

She waited a beat, then nodded and drained her drink, setting the empty glass on the bar. "I guess I'll head for home, then."

"See ya around."

She started to walk away, but she stopped and came back to put her hand on his arm. Her nails were long and painted a red so deep it almost looked black. Hooker nails, she'd always called them.

"Why don't you come home with me tonight, Ryan?" she said unexpectedly. "I'll cook you a homemade dinner. We can talk. You can stay the night if you want."

For longer than he would have thought, Ryan was unexpectedly tempted. Ginny had been gone eighteen months, and the idea of spending a night in a woman's arms was almost more than he could resist. He could only give her his body, nothing more, but Diane wouldn't want anything in return, wouldn't *expect* anything in return. She was that kind of woman—too generous with her heart. But before he could answer, he thought of Maria Worley. Of her damned white shoulders and her gleaming dark hair and her sparkling brown eyes. The image brought with it an instant sweep of guilt that he didn't understand. The idea of sleeping with Diane hadn't made him feel that way. What did that mean?

Diane read his reply in his eyes before he could speak. She raised one crimson-tipped finger and laid it across his mouth as if she didn't want him to say the words.

"Maybe another time," she said quietly.

He nodded slowly. "Maybe…"

A second later she left and Ryan turned back to his beer. He did so with a vague feeling of confusion. But Lena appeared at his elbow, giving him no time to sort out his feelings. She held a can of cola—the only thing most of the SWAT team could order since they were always on call.

"That was close." She nodded in the direction Diane had taken. "I thought she had you there for a minute."

"Mind your own business."

"Your business *is* my business," she shot back. "I'm your boss, remember?"

"How could I forget?"

She snorted lightly. "You can't, so don't even try. That's why I'm here, as a matter of fact."

He shook his head and pointed to the amber bottle sweating on the bar. "Lena, all I want is a beer and a little peace and quiet. What do you need with me that can't wait until tomorrow?"

"Tomorrow is Thursday," she answered. "I want to make sure you know that."

"Thursday, right. I got it." He picked up the bottle.

"You have an appointment with Dr. Worley."

He took a long sip from the drink and said nothing.

"You've got to be there. No excuses this time."

He stayed quiet.

"Do you hear me?"

He continued to stare into the mirror behind the bar. "Loud and clear."

"Good," she answered, "because if you don't show up, I'm going to have a real problem with—"

Her words were suddenly drowned out by the sound of a dozen or so beepers going off at once. Most of the men and half of the women reached for their waists. A united groan went up from what seemed like every throat but Ryan's. He stayed perfectly still.

Lena didn't bother to finish what she'd been about to say. She grabbed her purse, yelled for Bradley Thompson, her second in command, then strode from the bar without looking back. Ryan's gaze remained where it had been—on the bottles lining the counter above the mirrored back wall. He drained his beer and ordered another.

Thursday and Maria Worley. Thursday and Maria Worley. He tried to flush the words, but they wouldn't go away. Sitting in the now empty bar, he felt his life slip a little bit more out of control.

WEDNESDAY EVENING Maria drove Christopher to the karate center on the outskirts of Destin. Unlike the other parents who dropped off their kids then left, Maria always stayed and watched. Tonight though, she saw him into the building then got back in her car and headed east for Seaside. She'd called Jackson the day before and told him she wanted to see him. She needed to talk to him in person and she wanted to do it alone.

Chris had met with the juvenile officer Saturday morning. He'd denied everything and insisted he'd been nowhere near the warehouse, but underneath his coolness, he'd been rattled. Seeing his reaction, she'd been angry, but she'd also wanted to wrap her arms around him and protect him. In the end, all she could do was pray that an interview with a cop would make a difference.

It did. After the meeting, Chris was more sullen and uncommunicative than ever before. She was about to pull her hair out.

And tomorrow was Thursday.

She'd tried not to dwell on that fact, but as Thursday had grown closer, the reality began to make itself felt. Ryan Lukas was supposed to be in her office tomorrow at 3:00 p.m. Because she'd been so upset with Chris, she'd had little time to think of the man since Saturday but he would slip into her mind given the slightest chance. With the empty road ahead of her, she found him in her thoughts once again.

But she pushed him away.

He was a patient, for crying out loud. She didn't need to be wondering about him constantly. Tomorrow afternoon would be the time to think about him. When he was in her office and the city was paying her to concentrate on him.

Twenty minutes later, she pulled up outside Powell's Antiques. Jackson was sitting outside by the front door on a refurbished church pew. Maria closed her car door behind her and grinned. "You look like an escapee. Did Richard cut you loose for a bit?"

"I broke a vase," he said morosely. "Richard screamed and I ran out."

Maria sat down beside him on the polished wood. The bench was warm from the evening sun and the rich patina gleamed. "You broke a vase, eh? Was it a Freudian slip?"

Jackson laughed at her quip. "Probably so," he admitted when he finished chuckling. "It got me out of there, didn't it?"

"I wish I could do something that simple and solve all my problems," she said. Her eyes filled with tears. She had to blink hard to keep them in place.

Jackson's expression immediately went serious. "Tell me what's going on."

She talked for half an hour, explaining everything as completely as she could. Saturday with Christopher. The drawing Ryan had found. The interview between her son and the cop. She was growing more and more certain Chris was lying to her.

"What's your gut say?" Jackson asked when she finished. "Do you think Chris was out there?"

"I talked to the cop. I talked to Lena. I even asked my neighbor if she saw Chris leave the house that day. No one could say anything for sure, but I have to admit, I'm beginning to wonder."

"Are you going to punish him?"

"He's grounded right now as it is," she said. "I don't want to do anything else without being sure, but the officer who interviewed Chris couldn't shake him. I could see Chris was upset, though." She glanced up, confusion swamping her. "I don't want him hanging around with kids like that, Jackson. This is dangerous stuff."

"The cop, the one who brought you the drawing—Lukas—he's sure it was Chris?"

"He sounded as if he wanted to be sure."

"What do you mean?"

She stared out across the parking lot. On the other side of the highway, there were six perfect cabins, painted in various pastel shades. They were always rented, the upscale neighborhood a draw for people from across the world. They faced the ocean and came complete with a butler.

"It's typical transference of aggression and disassociation of the situation by substitution," she replied. "His life isn't perfect but mine is worse. If he can find something wrong with—"

"Oh, good grief, Maria, cut the clinical bullshit. Tell me the real reason."

She glanced sideways at Jackson. "That is the real answer."

"I don't think so."

"Well, what do you think *is* the real answer?"

"I think it's quite possible the man might be trying to help you. He obviously had a tough childhood himself and maybe he sees something in Christopher that makes him want to do something." He leaned closer to her. "You might want to think about this, Maria. This cop needs someone to care about right now. And Chris needs a man in his life. It could work to your advantage."

Maria felt a ripple of shock. "Ryan is a client. I hope you aren't suggesting I let Chris get to know him personally."

"If it would help both of them, why not?"

"You know why not. It's unethical for a therapist and a patient to be personally involved."

"Chris and Ryan Lukas aren't therapist and patient. You and Lieutenant Lukas are. As long as there's no personal interaction between the two of you, you'd be fine. You'd just need to be careful and make sure that doesn't happen."

"I understand what you're saying." She bit her bottom lip, her hair swinging back and forth in the evening breeze. "But I can't let Christopher get close to this man. No way."

He shrugged. "It's your call, you're the doctor. I have to say something, though...."

She held her breath. When Jackson started a sentence that way, it usually meant one thing. That she wouldn't like what he was about to tell her.

"You're not focused on the issue, Maria. Your brain is going in two different directions and that's why you can't decide what to do with your son."

"Two different directions?"

"When you have a problem and we discuss it, you're like a magnifying glass. You point that mind of yours toward the issue and you don't let up until you arrive at an answer. You're not doing that this time. You seem...I don't know, almost distracted."

"I'm not thinking of anything else," she protested.

He looked as if he didn't want to accept her answer, but he didn't press the issue. They talked for a bit more, then glancing at her watch, Maria realized she had to leave. Standing up, she leaned over and kissed her friend on the cheek. "Thanks for listening."

He put his hands on her shoulders. "You're welcome, sweetheart. I'm always full of advice, you know that. It may not be what you want to hear, but I'll tell you anyway."

All the way to town she considered Jackson's words, but she couldn't see the situation any differently. Chris was her responsibility and she had to be there for him. And it was the same for Ryan Lukas. His mental well-being was in her hands as well. The two of them couldn't help each other. That went against everything she stood for.

She picked up Christopher then drove home, but as she pulled into her driveway, she started to wonder about Jackson's other point. She'd denied what he'd said, but deep down she suspected he was right. She *was* distracted and she was pretty sure she knew why. Ryan hadn't even come in for a full session yet and she couldn't get him out of her mind. There was something deeply compelling about the man. She had realized that on Saturday but had managed not to accept the fact until this very moment. As usual, Jackson had forced her to open her eyes.

Ryan Lukas wasn't someone she wanted to help. He was someone she wanted to know.

CHAPTER SIX

IT'D ALREADY BEEN a hectic morning when Sher put the call through early Thursday. Just before he'd gotten on the bus at seven, Chris had informed her of his science project. The one that was due tomorrow. Before coming into the office, Maria had had to make a run to the hobby store for a magnet and then the art supply place for cardboard. She'd raced into the office with two minutes to spare before her first session. Now this. "It's the Hunk," the receptionist announced. "He's on line one."

Maria picked up her phone and answered as she always did even though her mouth had turned dry at Sher's words. "This is Dr. Worley."

"This is Ryan Lukas. Lieutenant Lukas," he repeated as if she needed clarification.

"Yes, Lieutenant. What can I do for you?"

"My appointment this afternoon—the one at 3 p.m.?"

"Yes?"

"I'd like to reschedule for tomorrow. And I want to meet somewhere other than your office."

She had known he would come up with something, but this twist wasn't one she'd anticipated.

Once again, he'd managed to surprise her. "Is there a problem with my office?"

"No."

She waited for him to elaborate but he didn't. "Why do you want to meet somewhere else?" she asked as the silence stretched out.

"I can't go into it right now. Can you do it or not?"

Her mind danced over the possibilities but settled on the most obvious, at least to her. If he came to her office, it was tantamount to admitting he had a problem. Relocating the session was another form of denial, another way for him to control the situation. On the other hand, if she did agree to meet him somewhere else, he'd have to start talking.

"It's not something I normally do," she said thoughtfully, "but I guess I could arrange it. Where would you like to meet?"

It took him a moment to answer. In that split second she realized he'd been counting on her refusal. Then he'd be relieved of the responsibility.

"How about The Crab Shack," he countered. "At seven? I'll buy you a drink."

A second challenge, she realized. A drink instead of a session.

She processed what that meant. If she was going to be out that late, she'd have to find a sitter. Maybe she could call Mrs. Lowe. Maria's elderly neighbor had often sat with Chris in the past. It would be worth it, though, to make progress with Ryan. After a heartbeat of hesitation, she called his bluff. "All right," she answered. "I'll see you at 7:00 p.m. tomorrow. At The Crab Shack."

She hung up the phone and instantly began to have second thoughts. Therapists sometimes did off-site work, but a meeting in a bar? That was definitely on the borderline between acceptable and questionable. What did she think she was doing? Better yet, what did he think *he* was doing? What if someone saw them and assumed the wrong thing? What if *Ryan* assumed the wrong thing? What if...

With a mental shake, she stopped buying trouble. She was meeting Ryan in an unorthodox setting but she was still the doctor. This was not a date, for heaven's sake. He was a client, a man she needed to help. She would deal with her attraction to him like she dealt with everything. Efficiently, professionally, quickly.

She spent the rest of the day worrying about her decision but remained unsure of how else she could have handled the problem. By five, when she got home and opened the front door, she had exhausted herself, emotionally and physically. Even if she'd been in perfect form, though, she couldn't have handled the sight that greeted her.

Christopher and four other boys were sprawled across the living room floor. Surrounded by a pile of chip bags and spilled popcorn, giggling and making noise, they didn't notice her until it was too late.

Too late to pick up the empty bags. Too late to

clean up the room. Too late to hide the can of beer Christopher clutched.

Silence descended when they saw her. Maria's reeling brain dredged up a memory she'd thought long gone. Just after she'd allowed Chris to play stickball at the end of the street without supervision, she'd been washing the dishes when she'd heard a horrible sound. The screech of a car horn, then tires squealing against slick pavement and finally the dull thud of a fender hitting something. She'd dropped the plate she'd been scrubbing—it shattered—and run out the door. The driver, dazed and disoriented, had stumbled from the car to stare at the magnolia tree he'd crashed into, going around the corner too fast. Her legs had barely carried to where Chris stood, her fright too overwhelming to contain as she'd wrapped her arms around him. It was the first time she'd realized she couldn't always protect him.

This was the second.

After a very long moment, she reclaimed her voice, and her brain, from the shock which had stolen them both. She kept her words level and calm. "What's going on here, Christopher?"

He scrambled to his feet, a bit unsteadily. "We were just…just having some fun, Mom. That's all." One of the boys laughed softly and another one poked him in the ribs. They both fell silent as her eyes raked over them. They'd obviously been passing the can around, sharing the drink.

"Where did you get the beer?"

No one said anything, but the boy all the way to the right, a neighborhood kid, looked down quickly. The sudden movement caught her eye. "Travis?" Her voice sharpened. "Did you bring that beer over here?"

He refused to look at her.

"Mom, it's not his fault, c'mon—"

"I wasn't speaking to you." Her eyes drilled Christopher's. "Sit down and be quiet."

He started to answer and she held up her hand. "Not a word."

Something in her voice penetrated the fuzzy layer of fog surrounding his brain. He dropped to the carpet and she turned back to the other boy. "Well? I'm waiting for an answer."

He mumbled a frightened, "Yes, ma'am." She felt a tiny tremor of relief that at least Christopher hadn't gotten it himself before realizing how shallow that thought was. Chris might not have obtained the beer, but what did that matter? She couldn't put the whole blame on Travis no matter how hard she wanted to.

One by one she got their phone numbers. One by one she either walked them home or escorted them to the cars of their equally upset parents. She tried to explain, but there wasn't much she could say. She closed the door an hour later and turned to her son. He sat on the floor, his head hanging down.

She didn't know where to start. She simply blurted out the first thing that came into her mind.

"What in the hell is going on with you, Christopher?"

He looked up at her and she couldn't believe the defiance in his eyes. "You weren't here," he said, as if that explained everything.

She felt her mouth drop open. "So you thought it'd be a good idea to drink? Just because I wasn't here to stop you?"

"The other guys' moms were home. We had to meet somewhere."

Maria sat down in the recliner. A crunching sound accompanied the move. She shifted slightly and pulled out a deflated bag of toasted corn chips. Dropping the sack to the floor where it joined six others, she shook her head. "I don't believe this," she said to herself. "I don't believe it."

She lifted her head and stared across the room at her son. "Christopher, have you done this before? I mean...do you drink?"

"Oh, God, Mom...c'mon—"

"No!" She screamed suddenly, losing her composure completely as she jumped to her feet. "Do you? Do you drink? You answer me right now, Christopher Worley, and you tell me the truth or you'll regret it!"

"No, Mom! I promise! I—I don't drink. Th-this is the first time." His brown eyes were the size of quarters. He'd seen her mad, he'd seen her upset, but he'd never seen her like this. Out of control. "Tr-Travis said he was going to sneak one out and then he brought it over here and we just…we just opened the can and passed it around. That's all.''

His quavering voice had the same effect on her as her scream had had on him. She blinked and sat back down abruptly, her heart racing inside her chest. She'd had parents in her office who had told her sad tales of going nuts like this, and she'd always wondered why they didn't realize their actions only made the situation worse.

Now she understood.

She stared at her son through narrowed eyes, her hands gripping the arms of the chair.

''Are you telling me the truth?''

He nodded with fast, short dips of his head. ''I am, Mom. Really. We were just trying it out. You know, tasting it to see—''

She held up her hand. ''How many times have we talked about drugs?''

''Drugs?'' He actually looked confused. ''We weren't doing anything like that—''

''Christopher, alcohol *is* a drug. It's a legalized drug. People who are *mature* enough to decide for themselves can use it but not anyone else. And even then, they have consequences to face when they drink, too.''

''But you drink! I've seen you have wine or—''

''I'm thirty-five,'' she answered. ''I'm old enough to know how to handle it. You aren't.''

He stayed silent. There was nothing else he could do.

She didn't know what to do, either. A sick wave of wondering just where she'd gone so wrong hit her head-on. This was all her fault. If she was a better mother, he wouldn't act like this.

"I want this room cleaned up," she said at length. "When you've finished, come get me. We'll discuss what your punishment is going to be." She looked down at his bowed head. "I'm very disappointed in you, Chris. We've had our problems lately, but this is a big one. I don't understand why you're acting like this and I don't know what I'm going to do about it."

He looked up. There were tears in his eyes.

She strode from the room before he could see them in hers.

IT TOOK REED an hour to return her call. Maria paced the kitchen floor and checked the clock every ten minutes. But when the phone finally did ring, she immediately wished she hadn't called him. What had she thought he'd do?

"Everyone experiments," he said after she finished explaining.

"Everyone exper—" Maria held the receiver out from her ear and actually stared at it in disbelief. "He's fourteen years old, Reed. Fourteen years old! Are you nuts?"

"I was younger than that when I had my first sip. It's no big deal, Maria. You're acting crazy."

"You're the one who's crazy if you think this is

acceptable. You need to talk to him, Reed. Dammit to hell, he needs a father!''

''And he's got one! I just don't happen to live there anymore.''

''Reed, you never come see him, you never call him. He misses you. He doesn't have anyone to look up to or talk to.''

''He has you.''

''I'm not his father! He loves you, Reed. He needs you just as much as he needs me. Don't you even care? Doesn't this disturb you just a little bit?''

''Maria, look—I'm busy, okay? I've got clients I have to meet in half an hour and Sandy's coming over later this evening. I don't have time for one of your hysterical moments. Handle this on your own. It's not as big a deal as you're making it out to be.''

Without waiting for her to reply, he hung up. She stood with the buzzing phone in her hand for a moment, then very carefully she replaced the receiver in the cradle.

He didn't care. He'd never cared. Christopher was nothing to him, but an inconvenience. Reed's job and Sandy, his girlfriend of the week, were both more important to him than his son.

She was on her own.

She turned slowly to go back into the living room, then stopped. Christopher stood in the doorway. He'd heard everything.

''Did you call Dad?''

''Yes, I did. Your father needs to know what

you're doing, Christopher. He and I may be divorced, but he's still your dad. He'll always be your dad, no matter what.''

There were magnets on the refrigerator, souvenirs of places they'd visited during happier times. Christopher reached out and palmed one, a pink, plastic seagull from Miami. Without looking at her, he spoke. ''Is he coming over?''

''No.'' Her heart tilted at the anxiousness in his voice, a big chunk of her anger falling away. ''He's not coming over.''

For a second, he tossed the seagull from palm to palm then he closed his fingers around it. Tightly. ''Well, what did he say?''

She took a deep breath. Lying wasn't something she liked to do. ''He said he was very disappointed in you, too. He…he told me I should handle this the best way I could.''

''What are you going to do to me?''

Leaning against the back of the kitchen counter, she folded her arms and stared at him sternly. ''Do you remember when I decided to let you stay at home after school by yourself? It was two years ago, when you started junior high. Do you remember what I said?''

''I remember.''

''Tell me.''

''You told me I had to act right or it wouldn't last.''

His version of what she'd said lacked the details,

but the basic principle was there. "That's right," she said. "And do you remember what I said would happen if you didn't 'act right'?"

His expression changed swiftly into one of horror. "Mom—no! I'm fourteen! You can't do that! The guys would—"

"Christopher, I don't care what your friends will say. If you don't straighten up, I'm getting Mrs. Lowe over here. And she'll stay with you until I get home."

"I'm too old for a baby-sitter!"

"Then act as if you are," she demanded. "Straighten up and fly right, Christopher, or that's what's going to happen. One more slipup and she's going to be over here, full-time. Until then, you're already grounded, so there's only one thing I can think of to do and that's take away your electronics. No stereo. No television." She paused. "And no computer."

He tightened his fist even more and the seagull's wings cracked loudly. Nothing meant more to Chris than his IBM. He'd mowed lawns all last summer to buy it. She carefully monitored his time on the high-powered system—he got an hour a day on the Internet and no more—but he looked forward all day to that one hour.

"Mom, you can't do that! I need it for school. I need it for—"

His reaction only confirmed her resolve. "No," she said. "You don't need it. There are plenty of

kids who don't have a computer at home. You're
going to be one of them, at least until I see some
improvement in your attitude and your actions.''

"But summer's coming! What am I going to do
all day if I can't surf?''

"I'm sorry, Chris. I told you last time you got in
trouble that your actions had ramifications. Obviously you didn't believe me. Maybe this will help
you learn the lesson.''

He almost looked panicky. "Well, when can I get
it back?''

"I don't know the answer to that question right
now.'' She gripped her arms above her elbows as if
holding herself in. "But I can tell you this—you're
going to have to earn the privilege of having your
things returned. A minute at a time.''

"But I paid for that stuff. I bought it all. You
can't do this—''

"No arguing,'' she said in a steely voice. "As
long as you live here, you're under my control
whether you like it or not. If you choose not to play
by my rules, then you're going to suffer the consequences. Take the computer and put it in my bedroom. Right now.''

She turned away from him and looked out the
window over the sink. A purple dusk was falling
over the backyard and a breeze rippled the oleanders
by the fence. "Go on,'' she said when she didn't
hear him leave. "Move the equipment then go to
your room and shut the door.'' She dug her nails

into thc cdgc of thc countertop. "I'll bring you a sandwich and you can eat it in there."

MARIA WALKED into the small, seaside restaurant a few minutes after seven on Friday. Ryan rose when he saw her enter and continued to stand as she made her way to his table. She wore a dark-blue suit with a soft blouse underneath, her brown hair curling around her shoulders in waves of gleaming silk. She looked even more appealing than she had the last time he'd seen her, and another guilty struggle came over him. This was not of his doing, he told himself. It was talk to her or lose his job.

The reasoning—as sound as it was—rang hollow.

They stared at each other in silence for a few seconds then he moved to her side and pulled out a chair. When she sat down, he bent over to push the chair in, and something light and floral wafted up to him. He wanted to freeze the moment, to stand there and simply drink in the scent of a woman's perfume, but instead he sat down on the other side of the table and spoke stiffly. "Thank you for coming out here."

The waitress appeared at the edge of the table. Maria looked as though she'd like to order something stronger, but she settled for coffee.

When the uniformed woman disappeared around the corner, Maria answered him. "I don't normally conduct sessions outside my office. I'd like you to tell me why you didn't want to go there."

A shaft of late-afternoon sunlight fell on the table between them. It painted a stripe across her fingers and highlighted a tiny heart-shaped ring on her right hand. Ryan stared at the piece of jewelry and wondered if her husband had given it to her.

He'd assumed she would ask him that question, but the fact was, he wasn't even sure *why* he'd done what he had. He repeated the answer he'd rehearsed beforehand. "I had to meet the owner of the industrial park out here, by his business. He couldn't see me until after work, and I wouldn't have had the time to get there from your office."

"Is that your only reason?"

"Of course," he lied. "What else could it be?"

The waitress brought a mug of coffee and placed it on the table between them. Maria added milk and sugar before she spoke again. "Everything we do, we do for a reason, Lieutenant Lukas. Nothing is random."

"Nothing is random? Then I guess your calling me Lieutenant all the time means something, eh?"

A pale blush appeared on each of her cheeks. His question flustered her and he realized a second later that was exactly why he'd asked it.

"What would you like me to call you?"

"My name is Ryan," he answered. "That'll do."

She removed the spoon from her mug and placed it carefully on the table. "I'll call you Ryan if you'll do me a favor, as well."

"What is that?"

"Stop trying to fight me." She lifted her gaze. "I've gone the extra mile for you each way. It's time for you to reciprocate."

"Reciprocate?" His chest tightened. "Don't you mean spill my guts to you?"

"You see this situation as adversarial. It doesn't have to be. It *shouldn't* be. I'm here to help you."

"I think we've been over this before, Doctor. I don't need your help."

"You aren't going to have a job if we don't talk, Ryan. You need me," she said bluntly, "or you're not going back to work."

"Is that a threat?"

"No. It's a fact of life."

The muscles in his legs actually bunched. He wanted to stand up and walk away, but he didn't.

He puzzled over his inability to leave for a few minutes, then through the haze of his anger—at himself and at her—something began to register. Something about the way Maria held herself. She sat stiffly, not with her usual grace but with tension. Narrowing his eyes, he studied her face. Slowly, the details began to emerge. The shadows hanging in the hollows of her cheeks. The weary cast behind her eyes. The pain peeking through her expression. Something was wrong, and all at once he wanted to reach across the table and take her hands, to ask her what it was and to comfort her even when he knew he shouldn't. He settled for simply asking the question.

"You're upset about something, aren't you?" he asked quietly. "What happened? Is it Christopher?"

Her eyes flew to his. "How did you—"

"Cops have insight, too. It's not the sole domain of therapists, you know."

She seemed to draw back. "My personal life isn't what we're here to discuss. We're here to talk about you—"

He leaned closer and halved the distance between them, willing her to speak. "Just tell me," he said.

She sat still for a second, then picked up the spoon beside her mug. Toying with the handle, she turned her head and looked out at the ocean. She was debating with herself, he thought, weighing the relief she would feel to share her problems against the strict code of how she thought she *should* operate. He wasn't sure which side would win, and then she spoke, surprising him.

"It *is* Christopher," she said after a moment more. "I came home last night and found him drinking with some of his friends." She met Ryan's eyes. "He's too damn young to be doing that."

"What did you do?"

"I got hysterical. I called his father. Then I took away his computer and threatened him with a baby-sitter." She shrugged. "I'm trying to decide what else I can do short of chaining him to my ankle."

Ryan remembered the quick glimpse of her legs he'd gotten at the picnic. He spoke without thinking. "That would be punishment?"

She surprised him by laughing. "For my son? Absolutely. We used to get along, but lately…" She shook her head. "Let's just say he avoids any proximity to me as much as possible." Her expression went sober once more. "I'm at the end of my rope. I don't know what to do with him. I don't know how to make him behave any more. It seems like all I do is worry about him."

The words almost sounded familiar. How many times had Ryan heard his own mother say something similar? "What did his father say when you called him?"

"Nothing useful. He's more concerned about his job and his new girlfriend than the life he left behind. He doesn't care about us anymore." Her voice held a hint of bitterness. Was it just for her son, or for herself as well?

Ryan knew he shouldn't ask, but he had to. "Do you wish that he did?"

"For myself, absolutely not. When we divorced, we divorced. It's over between us. But I hate how he acts toward Chris. Half the time Reed doesn't even show up when it's his turn to take him for the day. I don't understand how you can treat your own kid that way, especially one as great as Christopher really is."

A crazy feeling of relief went over Ryan at her admission, then he immediately wondered about it. Why did he care if Maria Worley no longer had feelings for her ex? He concentrated on Chris. "So he misses his dad. I guess it doesn't take a Ph.D. to understand why he's doing what he's doing?''

"No, I'm afraid not. I'd say he's reacting exactly how I would expect a kid his age to react, but I do feel, in his case, it's a little more complicated.''

"How so?''

"I don't know. I'm having trouble putting my finger on it and that bothers me, too. I'm not handling the situation too well.''

"What would you tell a client to do who was having this problem? Say, a single mom?''

She answered almost automatically. Obviously this wasn't an unusual problem. "I'd tell her to make sure the lines of communication were open. Not to be too harsh, but firm and consistent. To keep him talking, as much as possible. I might also ask if she had a brother or uncle—someone the boy could relate to who might act as a substitute father figure.''

"Do you have someone like that?''

"I have two brothers but they both live in Atlanta. I don't get to see them very often. My father and mother live in Miami. They're retired, but they're so busy they hardly ever come down. Chris needs someone who could be here for him consistently.''

"What about a friend?''

"I actually do have a great friend who lives out in Seaside. Jackson Maxwell. He's a professional associate. He and Chris used to get along great but

Chris is as sullen with him now as he is with me.''
Her expression shifted a bit, but he couldn't read
the change.

"How good a friend is this guy?'' Ryan asked
carefully.

"We're very close,'' she said. "He and his partner, Richard Powell, have been friends of mine forever.''

It only took a second for Ryan to understand. He
felt something loosen inside him, then she spoke
again.

"It's different when it's your kid,'' she said
softly. "I know what to do, but I'm not doing it the
right way. That's what's so frustrating. I get upset
and start yelling and everything goes downhill from
there.''

"My mom did the same thing.''

"With you?''

He nodded. "I gave her an awfully hard time after my father died. She deserved better.''

"You were grieving.''

"But so was she. I didn't realize that until later,
of course. I was too wrapped up in my own life.''

"What did you do?''

"Everything I shouldn't. Broke windows,
skipped school, gave my teachers hell. Worse things
that we won't go into. I was mad as hell. My father
had died and I didn't understand why.''

He fell into silence. She sipped her coffee and
waited for more but he said nothing else. After a

second, she asked, "Do you have brothers and sisters?"

"I have a brother in Mobile. He's a defense attorney. We don't see eye to eye on too many things."

"What about your mother? Is she still alive?"

"Yes." He felt his lips narrow. "She lives in Sarasota Springs."

"Do you visit her often?"

"We're not close anymore. She remarried a few years ago. I don't get along with the man she chose."

"What about Ginny's parents? Do you ever see them?"

"They live out west. They haven't been here since the funeral. They wanted the service held at the church and I didn't. When they got here, I gave in."

"Tell me about it," she asked in a subdued voice. "Tell me about the service."

It was his turn to look out the window. He took a long time to stare at the churning waves. "I don't remember much about it, actually. I tuned the whole thing out. There were flowers, I know. Daisies. Those were her favorites and I picked them out. There was music." He smiled without thinking. "'Amazing Grace.' She had a friend named Grace, and we always teased her about her name. Ginny would sing the song sometimes. She had a terrific voice."

"How did you feel when you heard the song?"

He thought for a moment about his answer, then without any warning, just like at the park, Ryan felt something crack open inside him. It wasn't a pleasant feeling. He couldn't catch his breath.

Maria leaned closer, her intensity something he could almost feel as it reached toward him. She said nothing, but words weren't necessary.

He didn't want to answer, but he did. "It made me feel like shit," he whispered above the pain. "Like warmed-over shit. Then I got mad."

She looked at him with what seemed like approval and nodded slowly. Her eyes were warm in the dusky light, warm and comforting, and he blinked as he succumbed to their sweet darkness. Then the realization of what she'd done ripped through him. He felt the tear go up his spine then straight into his heart as it laid him bare.

She'd gotten him to talk. About his dead wife. About his still-fresh grief. About his screwed-up emotions.

CHAPTER SEVEN

MARIA WATCHED Ryan struggle. She felt sorry for him, the unexpected grief as much a surprise to her as it had obviously been to him. She hadn't imagined he would have a breakthrough so quickly, even one this small. Especially since she hadn't been trying to get him there.

After a second he spoke, his voice tense, his jaw locked with anger. "You're very good," he said from behind gritted teeth. "I was told that you are but I didn't realize how good."

"I'm not sure what you mean by that, Ryan. You're the one who worked through—"

He stood and glared down at her. "I don't like being manipulated."

"Manipulated?" She jumped up as well and held out her hands in defense. "That's not what happened here, Ryan. You expressed yourself and you weren't prepared for it. I didn't orchestrate that—"

"The hell you didn't! It's your job to do exactly that."

"Helping you deal with your emotions is what I'm here for, not—" Sensing the stares of the people around them, Maria stopped herself in midsentence. This wasn't supposed to be a debate. It was a conversation—and meant to be private, too.

Taking a deep breath, she put her fingers on Ryan's sleeve. Under her touch, his arm was rock hard. She made her voice soft, nonthreatening. "Therapy isn't always a pleasant experience, Ryan. Feelings erupt that are hard to handle. That's why it's so important to deal with them in a controlled atmosphere, like my office. What if you'd been at work or in the middle of a call-out? The grief you have over your wife's death—"

He shook off her touch. "Ginny has nothing to do with my job. I've told you that before."

"And you're wrong. Our past *determines* our present. The sum total of who you are rests on your history. If you can't face where you've been, you can't do anything, including your job."

His eyes went hot with anger. "Forget the mumbo jumbo, Doc. I don't want it and I don't need it." Glaring at her a second longer, as if to make sure she understood, he grabbed the check from the edge of the table then he stalked away without another word.

Disappointment mixed with embarrassment as Maria sank back into her chair. She'd never had a client run out on her. Then again, she'd never agreed to meet one in a bar, either. She hadn't been thinking like a therapist, hadn't been in control of the situation from the very start.

She'd acted like a woman. Not a doctor.

She wrapped her hands around the now cold coffee mug and closed her eyes. Talking about Christopher should have been her first warning. She never discussed her personal life with a client. She'd been so shocked when Ryan had sensed her disquiet, she'd simply answered, the tug of his genuine interest and obvious concern too strong to resist. For a moment, he'd even looked as if he was going to reach across the table and take her fingers in his. She would have welcomed his touch, she realized with shock. He had hands that looked gentle.

The waitress's voice broke into Maria's thoughts. Her eyes flew open and she saw the woman standing at the edge of the table. She wore a sympathetic expression as she tilted her head toward the front door. "Have a fight with your boyfriend?"

"Oh, God, he's not my boyfriend. No, no. We can't go out, he's..." Unable to fill in the blank, Maria stopped.

The waitress's face didn't change. "Married, huh?" She filled Maria's mug and shook her head. "Men! They're all rats, aren't they?" She patted Maria on the shoulder then walked to the next table.

Married? It'd almost be easier if he was, Maria thought with disgust. Then she wouldn't even be here! She wouldn't look at him twice. His magnetism wouldn't have registered with her.

But he wasn't married. He was a patient. A fact that made him just as off-limits. What was it going to take for her to remember that?

HE POUNDED through the surf, the night dark and empty. Ryan looked neither left nor right, his feet slapping the sand as he ran across the beach. The waves were high and foamy, the breeze so humid it was liquid as it hit his skin. Out to sea, above the horizon, rain clouds threatened, their outlines split by lightning every few minutes. The weather had made the dog restless. He'd actually come off the deck and followed Ryan halfway to the shore, only turning back when Ryan had yelled at him.

Ryan's angry thoughts turned to what had happened that evening. He should have known better than to meet Maria. She had one thing on her mind, and that was helping him, whether he needed it or not. If she had to help someone, she ought to concentrate on her kid. The boy needed all the assistance he could get. If Ryan had a son like Chris, he'd do whatever it took to make his life okay.

Instead Maria had made him talk about Ginny. The good doctor had sliced and diced his emotions and laid them raw. Tricked him into discussing something he'd vowed to ignore. And for good reason. In the end, talking about it wouldn't change anything. Ginny was gone. Nothing would bring her back. It was over. The end. Th-th-that's all, folks. In the darkness, Ryan tried to conjure his dead wife's face, but the image refused to materialize. Another one came in its place. He struggled with what that meant, a hole opening up inside him.

When he reached the deck an hour later, his

cheeks were wet. The clouds were still in the distance, but he blamed the rain anyway.

SHE DEBATED for a long time with herself, but Maria was so frustrated, she didn't know what else to do. Saturday morning, she loaded Christopher into the car and headed for Seaside. Since their last conversation, Jackson had called twice to ask how things were going and she hadn't been able to tell him the full story. Her brain felt cleaved; one side concentrated on Christopher and the other side only thought of Ryan. Her other poor patients were getting what was left over, which wasn't much at all. She was getting nothing.

Rain the night before had cleared the air. As they pulled into the tiny resort town, the streets sparkled and the air was perfumed with the scent of the ocean and the roses Richard had planted in two huge urns by the front door. She stopped to admire the flowers and Christopher pushed past her to go inside. He hadn't said two words to her on the drive out. He hadn't said two words since Thursday.

She followed him into the store, the dim light forcing her to stop so her eyes could adjust. The air in here was scented as well, but the fragrance came from the potpourri Richard kept in crystal bowls on top of all the old furniture. It never quite worked, she thought, stepping farther into the shop. There was always a muskiness in the air. She liked the smell, though. It made her think of simpler times.

She heard Jackson's voice from the rear of the store as he emerged and greeted Christopher. He stopped to pick something up, then the two of them came toward her and she saw that Jackson was holding a huge kite. It was so big it filled the aisle where they stood.

"I just got this." He held up the brightly colored object so she could see it better. Green iridescent scales glimmered in the pale light. Wings and a long tail. At the other end, two red spots glittered malevolently. A dragon, she realized.

"Isn't it great?" he asked. "I went to a kite store on the Net. Chris helped me find the site."

"It's beautiful."

"We're going down to the beach right now to fly it." He tilted his head to one side and sent her a message with his eyes. He wanted some time alone with Christopher, which was just fine with her. "The slave master is back there. You two can run the place while we go have some fun."

She smiled and nodded. "I'll clean the crystal," she promised.

"You do that," he said over his shoulder. "And no streaks, either. There *will* be an inspection...."

In times past, Christopher would have added a smart-aleck remark of his own. As it was, he trailed the older man with his head down, silent and lost. Maria's heart filled with guilt and confusion. God only knew how much she loved him and wanted to help him.

For more than an hour, she and Richard worked together amid the shining antiques and precious artworks. Seaside had been started as an experiment sometime in the late eighties, and just like Richard's store, the community had done nothing but grow. The houses and all the businesses had to conform to a strict code of architecture. Mostly pastel, the buildings were painted in a variety of colors—pink, yellow, green, blue—and all were full of windows and light. The streets were closed to traffic unless you were a resident, the idea being to take the town back in years. The concept had worked. In the evenings, people sat on their front porches and visited back and forth. The low sound of a television set sometimes broke the quiet but more likely it was a child's laughter or the tinkle of wineglasses raised in celebration.

Maria stood up and stretched her back, the last of the crystal vases now gleaming under the fans.

"My word! You are one good cleaner, girl!" Richard picked up an etched bell, the soft chime filling the store as he held it to the light. "You are so much better at this than Jackson."

"I heard that!"

They both turned as the screen door opened. Jackson stood at the cash register and fanned himself. He held a dripping ice-cream cone, which he licked before speaking. "If you don't want me working here, I'll gladly move on."

"Is that a promise or a threat?" With mock anger, Richard glared at Jackson.

Maria spoke before Jackson could keep the rally going. "Where's Chris?"

"I left him down at the boardwalk. He wanted to play some video games so I gave him twenty bucks and told him to come back when he ran out."

"Jackson! That's way too much money—"

"Give him a break, Maria. The kid is suffering." He licked the cone a final time then dumped what was left into the nearby trash bin. Dusting his hands against his legs, he came to where she stood. "He's cranky and grumpy and confused. He almost started to cry when the kite crashed. He needs a little down time. Away from everyone. Away from *you*."

The sharp words stung, but she nodded.

Seeing her expression, Jackson put a hand on her shoulder and squeezed gently. "Let's go for a walk," he said in a softer tone. "I think you need some quiet time yourself."

They went out the back door and headed aimlessly down the nearest street. Paved with bricks and lined by a row of pine trees, the narrow passageway seemed to close in on Maria. She sighed heavily.

"Oh, come on now. It's not all that bad." Jackson glanced in her direction as he spoke. He wore a sympathetic look mixed with exasperation. "Christopher is simply doing his job. He's a teenager. He's *supposed* to drive you nuts."

"Drinking alcohol is too serious to ignore."

"I'm not suggesting you do that."

"Well, tell me what you do suggest," she countered. "I'm out of ideas. Completely out."

"Be consistent. Talk to him. Love him. Don't give up."

The litany was a familiar one. She had recited it to her own patients too many times to count. "I'm doing all that. It's not working." She hesitated for a moment, then spoke. "But I've been thinking...."

"Oh, no. That's not a good sign."

Maria smiled. He was more right than he knew, but for days, in between all her other concerns, Maria had found a theory developing. She might be reaching, but who could say? She might also be right.

She spoke slowly, still not sure herself. "It's so obvious, I can't believe it's the reason, but do you think...well, that he might be trying to get Reed and me together again? You know, by acting out?"

Jackson pursed his mouth. "It's a possibility. Like you say, he certainly wouldn't be the first kid to ever come up with that scheme. Did you ask him?"

She shook her head. "He'd just deny it."

"You never know. If you surprise him, catch him off guard, he just might break down and tell you the truth. I do know one thing. Unless you ask, you won't find out."

They took a few more steps, Maria lost in thought. If Chris *was* working a plan like that, he was going to be extremely disappointed. There was nothing that would get her and Reed together again. Nothing.

Jackson seemed to read her mind. "I take it you've spoken to Reed?"

She nodded but said nothing.

"Useless conversation?"

"Exactly. He doesn't care, Jackson. At all." She pointed toward a nearby palm. "I could talk to that tree and get more of a response. How could I have married someone like him? A man so indifferent to his own son?" She shook her head and thought of Ryan. "It makes me scared to even think about trying again."

They had reached the end of the street. Jackson stopped in the shade and looked down at her. "Did you see your sniper?"

She looked up sharply, suspiciously. "Why do you ask?"

"You seemed worried about him last time we spoke." His face was a mask of innocence. "I was just wondering, that's all."

"I saw him." She forced her shoulders to relax. "Off-site. He called and said he couldn't get into the office. When I agreed to meet somewhere else, it threw him."

"And where did he want to meet?"

"At The Crab Shack. For a drink."

She waited a beat. "I know," she said evenly.

"Don't tell me how big an idiot I am, okay? I know already."

"Maria…" He said her name softly and shook his head. "You, my dear, are your own worst critic. It's not idiotic to accommodate a reluctant client. That's being a good doctor."

"Not when you forget you're the doctor."

His expression shifted. "That's not good, you're absolutely right. Did that happen?"

"I'm afraid so," she answered with reluctance. "He got me talking about Chris, something I would never have done if I'd been at the office, and things got worse from there."

"Worse?"

"He started to open up about his wife. I wasn't even trying to get him there. He managed it all on his own. Then he realized what he was doing and got furious. Told me it was my fault. Said I was manipulating him. He left the restaurant in a real huff."

"I'd call a breakthrough like that a good turn."

"I would, too," she said, "if I'd brought it about. I was just letting him talk. As a friend would." She shielded her eyes from the sun and watched two little boys fly by on roller skates. A woman trailed them, pushing a baby stroller. Lifting her gaze, Maria met Jackson's eyes. "Not as a doctor would."

He studied her face, then said, "I see."

They started walking again. Jackson broke the thick silence. "You're attracted to him."

Maria let the question roll around in her head. The words felt like rocks. "Yes," she said after a while. "I am attracted to him. He's very…"

"Very?"

She searched for the right word, then gave up. "I don't know. Just very very. There's something about him that's different."

"Well, he kills people for a living."

"There is that."

"He puts his life on the line every time he goes to work."

She nodded.

"And he's not too hard on the eyes."

She grinned. "Yep, that, too."

"But a client."

"I know." She stopped, her sandals scuffing against the sandy brick. "I *know* he's a client. And I know that means off-limits. I know…but my body doesn't."

"It's okay if you're attracted to the guy. It's when you start to act on that attraction that you get into trouble. You can't let that happen."

"Of course not. I know I *can't* work effectively with someone I'm attracted to."

"Actually, you may have even more empathy, but you have to be careful with it."

"And if it goes past empathy? One thing can lead to another, you know."

"It's your responsibility to make sure that doesn't happen." Jackson spoke sternly. "You're the doctor. He's the patient. The line is drawn by you, Maria.''

Jackson wasn't going to help her, she realized. Like all the other problems she'd worked through with him, she had to make this decision on her own. He could only ask the questions. She had to find the answers.

Regardless of that knowledge, by the time she and Christopher left early that evening, Maria felt better. Talking to Jackson always did that for her, even when his words were as strong as they had been tonight. Chris's mood seemed a little lighter, too.

But the improvement only lasted until they got home. The light was blinking, furiously it seemed, on the message machine. Maria hit the play button and Ryan's deep voice filled the living room. Her peace of mind disappeared.

RYAN WAS OUTSIDE on his deck when the phone sounded inside the house. Since he wasn't on call and Maria was the only person he'd telephoned, he knew exactly who was on the other end. His fingers tightened against the dog's fur, and Ryan realized he'd been stroking the animal's back without even thinking about it. He pulled his hand away and the phone rang again. He didn't jump up to get it, though. He was already having second thoughts.

He'd called Maria's house in a fit of something,

angcr, maybe, and left a message. *Call me when you get in. I want to talk to you about your son.*

Now he was wishing he could take the words back. Yeah, the kid needed help, and yeah, Ryan could do something that would probably be constructive, but what had he been thinking? Christopher Worley wasn't *his* problem. Ryan had enough to deal with as it was.

A little voice mocked him. *You know exactly why you called,* it jeered. *It's not Christopher you're so concerned about. It's Christopher's mother.* Despite the way their last encounter had ended, he couldn't quit thinking about Maria. About the only face he'd been able to see in the darkness the other night. It bothered him tremendously yet he couldn't seem to stop that train of thought.

The dog whined as the phone rang once more, and Ryan cursed. Rising from the chaise longue he made his way into the kitchen and yanked up the receiver.

"This is Maria Worley," she said to his curt hello. "I just got your message. We've been out."

With whom, he wondered, illogically. And doing what?

"I'm not sure I understand," she continued when he didn't speak. "You said something about Christopher?"

She had the smoothest voice he'd ever heard. Low and lulling. How would it sound coming from the depths of tangled sheets? The guilt he had now come to expect shot through him.

He issued the invitation he'd vowed earlier he wouldn't. "I've got some free time next weekend. I was wondering if Chris might like to go out to the training field. He seemed interested in the facility during the rally. I could show him around a bit more, let him see what we didn't open to the public."

Her silence held surprise. "That's very generous of you," she answered after a moment. "Frankly I'm shocked you'd call, much less offer this help. I—I didn't think our session ended too well."

"It didn't," he answered. "But this isn't about us. It's about Christopher."

When she didn't speak, he continued. "I just thought he might enjoy going out there. And frankly, it seems as if you could use a break."

"Maybe so, but I shouldn't have dumped all my problems on your shoulders as I did the other evening. It wasn't professional, and I'm sorry. I—I've felt badly about it ever since."

"Don't worry about it. I knew something was wrong. I would have kept up until you told me. You didn't have a chance."

"That sounds ominous."

"It is," he said. "But only if you're a bad guy."

She chuckled. The sound of her amusement was as smooth as her voice, only it held another tone as well. Something sexy. He didn't fight his reaction, he simply gave up and the conversation continued.

Ten minutes later, they were still talking. He wasn't sure about what. He'd only listened to her voice, not the words. When he realized she had started to say goodbye, he focused again. "I'll see Christopher on Saturday then?"

"You are persistent, aren't you?"

"Only when it's important."

"I don't know," she answered. "Let me think about it a bit, Ryan. It's not something I'd usually agree to, but..."

"Why not?"

She seemed to hesitate. "You're a client. It's not acceptable."

"Neither is a fourteen-year-old drinking."

"That's true."

"Look," he said. "I was a lost kid once and if someone had done this for my mom, who knows? We might be closer now. I just want to help, that's all. If you don't feel comfortable with the offer, that's certainly your decision."

"I'll consider it," she said. "How about I call you next week sometime and we talk about it then?"

He hung up a few seconds later and went back to the deck. The stars had come out while he'd been on the phone, and the night sparkled. He looked down at the dog and ruffled his head, a feeling of calmness coming over Ryan that he hadn't experienced in quite a while.

It was shattered a second later.

From somewhere inside the house, the shrill sound of his beeper cut into the silence. He whirled and ran for the patio door. He wasn't sure where the device was but the persistent noise led him into the living room. He'd dropped the damned thing on the sofa when he'd come home earlier. Seizing the black box, he read the numbers now pulsing in its window. The flashing address was within a mile of his own home—501 West Grayston. The debate only took a second. He grabbed his jacket and gun and headed out the back.

He arrived before the team did, the swirling red lights of two black and white units leading him to a side street. Parking his truck behind the marked police cars, Ryan sprinted toward three Destin cops who had crouched behind the open doors of the vehicles.

He knew them all and greeted them by name. "What's up?" Kneeling beside the oldest man, a sergeant, Ryan looked in the direction they faced, toward a small frame house that sat across the street.

"Bad warrant on a dope dealer." Charlie Jacobson, the sergeant, tilted his crew cut toward the dwelling. He'd been with the force for as long as Ryan could remember. He was smart and savvy, the kind of cop Ryan's father had been. "We didn't think there would be any trouble, but we thought wrong. Guy's holed up inside there. Tried to serve 'em and the son of a bitch took a shot at us.''

Ryan nodded, but before he could say anything, the older cop took his eyes off the house for a moment and stared at him in the darkness. "Hey, whaddaya doing here? Aren't you on leave, Lukas?''

"Yeah, I'm on leave, dammit," Ryan answered with chagrin. Had everyone in the department seen him come out of Maria Worley's office? "But I live right around the corner. I heard the page and just thought I'd see what was going on.''

"Well, now you know." Charlie's gaze held a moment of compassion, then it hardened. "So get outta here," he said roughly. "Before you get into deeper shit than you already are.''

A sudden shot sounded from inside the house, and the men all tensed, including Ryan. His hand went to the back of his jeans where he'd tucked his service revolver. The noise of the single discharge was still in the air when the War Wagon rumbled into the street behind them.

Bradley Thompson, Lena's right-hand man, jumped from the still-moving Winnebago and dashed to where the other cops waited. His startled glance took in Ryan's presence then dismissed it. "Give me an update," he demanded, looking at Jacobson.

The sergeant repeated the story he'd told Ryan, Thompson nodding all the while and injecting several questions. Using the microphone and headset all the SWAT members wore, the big cop relayed the information back to the command post, including a report on the last shot fired. When he finished, Bradley turned to Ryan. "You'd better leave."

Ryan looked at him steadily. "The shot we heard came from a rifle, Brad. Maybe a Universal, I'm not sure. You don't want to send anyone in there."

"I'll give Lena that information."

"Is Chase with you?"

Brad's gaze flickered at the mention of the other sniper's name. "Lena didn't call him. His wife is due almost any minute. J.L.'s third backup and he's here, though. She wanted to see what was going on first—"

He broke off abruptly as Ryan shook his head. "J.L.'s a good man, Brad, but he's the *backup* for a reason. Chase should be there. Chase...or me." Ryan managed two steps away from where they stood, then Brad's voice stopped him.

"Ryan—stop! Lena will kill you if she knows you're here."

"Maybe so, but the team needs me." With that, Ryan sprinted into the dark toward the War Wagon.

Lena stared in disbelief as he opened the door and entered the command post two seconds later. "What the hell!"

"I heard the page." Without giving her time to ask any more questions, he pressed forward. "The shooter has a rifle, Lena. I heard it. Don't place anyone closer than you are right now or you're asking for trouble. You're going to need a long-range solution.''

"That may be so, but you aren't it.'' She glared at him from the other end of the narrow aisle. Sarah Greenberg, the team's information officer, sat at her desk tucked into one corner. Her eyes bounced from Ryan to Lena then back again as Lena spoke tightly. "Get out, Ryan. You're on leave.''

"You need me, Lena—''

"I've got J.L.—''

"And did he tell you what I just told you?'' Ryan didn't wait for her answer. "No, he didn't. Because he's not experienced enough to recognize what's going on. I am. The guy inside that house has a long-range rifle and he's already fired it more than once. Are you willing to risk lives just to punish me?''

Her expression flattened, her lips going into a single line. He'd gone too far.

"I'm not punishing you, Ryan. You are on leave pending therapy with a qualified professional.''

"It's the same thing,'' he said bitterly.

"No, it is not the same thing.'' Lena spoke each word with a deliberate distinction. "We are talking about your mental health. Please leave now. Don't make me do something more or you'll regret it.''

"I can help—''

"Get out.''

"Lena, listen to—''

Her eyes glittered suddenly. "One week."

"What?"

"You just added another week to your leave for disobeying a direct order. *That's* punishment! Do you want to add a second one?"

"Dammit, Lena, you can't do that!"

"I just did." She put her hands on her hips. "Do you want another one?"

He stared at her wordlessly. After a second, she lifted her finger and pointed to the door. An angry mist filled his vision. He spun around and slammed out of the Winnebago.

CHAPTER EIGHT

MONDAY MORNING, Maria saw two clients before lunch and only had a single one scheduled afterward. She used the time to call Christopher's school and talk to his counselor. Since the forgery incident and their subsequent visit, Maria had phoned the woman once a week to check on his progress. She always answered Maria's questions patiently, but it was obvious she thought Maria was going overboard.

Maria didn't care. She rocked back in her desk chair and stared out at the harbor. It was the end of May and in another few weeks, the kids would be out of school. She was worried; she couldn't leave Chris totally unsupervised and Mrs. Lowe had obligations, a part-time job and grandchildren of her own. Despite Maria's threat to the contrary, Mrs. Lowe couldn't stay with Chris every minute Maria was gone.

In the past, she'd structured his vacation time, filling June and July with camp and trips to her parents' house. She took off every day that she could and tried to spend extra time with him herself, as well. This had been the first summer she'd thought he could manage on his own. Now she was going to have make arrangements for him, but she didn't know what, and with that realization another round of guilt hit her square on. He wouldn't be having the problems he was if she was a better mother. If she had more time. If she had more patience. If she just tried harder...

She thought back to the conversation they'd had a few days before. After giving it a lot more consideration, she'd flat out asked him if he was trying to get her and Reed together again by acting unruly.

He'd stared at her with eyes full of shock, then he'd turned around and stalked away without a word.

The thoughts brought her back to Ryan's offer, which had been on her mind since he'd called on Saturday evening. Before she'd even hung up the phone, Christopher had begged her to let him go.

Her chair creaking, Maria stood and crossed the office to her window. Even if Ryan had not been a patient, she wasn't sure he was the kind of role model she'd select for her son. He was a sniper, for God's sake. Ryan was trained to kill people. How could she ignore his career choice? His job colored everything, even though she'd told him otherwise on the first day they'd met.

She closed her eyes against the sparkling sunshine but she couldn't shut off her mind. The opposing argument came to her swiftly. Ryan Lukas was more than the sum of his parts. Bright and articulate, he personified the type of individual who functioned best on a SWAT team. He clearly cared about his job, too much, it seemed, and had loved his wife with the same passion. Underneath the anger that simmered inside him now, he was a kind, decent person. Maria thought she could find that man again...but she wasn't sure.

A soft knock interrupted her thoughts. Maria turned just as the door was opened. Lena stood on the threshold. "Mind if I come in? Sher said you had some free time."

Welcoming the disturbance more than Lena could know, Maria waved her into the office. "I've always got time for you," she said with a smile. "Come on in."

It wasn't unusual for Lena to drop in unannounced, but the deep creases around her eyes and the weary droop to her shoulders *was* different. She shut the door and headed for the couch as Maria stared at her in concern.

"I need to crash here for a while." Lena collapsed on the sofa and closed her eyes, leaning her head against the cushion. "It's either that or I run away and join the circus." She stopped and laughed hollowly. "Actually I feel as if I've already done that."

"What's wrong?"

Massaging her temples, Lena stayed quiet for a second, then she opened her eyes and met Maria's sympathetic gaze. "It's Ryan." Her stare held anger mixed with concern. "He showed up at a scene Saturday night. We argued. I had to give him hell and an extra week of leave to get him out."

"Oh, dear." Maria sank into one of the padded armchairs in front of the couch.

"Oh, dear is right," Lena said with a weary groan. "Before Ginny died, he would no more have disobeyed an order than fly! I could depend on him the way I depend on myself." She dropped her fingers but her frown told Maria her headache was still there. "What am I going to do?"

"Tell me exactly what happened."

A few minutes later, with the details behind them, all Maria could do was shake her head. "You're right. This doesn't sound good. He's losing sight of his boundaries."

"Can you fix it?"

Maria laughed, in spite of the gravity of the situation. "He's not a leaky faucet, Lena! I can't just go in there and tighten a few bolts."

"Well, something's got to be done. Don't you have any ideas?"

"We've really only had one session and it didn't go too well. You've told him what's going to happen if he doesn't complete his therapy. The responsibility is his."

"But he was so good." Lena pulled her fingers through her hair, the ends standing straight up as her voice filled with agony. "He was the best! Can't you help him be that again?"

If Maria hadn't already known how much the men meant to Lena, she could have read the emotion in the other woman's expression. Lena was really upset. These guys were her second family, the team a unit that she'd handpicked and worked with for years.

"I *can* help him," Maria answered in a consoling voice, "but he has to want it himself. You know that as well as I do." She paused. "He has to come to me."

Lena fell back against the sofa in defeat, but Maria didn't notice. She was thinking instead, thinking of what she'd just said. *He has to come to me.*

Something on her face must have given her away. Lena spoke sharply. "What?"

"Ryan called me Saturday. Before the incident, I assume," Maria said hesitantly. "He asked if he could take Chris out to the training camp next weekend. To show him around."

"He did?" Lena's eyes widened. "What did you say?"

"I told him I would think about it, but frankly I've pretty much decided against it. It's not a good idea."

"How come?"

"He's a client. That kind of personal contact would be frowned upon by any ethics board." She paused and felt Lena's stare. "But..."

"But he asked." Lena moved to the edge of the

couch. "He came to you and asked if he could do this for Christopher."

"That's right."

They stared at each other across the low coffee table separating the sofa and the armchair.

"So he did come to you. In a way."

Maria nodded.

"Then you don't have a choice. You have to let him connect. It might be exactly what he needs."

"It's not that simple. I'd have to think about it some more."

"Well, I don't," Lena said abruptly. "Ryan has always loved kids, and they love him. He attracts them almost magnetically. Ginny was trying to get pregnant when she died. If Ryan wants to help you with Christopher, I think it's a step forward." She held out her hands. "How could you see it any other way?"

"But ethically speaking—"

"Ethically speaking, your responsibility is to help this guy." Lena leaned forward again, her coiled energy forcing Maria to meet her eyes. "*That's* what you have to do."

"Yes, but—"

"But what?"

But I shouldn't, Maria argued silently. *I shouldn't want to look into those sad eyes and see right down inside him. I shouldn't want to kiss him and taste those lips that never smile. I shouldn't want to make him feel like a man again.*

"I need to think about it," Maria finally said, setting aside her traitorous thoughts. "I have to do what's best for Ryan. The easiest answer isn't always the best one."

Lena stared at Maria for a moment longer, then she jumped up, her hands on her hips, her mind clearly made up. "You have to do whatever it takes. Ryan's a good guy and I don't want to see him go off the deep end, especially now when he's asking for help." Her gray eyes turned stormy. "If you don't take advantage of this, Maria, you aren't the doctor I've always thought you were."

SHE WAS NUTS. Absolutely nuts.

Late that afternoon after she'd checked in with Chris and knew he was already home, Maria headed out on the Beach Road. Gripping the steering wheel of the Toyota, she told herself *she* was the one who ought to be in counseling.

Surprising Ryan at his house, interfering in his life, telling him what to do! Those were not the actions of a professional therapist. She was acting like a...like a woman, dammit! She should have never let Lena talk her into this, but one look at her friend's face and Maria had known she didn't have a chance. She'd tried to argue but had given up. Lena was relentless.

She'd scribbled Ryan's address and handed it to Maria before leaving. "All he has is a cell phone," she'd said. "He's supposed to turn it off on his free day. If you want to talk to him, you'll have to go out there.''

''Doesn't he have a beeper?''

''That number's only for call-outs.'' Lena had shook her head. ''Go see him.''

Agreeing reluctantly, Maria knew now she was insane. She'd tried to call him first, but just as Lena had said, she'd gotten a recording. In the solitude of the car, Maria let out a curse she didn't normally use.

But she kept on driving.

THE DOG'S EARS went straight up. He jumped to his feet on the wooden deck, his toenails digging into the soft, weathered cedar, and began to growl. The sound of warning rattled inside his deep chest, and Ryan responded without thinking.

''Hey, boy, what's wrong?'' He reached out from where he sat in his patio chair and spoke to the animal, dropping the newspaper to gently touch his stiffened back. ''What's the matter?''

With his unfathomable eyes, the shepherd looked at Ryan, then a second later, Ryan heard the vehicle, too. He went as tense as the dog at the crunching sound of tires on his driveway. The engine cut off, a car door squeaked open then closed. Ryan's was the only house at the end of the road. There was a little breakfast place nearby and a plant nursery, but they were both closed this late in the day. Whoever was walking up his driveway had come to see him.

Ryan didn't move and neither did the dog.

A minute passed, then more footsteps, these coming up the stairs on the back deck. When he saw who it was, Ryan couldn't believe his eyes. Before he could even register the emotion, it automatically changed into pleasure.

Maria.

She hesitated on the top step. He wasn't sure if she stopped because she saw the dog or because she saw Ryan. Either way, she didn't advance.

He said nothing because he wasn't sure what to say. Apparently, she felt the same. They stared at each other for several seconds, the only sounds the surf as it hit the sand and the breeze brushing through the sea oats at the foot of the deck.

Finally, Maria spoke. "I hope I'm not intruding...." Her voice died out uncertainly, then she seemed to gather herself. "I'd like to talk with you if that's possible. Do you have a moment?"

Without answering or even rising, he let his gaze drift over her body. As usual, she was dressed in a suit. It was black, a short skirt and a jacket molded over a white V-neck blouse. She had on high heels, too. Women didn't wear heels that much any more, he'd noticed, and seeing her legs, he wondered why. There was something incredibly sexy about a woman in high heels and no hose.

It didn't really matter, though. She would have looked just as good if she were standing before him barefoot.

She lifted her hand and tucked a strand of hair behind one ear. It was the same gesture she'd made when he'd seen her in the hallway talking with Lena. Was it habit or nervousness? "Do you have the time? We need to talk."

The low timbre of her words was even more sexy than her appearance. His awareness of that fact, and the pleasure he'd felt at seeing her, upset Ryan. What was he doing? His chair screeching across the wood, Ryan stood and glared at her, the dog beside him taking a step backward. All at once he understood why she was there; Lena had told her he'd shown up at the call-out.

"I have plenty of time," Ryan said. "But if you're here because of Saturday night, you can turn around and leave. Tell Lena I was rude and obnoxious and I sent you packing. Tell her I made you cry."

"I'm not the one who needs to do that."

Her softly spoken answer made him even more angry. His eyes locked on hers. "I don't want you here."

"I know that."

The dog suddenly trotted across the deck to sit at Maria's feet. She dropped her glance in his direction, then held out her hand for him to sniff. He arced his neck out delicately, smelled her fingers then lowered his head for her to scratch. She went one better. She knelt down and put her arms around him, her fingers easing behind his ears with instant familiarity.

Traitor, Ryan thought.

"He's gorgeous." She raised her eyes to Ryan's. "What's his name?"

Ryan wanted to yell at her to leave, to scream and tell her he didn't want her there. But he didn't. He answered her instead. "He doesn't have a name."

Expecting her to ask him why, Maria simply nodded. "I'll call you Star," she said to the waiting animal. "I had a shepherd when I was kid and that was his name. He was the best dog in the world."

To Ryan's amazement, the animal made a sound in the back of his throat that could have passed for approval. Maria fondled his ears a bit more, then stood up. Her brown eyes held compassion and he hated it.

"I'm not here to give you a hard time, Ryan. Lena *did* tell me what happened but that's not why I came. I came because—" she looked down at the boards beneath her feet, then lifted her eyes "—because I care about you," she said quietly.

He almost believed her. He *wanted* to believe her. Another series of emotions tumbled through his brain. Surprise. Pleasure. Guilt. Then he realized how he felt and he stopped himself. She cared because it was her job to care, nothing more.

"I don't need the emergency visit, okay? And

I've learned my lesson, too. I won't be seen at any more call-outs.''

She didn't miss his phrasing. "You won't be seen? Or you won't be there?''

He turned sharply and walked to the edge of the deck. The railing he gripped was rough and splintering. It bit into the palm of his hand, just like her words.

She materialized at his side, her persistence something he would have admired had it not been directed at him. "You're on a path of self-destruction,'' she said calmly. "You're going to lose your job and it's all you care about right now. It's the *only* thing you've got in your life, and if you don't get a handle on your actions, you're going to find yourself with empty nights *and* empty days. I don't think you need me to figure out how that will feel.''

He didn't expect the candidness. She read his surprise.

"I'm not talking to you as I would a patient,'' she explained. "I'm trying to give you a break. I'm talking to you as a friend.''

Her voice reached deep inside him and tugged at a string that seemed to be directly connected to his heart. He fought the pull but lost. "I don't want you as a friend.'' He spoke hoarsely as he turned and stared at her.

"I'm sorry you feel that way.''

Behind her the sun was about to go down. The

last red rays reached out to set her hair aflame. Cursing himself but unable to stop, he lifted his hand and took a strand between his finger and thumb. She looked startled but she stayed right where she was, a carved statue of ivory skin and secret promises. The chestnut curl was as soft and silky as it looked, and the smell of strawberries rose in the heated evening air. His words slipped out before he could stop them.

"You're not the kind of woman a man wants for a friend."

"You hardly know me. How can you say that?"

"I don't have to know you to know that." He rubbed his fingers together and her hair whispered in the dusk. "It's how you look. It's how you smell. It's who you are."

She raised her hand and covered his fingers with her own, as if to stop him. Instead Ryan captured her hand and twisted the ribbon of hair around both their hands. Trapping them. Without thinking of what it meant, he lowered his head to hers.

HIS LIPS barely brushed her mouth before Maria jumped back.

Ryan didn't look surprised. He stood where he'd been and simply raised one eyebrow.

"Wh-what are you doing?" She stammered as though she were fifteen. It was an appropriate response considering the way her heart was racing.

"I was about to kiss you," he answered. "Obviously a big mistake."

"Y-yes," she replied. "That would be a big mistake. A major mistake, in fact."

His mouth, that same smooth mouth that had just grazed hers, turned up slightly at one corner. "I'm not *that* bad a kisser."

"That's not what I meant," she said. "You're my patient. I'm your doctor."

"Then it won't happen again." His eyes locked on hers.

"That's right," she said. "It won't happen *again.* It won't happen ever."

She took a step backward as she spoke. She needed to get away from the energy pulling her into his orbit. "In fact, I think I should leave. I shouldn't be here in the first place. I should have waited for you to come to my office. Lena insisted I come out here, and I just thought I could help and that's all I wanted to do." She knew she was babbling but seemed incapable of stopping. "I thought since you'd called about Chris, it meant something and—"

He interrupted her. "It *does* mean something," he said. "I want to help him, Maria, or I wouldn't have made the offer."

Despite the crazed moment that had just occurred between the two of them, Maria read the earnestness in his eyes and in his words. Ryan did want to help her son. And even though she wanted to deny it, the possibility still existed that there was more to his offer than what appeared on the surface. He might be reaching out. If she rebuffed him now, what kind of repercussions could it have on his emotions later?

The questions warred inside her, the push and pull too much to handle. "I appreciate what you're trying to do, but I don't think it's a good idea."

"I understand." His words were stiff, and his eyes shuttered almost instantly, a curtain of denial falling to cover his hurt.

Witnessing his raw reaction, Maria felt her heart go tight.

"I don't think it's a good idea," she repeated, "but Chris would kill me if I didn't let him go. He heard us talking on the phone the other night, and I had to tell him what you offered. He begged me to say yes. I think if I refused, he'd probably thumb a ride out there and meet you anyway."

He stared out at the water. "It's your decision."

"I know," she said. But looking at his carved profile, she suddenly knew the opposite was true. It was *his* decision. He'd made the offer. He'd made the first step.

She was an idiot to say no.

And she was crazy to say yes.

He didn't look at her as he spoke. "I'll pick him up at ten on Saturday."

She nodded. "He'll be ready."

THE PHONE was ringing when Maria stepped into her office. She'd left in such a fog for Ryan's, she'd forgotten some reports and had been forced to go back to pick them up. She'd called Christopher from the car and told him she'd be late. She picked up the phone now, half expecting him to be on the other end.

"What did he say?"

Maria shook her head at Lena's anxious question. It wasn't what Ryan had said, Maria thought, it was what he'd done. Or almost done, she corrected. Still in shock, she stared at the lights twinkling in the harbor. Nothing like this had ever happened to her before. Before Ryan, she'd never been attracted to a client, never even given one a second glance. But she'd told him the truth when she said she was talking to him as a friend.

Everything about Ryan—from his dark-blue eyes, so full of grief, to the wall of pain that he hid behind, even the dog he couldn't bear to name for fear it'd abandon him, too—all these things made her want to pull him into her arms. She wasn't accustomed to the need to comfort him and didn't know what to do with the feeling. In that brief second, when she'd felt the warmth of his lips sweep over hers, she'd realized just how much she wanted to do that, and more. From the look on his face, he'd felt the same.

She pushed aside her thoughts with sheer determination. "He and Christopher are getting together Saturday morning," she said briskly. "I'm not sure it's the right thing to do, but he offered again so I said yes.''

''So we were right! He is making the first step—''

In spite of her revelation, Maria protested. ''He's offered to do something with my son, that's it. I can't tell you if it's a first step or a step at all. I don't know the man well enough to say that, Lena.''

There was a small silence. ''You sound upset.''

Maria sat down heavily in the chair behind her desk. ''I *am* upset,'' she said. ''This doesn't feel good, okay? I'm totally caught in the middle. I don't know if I'm doing the right thing as a mother and I seriously doubt if I'm doing the right thing as a therapist. Letting these two get together goes against everything I've been taught. It's a personal dilemma that's eating my lunch.''

Another silence rolled down the telephone line. Lena didn't often take this much time to think before she spoke. It made Maria nervous. ''What are you telling me, Maria? That you can't do your job?''

''I'm telling you I'm confused.'' Maria said after a long moment. ''I'm just not sure I'm doing the right thing, that's all.''

Another hesitation came over the phone, then Lena spoke. She sounded confident, maybe too much so. Was she trying to convince herself as well as Maria? ''Stay the path,'' she said. ''I know Ryan and I know you. You're the best there is. If anyone can help him, you can, I'm sure. Trust me on this one.''

They said their goodbyes, then Maria hung up the phone and crossed her arms, hugging herself in the empty office. Trusting Lena wasn't the problem.

It was trusting herself she wasn't sure about.

CHAPTER NINE

RYAN SAT at his desk Wednesday morning and stared at the report he was supposed to be reading. The words blurred, but his eyes weren't the problem. He couldn't concentrate. All he could think about was Maria Worley.

It was a cruel trick that he couldn't get her out of his brain. She was the only woman he'd been truly attracted to since Ginny's death. The irony didn't escape him.

Before she'd left his house Monday evening, Maria had told him she was booked the rest of the week but she expected to see him the following Thursday. He'd grunted a reply that wasn't really an answer, then she'd left him, but not in peace. The dog had stared at him after she'd gone. Ryan had read his gaze, too. *What are you?* it'd asked silently. *Some kind of idiot or what?*

Lena passed by his desk and tapped the corner, jerking him into awareness. "Staff meeting in ten minutes."

He nodded, expecting her to move on, but she didn't. She waited with speculation darkening her gray eyes.

"What?" he finally asked.

"You talked to Maria?"

He nodded again.

"Everything okay?"

"I'm taking her son out to the training camp this weekend. She's been having some problems with him."

"She told me. That's really good of you."

Ryan shrugged. "He's a kid with problems and that's something I understand. Just thought I'd help if I could."

"It was generous of you to offer."

He stared at her wordlessly, then after a moment she drummed the edge of his desk again and nodded briskly. "Okay, then. See ya at the meeting."

Ryan watched her leave. She looked as if she knew about the almost kiss, but who cared? It didn't matter one way or the other if she did, as far as he was concerned. Maria had spouted something about ethics, but to Ryan that wasn't important. There were other issues he'd had to handle. He'd sat on the deck long after Maria had left and thought about the brief encounter, myriad emotions bombarding him, one in particular standing out. The guilt he felt almost every time he saw Maria was something he'd fought, ignored, and now had to deal with. Only trouble was, he didn't know how.

A few seconds later he followed Lena into the staff meeting and took a seat in the back. They debriefed the call-outs of the previous week; a domestic disturbance on Wednesday, a suicidal factory worker on Friday, the bad warrant on Saturday. Once Ryan would have listened intently, but today the words were simply noise.

For some reason, all he could think about was the first time he'd gone out with his wife. They'd both been in high school in Pensacola. She'd been a freshman, he'd been a senior. It'd been a blind date, set up by her best friend. Ginny's mom wouldn't let her go out by herself so the only way she could date was to double.

As silly as it sounded, he'd taken one look at her and fallen in love. She'd felt the same way. He went ahead with his plans to join the Marines and she promised to wait. When she graduated, they'd married, their whole lives ahead of them. Long, they'd thought, and prosperous, each of them wanting the whole enchilada: a crowded house, bills to pay, three—maybe even four—kids. Dogs with names.

She'd been thirty-two when she died. A heart attack. No warning, no advance notice, never a problem until that very moment. A congenital defect, the doctor had said. A time bomb waiting to detonate.

It'd been a bomb, all right. A bomb that had not only taken Ginny's life, but their future together. Blinking furiously, Ryan stared at the blackboard at the front of the room. He kept his face a stony mask, but inside, his heart crumbled. Again.

MARIA STARED at her son from across the breakfast table. "Don't you have anything else you can wear?''

He looked down at his black T-shirt. A band's logo was spread on the front—something about Crows—but the writing was so faded it couldn't be read. A blessing, most likely.

''It's my favorite,'' he said stubbornly. ''It feels good. I wanna wear it.''

Maria didn't press the issue. There were battles worth fighting and some you simply skipped. This one was the latter.

''I want you to be careful today,'' she said. ''And mind Lieutenant Lukas. Don't get smart with him.''

He didn't say anything.

She sipped her coffee. ''I mean it, Chris. He's spending personal time with you and that's very important.'' *It's something your own father can't manage,* she added, silently.

''Okay.'' He spooned the rest of his cereal into his mouth then jumped up and started out of the room.

''Excuse me?''

He turned around and she pointed at the bowl. ''This isn't Denny's. Take that to the sink, rinse it and put it in the dishwasher.''

He rolled his eyes but came back and did what she said without comment. A miracle, albeit a minor one.

Ever since she'd told him she was going to allow the outing with Ryan, Chris had been the model son.

Jackson had said, "I told you so."

Maria finished her coffee and began to clear her own dishes. When the doorbell rang a few minutes later, she took the nearest tea towel and dried her hands slowly. She didn't want Ryan to get the wrong impression. She'd acted stupid enough at his house. She wasn't about to meet the man at the door, bouncing up and down like a schoolgirl. He wasn't there to see her anyway, she reminded herself. He was there for Christopher.

A fact that didn't stop her from glancing in the mirror beside the refrigerator to check her hair before she went into the living room.

Ryan was standing by the front door, Christopher by his side. Her son was trying to look cool, but she could tell how excited he was.

"I guess we're ready," Ryan said as she drew close. "Do you have my cell phone number? Just in case?"

His thoughtfulness immediately touched her. On the rare occasions Reed actually did come by and get Chris, she'd watch them drive off and have no idea where they were going or how to find them. It always made her nervous.

"That'd be great. Lena gave it to me the other day but I left it at the office," she answered. "Come into the kitchen and I'll write it down again."

He turned to Chris and tossed him his car keys. "I'll be right there."

Chris's eyes rounded, and Maria felt another stab.

Reed drove a BMW. He hardly let Chris sit in it, much less unlock it and climb inside by himself.

Her son didn't even say goodbye. He shot out of the living room before Ryan had the time to change his mind. The front door rattled the house when it slammed behind him.

Maria couldn't help herself; she laughed. "I think he's a little excited," she said. "You might have to slow him down a bit."

Ryan smiled easily. "Not a problem. We'll work it out."

In the kitchen, she found pen and paper then jotted down the number he gave her. She'd expected to feel awkward around him, but she didn't. Maybe he'd accepted her pronouncement that nothing would happen between them. She felt a catch at the thought and told herself it was not disappointment.

"What time do you think you'll be back?" she asked as they headed toward the front hall.

"I'm not really sure. Is there a certain time you'd like?"

"Don't ask me that," she laughed. "I might say take your time!"

He smiled again, and she noticed how different he looked when the expression reached his eyes. Younger and more carefree. "It wouldn't be a problem if you did," he said. "I've been looking forward to today."

"Do you know what you're going to do?"

"I'll take him out to the training field and show

him around. I've got some things planned but I think
I'll see how it goes. It'll depend on him."

Nodding, Maria opened the door and leaned
against the edge. He stood close to her in the small
hallway and she could smell the soap he'd obviously
used that morning.

"I think he'll be okay. He's a fantastic kid," she
admitted. "Just confused. And that's my fault, not
his."

"Your fault or his daddy's?"

She shrugged. "Both, I'm sure."

He waited a second in the sunshine that fell
through the open doorway. "What are you going to
do today?"

"I don't know yet," she said. "I might take in a
movie. I haven't seen anything without guns and
space ships for the past fourteen years."

"The last movie I saw was *Green Dolphin
Street*." He said the words as if they surprised him.
"Do you know it?"

Maria felt her eyes go wide. "With Lana Turner?
My God, my mother loved that movie. I wouldn't
have guessed you were an old movie fan—"

"I'm not. But Ginny refused to watch anything
made past the fifties. She loved old films."

An uncertain flicker passed over his face as he
spoke. Maria thought he was going to blame her
again for making him talk about his past, then their
eyes met and she read the painful truth at the same
time that it came to him.

He'd brought up his wife's name all by himself and there was no one to fault, *but* himself.

RYAN PULLED the truck into the training facility twenty minutes after leaving Maria's house. On the drive out, he'd concentrated on Christopher's chatter; it kept him from wondering why he always ended up saying something he didn't want to when he was near Maria. He turned his attention back to the boy beside him. He'd seemed shy at first but once Ryan had got him started, Chris had warmed up quickly. It was hard to reconcile the articulate, intelligent kid now climbing out of the truck with all Ryan had heard about him.

Why would Chris even be friends with the punk they'd arrested at the industrial park?

Ryan followed the youngster out of the vehicle and answered his own question. Chris and the teen with the air gun probably hung out together for the same reasons Ryan had associated with a similar guy when he'd been fourteen. You weren't really friends; you were just guys with nothing better to do than sit around and shoot the shit. You did what they did and went where they went because to voice a different opinion meant you didn't really belong

And not belonging was the worst thing imaginable at that age.

Ryan led Christopher directly to the gym where they stepped inside the mirrored weight room. "I thought you might like to work out some," Ryan said casually. "I have a routine I do three times a week. I could show you some of it if you're interested."

Ryan hadn't thought Chris's eyes could get any bigger, but they did. Dark-brown and soft, they reminded Ryan too much of Maria's. "That'd be cool," Christopher said. "My dad used to lift weights but he never would let me mess with the dumbbells. And he took all that stuff when he left."

Feeling a stab of anger toward this unknown man, Ryan nodded. What kind of man would treat his son like that? What kind of man would leave a woman like Maria? Ryan headed for the locker room, Chris trailing along behind him. They found an extra pair of shorts and a T-shirt for him to wear. The shirt was black and had SWAT written across the chest in foot-high letters. The gear swallowed the boy; you couldn't even read the word, but he didn't appear to care. Especially when Ryan ferreted out a spare pair of weight-lifting gloves, as well. Outfitted for work, they returned to the gym.

A few other men had come in while they were in the back and Ryan introduced Christopher to them, each cop nodding in his direction and grunting a vague hello as they lifted the heavy weights. Some of them had sons they occasionally brought with them so Chris's presence wasn't unusual. Mostly they didn't even notice. They were there to train, each officer expected to fulfill a set list of exercise goals every month. Four times a year, Lena held physicals. If you didn't pass, you didn't play.

Without making it obvious, Ryan located the lightest weights he could and got Christopher started. He barely knew which part of the dumbbell to hold and they struggled for a while. He caught on fast, though, and once Ryan pointed out what muscles they were building and how the exercises would help him, Chris didn't stop. For more than half an hour, they worked in unison, Ryan's weights much heavier, but Christopher working the harder of the two. The sweat was rolling off his forehead when Ryan finally called a halt. They'd done less than a quarter of the routine Ryan usually went through, but Chris had had enough, whether he knew it or not.

"What do you say we clean up and get something to eat, then I'll take you out to the range?"

Christopher nearly dropped the fifteen-pounder he'd been struggling to lift with both hands. "Th-the shooting range?"

Ryan pulled off his sweatband then dipped his head to the sleeve of his shirt, wiping his face. He looked up. "I've got to get in some practice. It won't be exactly like the real thing, but I think you'll enjoy it. Sound okay?"

Without a word, Chris nodded.

Thirty minutes later, they'd changed and gulped down two ham sandwiches apiece. Heading for the back of the facility, Ryan chanced a quick glance at

Chris as they walked. He could hardly contain his excitement, and suddenly nostalgia, edged with sadness, hit Ryan hard.

When his father had been alive, they'd spent every weekend they could together. Hunting, fishing or just repairing the broken-down lawn mower, it hadn't mattered to Ryan. The time was always special. His dad's death had left Ryan lost. All the "guy" activities, as his mother had always labeled them, suddenly ceased. He'd filled the void with trouble.

They entered the shed a few minutes later. It wasn't much to look at, but the building served its purpose. A row of covered stalls lined one side, each divided by an open partition. They faced south to a low berm with hay bales situated in front. Overhead a mechanical array of chains and pulleys allowed for moving targets. Ryan passed everything without a glance, Chris trailing along behind him at a much slower pace.

At the end of the shed there was a bigger stall. Stretched out on the hard concrete floor were two dark mats made of egg crate foam. Ryan kneeled down on the first one and unzipped the canvas bag he'd brought with him. He pulled out two black guns and carefully laid them out beside him. They were wicked-looking weapons with long barrels and large canisters on one side. Opening the bag a little wider, he removed two hard plastic masks. They looked as if they belonged in a chain saw movie.

Chris watched his every move and when Ryan handed one of the masks to him, he started to step backward before he could stop himself.

"I get to shoot?"

"They're paint guns," Ryan explained. "I thought you might get a kick out of trying one. I use them sometimes for training purposes."

Chris's face was suddenly transformed, and Ryan forgave himself for stretching the truth. Actually, he rarely used the weapons. They were no good for fine-tuning his aim and their pull was nothing like his real rifle. He wasn't about to tell Chris any of that, though. He'd wanted to do something fun for Chris, and this had seemed like a good solution.

"Oh, man…" was all the kid could say.

Ryan showed him how to put on the mask to protect his eyes and face, then they loaded the CO_2 cartridges that acted as the propellant for the guns.

The weapons were semiautomatics and Chris had a hard time at first getting comfortable. He didn't seem to care, though, and soon enough he got the hang of it, just as he had in the gym. In no time, he was stretched out on the mat, happily firing away.

Ryan stood a short distance behind and watched. When Chris ran out of paint balls, Ryan opened a new can and tossed them to him, showing him how to reload. The boy only stopped to change targets.

Ryan joined him after a while and with different colored paint in his gun, they held a sharpshooter contest. Chris won once and Ryan won once. They agreed to one last competition and Ryan triumphed, but only by a single shot.

They cleaned up again, themselves and the weapons, then headed for Ryan's truck, the afternoon sun slanting through the pine trees as they trudged toward the parking lot.

"Man, that was awesome!" Chris danced ahead of Ryan and walked backward, facing him as he spoke. "Those paint ball guns are cool!"

"There's a park close to Pensacola. Some of the guys go there on the weekends for games and they take their kids. Think your mom would let you go sometime?"

"I hope so. She'd probably think it was dangerous or something, but maybe..." He stopped, his words dying as he stared at Ryan with sudden speculation.

"Maybe what?"

He hesitated, then spoke. "Maybe you could convince her for me?"

"Sure," Ryan said. "I'll talk to her for you. I don't mind at all." They opened their respective doors and climbed inside, but Ryan didn't start the truck's engine. Instead he looked through the dusky light at Chris. He made his voice more serious than it had to be, deep and husky with warning. "But guns *can* be dangerous, especially when there isn't supervision. I've seen men seriously injured with air rifles."

A wariness came into Chris's eyes. He struggled to hide it. "Air rifles? Really? Hurt how?"

"You can blind someone with them, mess up their hearing, hell, I guess you could probably kill somebody if you hit 'em just right."

From the other side of the car where he sat, Ryan could hear Chris swallow. "I—I didn't know that. I thought air rifles were just like, you know, for fun...."

"They can be. But anything you shoot, from a regular weapon to a pellet pistol, has the capability to hurt somebody. It depends on the person whose finger is on the trigger." He paused. "You know what I mean?"

Chris looked out the window of the truck, a sudden overwhelming interest in a nearby pine tree holding his attention.

Ryan played it cool. "We actually arrested a kid close to your age not too long ago for firing at an officer with an air rifle. He could have really hurt someone with it."

He didn't think Chris was going to answer he took so long. Finally he turned and looked at Ryan. "What's gonna happen to him?"

"I don't know yet. He'll have to go through the court system. It's up to the judge." Ryan reached over and started the truck's engine, backing up the vehicle as he spoke. "He's bound for trouble, though. If I knew someone like that, I'd stay away from him, that's for sure...."

MARIA RAN her finger along the inside of the frosting bowl, then licked it clean. Chocolate. Her favorite. She hadn't had the time to bake in weeks and with the house empty and silent, the sudden urge for brownies had come over her. She'd run to the store and picked up everything she'd needed, plus some chicken to grill for dinner. Glancing at the clock, she was shocked to see it was almost five. Ryan and Christopher would probably be back any minute.

Sure enough, as she washed the last spoon, she heard the door fly open. Chris's voice followed a second later. "Mom?" he bellowed. "Mom? We're home...."

She walked into the living room and almost collided with her son. His face was animated and happy, with red streaks down one side. She reached out and touched one. "What in the world is this?"

He mimicked her movement then stared at his fingers and laughed. "It's paint," he said. "We went to the camp and we worked out and then we ate lunch and after that we—"

"Whoa, whoa," she said, "this is too much information all at once and I'm sure Lieutenant Lukas doesn't need a recap, too."

Standing on the edge of the entryway, Ryan smiled at her over Christopher's head. Something sounded inside Maria's heart as she smiled back at him. It was a warning bell, a signal to beware, but she acted as if she were deaf and ignored it completely. There were too many other things going on anyway, things she couldn't ignore. Like her pulse suddenly accelerating and a flush coming over her body.

Ryan wore the relaxed look of a man who'd spent the day enjoying himself, his dark hair ruffled, a smear of crimson down his shirt the same color as the one on Chris's face. The paint wasn't the only thing that matched Christopher, though. Ryan appeared as relaxed and happy as her son. From the time he'd left her that morning to now, he'd lost five years from his expression.

"You look…as if you had fun," she said.

"We did, Mom. It was sooo cool. Lieutenant Lukas said we could maybe go…" Christopher kept talking, but she didn't listen. All she could do was stare at Ryan.

"Can we, Mom? Can we?"

Chris's voice brought her back and she gave him a mother's standard answer. "We'll talk about it later," she said with distraction. "I've got chicken to grill, and I'm sure Lieutenant Lukas has plans—"

Before she could finish, Christopher spun around and looked at Ryan. "Chicken! Oh boy, you'll love it. She makes it with this hot sauce that'll curl your toes—"

Maria held up her hand to stop Chris, but Ryan answered first.

"I do like grilled chicken." His eyes captured hers and held them. She couldn't have looked away if she'd tried. "It's my favorite dinner, too."

CHAPTER TEN

THERE WAS NOTHING Maria could do. She thought briefly of trying to explain why this would not be a good idea, but Ryan *had* taken Chris out so she told herself she had an obligation. She sent Christopher to his room to clean up and directed Ryan to the guest bath so he could do the same. By the time they both returned, she had the grill hot and the salad mixed. She'd never invited a client to dinner at her home before; then again, she'd never had a client like Ryan before.

He came into the kitchen smelling of soap with his hair slicked back and his hands scrubbed. She stared at those hands a second too long as she handed him a beer from the refrigerator.

He took an appreciative swallow, then set the bottle down, obviously sensing her second thoughts. "Look, if you don't want me here, I'll leave. I know I shanghaied you into this invitation."

She'd been cutting a tomato, but at his words, she stopped the knife in midair. She could be honest or she could be diplomatic. She tried a little of both. "It's okay. I really appreciate what you did for

Chris today and a piece of grilled chicken is hardly payment for all your time.''

''You don't owe me anything,'' he said.

''No,'' she said. ''You're wrong. I do owe you something.'' Deciding to be blunt, she laid down the blade and wiped her hands then met his gaze. ''I owe you what any good therapist does—my full attention. But I hesitated because I'm crossing a line here—something I've never done before. I took the first step when I let Chris go with you. Now I'm taking another and it's not something I feel comfortable doing. I've never mixed my private life with my professional one.''

''Is that what you think you're doing?''

She held out her hands. ''You're in my kitchen, drinking a beer. We're talking about everything but why you were sent to me. I think that pretty much covers it, don't you?''

He opened his mouth to answer, but Christopher's steps in the living room silenced him before he could speak. A second later, her son burst into the kitchen. Maria didn't know whether to feel relieved or upset. Either way, something was going to have to be done, she decided. She couldn't continue this way. The sparks between her and Ryan had to be put out. Right now.

They'd eat, she'd send Chris to bed, then she would tell Ryan this.

They moved outside to the patio a few minutes later, Chris keeping up a line of bubbly chatter. She was grateful for his nonsense—it made the tension between her and Ryan less noticeable—but just hearing him talk like that made her smile, as well. She hadn't seen him act so silly in months.

She served their plates and Ryan poured the wine as Chris launched into a blow-by-blow description of the gym. "And it's got these huge mirrors all the way around the room so no matter which way you look, you see these weights and stuff. It was really cool. And Ryan gave me a shirt, too. It says SWAT on it and I wore it while I worked out. You might need to wash it, though. I got pretty stinky...."

Maria cut into her chicken and raised one eyebrow. "Let's save that for later, shall we?"

With a full mouth, he nodded. "That wasn't the coolest part, anyway, Mom. We went to the range!"

"The shooting range?"

"Yeah! And Ryan had these really great paint ball guns and we shot and shot and I won one round, too!"

Maria turned and met Ryan's eyes. "You let him shoot a gun?"

"They were paint guns," he replied. "Kids use them all the time. They're safe."

Maria nodded but her disquiet about Ryan, about dinner, about the whole situation, began to grow. How could she have *not* realized Ryan would expose Christopher to his world? Wasn't that what this whole trip had been about? She hadn't really given

serious consideration to what showing Chris the
training facility meant. Now she knew.

It meant guns. It meant violence. It meant everything she worked day after day to help these men
overcome.

She didn't say anything, and Christopher continued his explanation. By the time they'd finished des-
sert, she knew she was going to have to wind him
down herself. She stood and picked up his plate.
"You've had a pretty exciting day. I think it's time
to thank Lieutenant Lukas and head for bed."

She expected an argument. Instead he nodded and
stuck out his hand in Ryan's direction. "Thanks for
taking me. It was fun."

Ryan took Christopher's hand and shook it once.
"I had a good time, too. Thank you for going with
me."

Chris started toward the door, then he stopped
abruptly beside Maria, his tennis shoes squeaking.
"Thanks, Mom." He squeezed her waist in one
quick motion then turned loose before she could really think he was hugging her. "Thanks for letting
me go."

She watched him disappear inside the house then
Ryan's voice broke the evening's stillness. "You
have a problem with what we did, don't you?"

She turned to face him. The candles on the table
between them flickered in the breeze. They painted
uncertainty onto his hard expression. "I guess I

do,'' she answered reluctantly, as she put the plates back on the table.

He leaned back in the canvas chair and stared at her. ''Tell me about it.''

''It's not you,'' she began.

''Yes, it is,'' he interrupted. ''If I weren't a cop, if I weren't a sniper, if I were someone else, we wouldn't be having this discussion.'' His eyes glowed in the candlelight and his voice turned mocking. ''Don't lie to me, Doctor. It isn't professional.''

''You're right. It isn't professional. Nothing about this situation is professional and it's no one's fault but mine. That's exactly what I was about to say in the kitchen, before Chris came in, but now I feel that way even more so.''

''Why? Because I let him shoot a paint ball gun, for God's sakes? The kid needs to do stuff like that! That's what he's missing in his life.''

''He's missing his father,'' she said. ''Exposing him to what you do is not something he needs. At the very least, you should have told me what you had planned for today. Specifically.''

''Maybe I should have.'' He conceded the point, but she could tell he thought she was overreacting. ''Frankly, it's such an innocent activity I didn't even think about asking your permission. I was standing right beside him the whole time.... They're paint ball guns, Maria, nothing more. I borrowed them from another cop. They belong to his ten-year-old daughter.''

She shook her head. Her words had as much to do with her feelings about Ryan as anything else but she couldn't back down now. ''They look like real guns. I don't want him seeing things like that.''

His irritation overcame him. ''Well, you're too damn late for that, and I'm not talking about simple paint guns, either.'' Ryan's voice went harsh. ''Have you already forgotten his friend we arrested?''

''He told me he didn't know that boy!''

''Then why did he ask me today what was going to happen to him?''

His question stopped her cold. She sat back down in the metal chair, suddenly less secure in her belief of Chris's truthfulness than she had been before. ''He...he asked you that?''

Ryan nodded. ''It's one of the reasons I wanted some time with him. I wanted to make sure he knew hanging around that kid might not be such a good idea.''

''Wh-what did he say?''

''He didn't say anything.''

Maria looked into the backyard, into the darkness. The house behind her had a swimming pool and the light was on. A watery blue glow lit the trees that lined the fence between them. Ryan's pronouncement had thrown her for a loop, but she gathered her composure and spoke. ''I appreciate you spending time with Chris, okay?'' She turned in her chair and looked at Ryan. ''You're a good man and you have the toughest job in the world. But you've got some issues you need to work on. And that's what you and I are supposed to be doing together. Not having dinner. Not discussing my child. Not sharing a bottle of wine.''

''You're being ridiculous,'' he said. ''Nothing wrong happened here—''

''No,'' she said, rising abruptly. ''You don't understand. It *is* wrong. I'm not allowed to have a personal relationship with a client. It just isn't done.''

He stood, too. ''Is that what you think we're having? A personal relationship?''

She should have known what was going to happen, but Maria was too caught up in her argument. She started to nod, but stopped abruptly as he reached out unexpectedly and gripped her shoulders. His hands were huge; they spanned the top of her arms and went almost to her neck. He held her gently but there was no mistaking the strength in his fingers.

A second later, he bent his head and kissed her.

SHE STRUGGLED, but only for a moment. Ryan could feel the exact minute Maria gave in and allowed herself to enjoy the kiss. Her mouth, as sweet and soft as it looked, relaxed and he brought her closer to him.

She smelled like vanilla and tasted like brownies. He'd never wanted a woman so badly.

For much too brief a time, the kiss continued. The feel of her arms beneath his fingers, the silky whisper of her hair, the way she murmured in the back of her throat. The details registered then she pulled away. In the aqua light that bathed them both, her eyes were huge.

"What in the hell are you doing?" she gasped.

"I kissed you," he said harshly. "*That's* having a relationship."

She swayed inside the circle of his arms and he automatically tightened his hold. Her hands gripped his arms and he couldn't help himself. He lowered his head again and tasted her lips, then he let her go. She stood beside the table and stared at him.

"I'll show myself out," he said. "Thanks for dinner."

THE KISS was a summer storm. Brief and violent, it left Maria so shaken all she could do was nod. Ryan didn't see her acquiesce. He'd already pivoted and vanished through the back door. A few seconds later, she heard the front door close as well. When the engine of his truck started, she realized she'd been holding her breath. She let it out in a rush.

Now she'd done it. She'd really done it.

Jackson's warning echoed in her mind. *You're the doctor. He's the patient. The line is drawn by you, Maria.*

But the feel of Ryan's lips had been unlike anything she'd expected. Hard and demanding, yet
warm and sexy. And beneath her hands, the muscles
in his arms had been like iron. What did he do to
make them like that? She tried to rope in her emotions, to corral the stampede that was threatening
her, but she could have just as easily stopped her
heart from beating. It wasn't going to happen. She
closed her eyes and touched her mouth with her
fingers.

What on earth had she let happen tonight?

She sat down in a daze. Finally, after a few
minutes, she stirred herself and took the dishes inside. Dumping them into the sink, she went upstairs
and took a cold shower.

It didn't help.

She spent the entire night inside the circle of
Ryan's arms, feeling his caresses, tasting his kisses.
He was the kind of lover every woman wanted, slow
when he should have been, fast when she was ready.
The words he whispered in her ears were just what
she wanted to hear, as well. Warm and loving, then
hot and wild, bringing her to the point of exhaustion
then taking her beyond.

When she finally woke up from the dream, some
time in the middle of the night, she actually looked
to the other side of the bed. It was empty, of course.
She rolled over and groaned.

RYAN'S PHONE woke him at 2:00 a.m on Monday
morning. The dog had started sleeping with him,

and the sound disturbed him, too. He sat up and barked once then watched Ryan roll over and grab the receiver. "Lukas here."

"This is Thompson. You wake?"

"I am now." Running a hand through his hair, Ryan swung his legs to the side of the mattress. The dog jumped to the floor and trotted out of the room. "What's up?"

"We're getting a call," the big cop said. "It's gonna hit the beepers in about two seconds. There's a sniper out at Rosemary Beach."

"Are you kidding?" Rosemary Beach was an exclusive subdivision on the outskirts of their territory; it was on 30-A, almost to Panama City Beach. The houses were beyond pricey, the architecture unique. Ryan stood. "What in the hell is a sniper doing out there? Are there uniforms on-site? What's—"

"Shut up and listen, Lukas, I didn't call to give you a personal report."

Ryan winced at the cop's response. He was one of the nicest men on the team, but he hated to be woken in the middle of the night. "Okay, okay...so why did you call?"

"Two reasons, so listen close. One—I knew you'd hear the beep and come out since it's close to you. Don't do it. If Lena sees you out there, she's going to fire you, okay?"

Ryan sat back down on the bed. "She tell you that?"

"She didn't have to," Thompson retorted. "The other time you showed up, she cussed for about an hour after you left, then she got real quiet. I don't need to remind you what happened to the last guy she got that upset with—I'm sure you can remember on your own."

Ryan nodded to himself. A year before, Lena had canned another sniper. He'd deserved it, of course. The man was a loose cannon; he couldn't control his weapon or his mouth. He and Beck Winters, the team's negotiator at that time, had fought constantly. Ryan wasn't anything like Randy Tamirisa but he was in trouble and Lena cut no one any slack.

"What's the second reason?"

"I want you on alert," Bradley answered. "If something goes down out there we can't handle, I didn't want to have to hunt you down and drag you out of some chick's bed."

She was the last person Ryan would have described as a *chick* but he instantly thought of Maria. He dismissed the notion, not wanting the picture Bradley's words had conjured...her dark hair spread over his pillow, her brown eyes looking into his. "Where's Chase?" he asked roughly.

"He's at the hospital. Judy had the baby but it's sick. He'll get the call, but honestly, he's not at his best. He's worried about his kid and distracted. And this is out of J.L.'s league. I'd rather have—"

He broke off in midsentence, but Ryan didn't need the assistant commander to finish for him to understand. Brad wanted someone he could depend on, not just a backup who hadn't had enough experience.

"I understand," Ryan said. "Why don't I head that way? There's an all-night convenience store right there on the corner. I'll park there and wait."

"That's good." Bradley paused. "But keep your damn head down, okay? Lena will kill both of us if she finds out I've called you."

"I think she might know the truth if you do have to bring me in."

"Yeah, but by then she'd be grateful. If we don't need you and she sees you, then we're going to have to explain it all to Lena...and I don't know about you, but that's not something I enjoy doing."

They said their goodbyes after that, Ryan throwing on his uniform and grabbing his gear. The dog watched his every move. When Ryan finally started for the garage, the animal trotted ahead of him, then stopped before him and pawed at the door. He'd never done that before and Ryan stared in amazement. "What?" he asked. "You wanna go, too?"

The dog just stared at him, of course, but Ryan felt something stir inside him. "I'm sorry, buddy," he muttered. "Maybe next time, okay?"

Twenty minutes later he was at the "Stop-and-Rob" on the corner nearest the subdivision. Ryan went inside and grabbed a cup of stale coffee and, at the last minute, a bag of dog treats. He went back out to the truck and prepared to wait.

From where he sat, the road that led into the enclave of overpriced homes was only a half mile away or less. In the darkness he could see nothing beyond the flash of the patrol cars but he knew the area well. The style of the houses was supposed to be quaint, yet they all looked the same to him—overdone. Painted a variety of colors, their wooden fronts were trimmed with elaborate shutters, porches and decks.

Ryan reached for his coffee. The house he'd shared with Ginny had been modest, but she'd kept it decorated and filled with flowers. She'd loved to bake, too. All at once he remembered Maria's house on Saturday. He'd walked in there with Chris and it'd smelled like a home.

His heart had locked up so fast he hadn't been able to breathe, but when he'd kissed Maria, he'd thought it was going to erupt from his chest. He wasn't sure why he'd kissed her, but he didn't regret it, not for a minute. There was something unique about her, something he couldn't wrap his mind around but that spoke to him regardless. The realization brought two emotions with it: the usual sweep of guilt, but also confusion. How could he think of Ginny one second and Maria the next?

The complicated reaction hardly had time to register; the cell phone beside him suddenly sounded. Ryan grabbed it up, nearly spilling his coffee.

"You there?"

It was Brad and he was clearly tense.

"I'm at the store," Ryan answered. "What's going on?"

"All we know is there's a guy in one of the beachfront houses. He has a gun—"

"Hostages?"

"None that we know about. His wife says he started drinking this afternoon and kept going till he passed out. He's just left the hospital after being treated for depression. He woke up around midnight, popped her a few times, then grabbed his rifle and started shooting it off the porch."

"Toward the water?"

"Yeah. There were some kids down there, too. They got away—nobody was hit, but the guy's refusing to talk to Diego. It doesn't look good."

"Is Chase there?"

Bradley started to answer then his voice turned muffled. He was obviously talking to someone else or speaking into his headset. He came back a moment later. "He's here," His voice went grim. "But he's a wreck. He can't even give us any recon, and he's in the house right next door. Hell, they're so close together, he ought to be able to hear the guy breathe."

Ryan's pulse stayed steady. He was too much of a professional for it to do otherwise, but he did feel a jolt of anger. He should be there, not down the road getting a secondhand recount and sipping a cup of cold coffee. He decided right then and there he would be at Maria's office in the morning when she opened to convince her—somehow—to release him. She had to.

He knew it was pointless but he spoke. "Let me come down there, Brad. I can help—"

"Not yet. My butt's in a sling if Lena finds out I even called you. You sit tight and I'll phone if we need you. Otherwise, don't come down here, and that's an order from *me*."

Bradley rang off without another word, and Ryan cursed loudly.

Two hot humid hours later, the phone sounded again. Ryan was accustomed to waiting long hours on stakeouts but not from the plush front seat of his truck. He was startled from a doze by the ringing.

"Get down here, Lukas, right now."

Fully wakened by these words, Ryan threw the phone to the seat, started the engine and tore out of the parking lot. In just a few minutes, the truck slid next to the War Wagon and Ryan jumped out. Lena met him at the door.

"Bradley told me what he did," she said in a tight voice. "We're not discussing his—and your—actions right now because Chase is exhausted and J.L. doesn't have enough know-how for this one. I need *you,* but don't consider this a pardon. You are back on leave the minute this is over!"

Ryan nodded. "I understand."

"Then understand this, too. You dot every *i* and cross every *t*. Take absolutely no chances whatsoever on *anything*. I'm leaving myself—and everyone else—wide-open by using you when you're officially on leave. If something goes wrong, you can bet I'll be the first one sued, then you, then the city. We all lose our jobs and nobody will be happy but the lawyers. Got it?''

He nodded. ''Just tell me what's going on.''

She outlined the scene. The house fronted the beach and they thought the shooter was still on the porch. In another hour, dawn would break and the early joggers and shellers who frequented the beach would begin to show up. Lena had blocked off the shoreline for half a mile on either side of the house, but she couldn't afford to leave the situation alone much longer.

She pointed to an architect's drawings of the street. ''We don't have any floor plans of the houses, but we know these two are mirrors of each other. Chase is in the one next door to the shooter. Come up from the east side, go in through the front. He's on the second floor and he knows you're coming.''

Slipping on his headset, Ryan jutted his chin to the nearby houses. ''Are they empty?''

''No.'' She sighed heavily and tapped the plans again. ''This one has the owner in it. These two are rented. We couldn't get everyone out. You'll have to watch for civilians.''

Grabbing his helmet and headset, Ryan asked a few more questions, then started out the door of the

Wagon. At the last minute, Lena called out. Ryan stopped to look at her.

"Be careful, okay? This guy's been very unpredictable. He shot off a lot of rounds at first but we haven't heard anything in an hour or so." She gripped the edge of her desk and stared at him with a worried expression. "He could be gearing up for the end."

IN LESS THAN five minutes, Ryan had jogged down the deserted streets of the tiny subdivision and reached the darkened house on the beach. Entering through an unlocked mahogany door that faced the front, he spoke softly through his microphone. "It's me, Chase. I'm coming up."

"Ten-four."

He picked his way through the elegant residence to the oak-lined stairs, gingerly passing a gilt-edged table in the entry that held a porcelain vase of fresh flowers. The homes at Rosemary Beach weren't typical beach houses. Nothing sold for less than a million dollars, not even an empty lot.

Ryan hesitated on the landing.

"Turn right." Chase's voice sounded in his headset. "I'm in the master bedroom. It's at the end of the hall."

With his weapon ready, Ryan slipped silently down the corridor. The carpet was so thick, his boots slid through it, leaving a trail. He passed several open doors then came to the last one. Ryan dropped to the floor and belly-crawled to the window where the other sniper waited by the window. They exchanged nods in the stifling silence. Lena had cut the power to the street hours ago; without the background hum of air conditioners and refrigerators, the quiet felt thicker than normal.

"Seen anything?"

Chase Mitchell shook his head with an almost imperceptible movement. "Nothing," he said hoarsely. "He fired several times about three hours ago and that's it. Total silence since then. I guess he's still on the porch but I can't see past the privacy fence. I wouldn't bet my life he hasn't moved."

"Heard anything from Diego?"

"Nada." He made a circle out of two fingers then dropped them. "If the guy ain't talking to Diego now, he ain't gonna talk ever." Chase cut his eyes in Ryan's direction. "I think he's gone, man."

Ryan nodded slowly. It wouldn't be the first time the team had been held at bay by a dead man.

"I'm outta here." Chase started squirming backward, but halted his progress when Ryan spoke again, his eyes never moving from the window.

"Hey—you going back to the hospital?"

"Yeah." Chase's voice became tense. "Lena tell you about the baby?"

Ryan nodded in the gloom. "I'm sorry, Chase. Tell Judy—" He stopped abruptly. He didn't know what to tell Chase's wife. If Ginny had still been alive, she would have been there already—waiting, praying, doing whatever women did at the hospital when they needed each other.

After a second he decided that was all he *could* say. "If Ginny was here—"

Chase interrupted before Ryan could stumble any more. "I know, man, I know. I'll tell Judy you said so."

In the heavy darkness, the silence stretched out, then a second later, with a whisper of breathless air, Ryan sensed more than heard Chase's departure.

He looked through the scope of his rifle at the house next door and settled in to wait.

THE SKY was still dark but in a few hours, dawn would break. Lena had been vague when she'd called Maria and told her to come out, but that wasn't unusual. Lena didn't always have the time for an explanation and Maria didn't need one. More than once, her expertise had been required at the scene and she was prepared. She'd rung Mrs. Lowe, and the older woman had come right over to be with Chris. She'd stay as long as she had to and even get him off to school if necessary, but Maria hated knowing she wouldn't be there when her son woke up. She'd call, if she could, about the time he was scheduled to leave.

Maria stood in the middle of the War Wagon and looked at Sarah. "Tell me what's going on."

"At this point, our information is sketchy. All we know is the husband and wife had a fight, the husband started drinking, then he pulled out the rifle. She fled the house and called their minister, who then called the P.D. There aren't any children involved, thank God.''

"Well, that's one good thing, at least.''

Nodding, Sarah turned back to her laptop computer and began to hit the keys.

Maria hardly noticed. All she could think about was the words she'd exchanged with Lena. Maria had just gotten there when the door at the front of the War Wagon had suddenly crashed open. Lena had poked her head in, then stabbed a finger in Maria's direction. "I need to talk to you. Right now!''

Maria had dropped her notes on a nearby table and clattered down the steps to the sandy parking lot where Lena waited.

The other woman's gray eyes were darker than usual. With short, terse sentences Lena had explained the real reason she'd called Maria.

"I had to put Ryan in the house next door. Chase Mitchell's wife is in the hospital and the baby she just had is very ill. I kept him as long as I could but I had to relieve him and I couldn't use J.L. He just doesn't have the experience. Ryan was my only option.'' The predawn air was heavy and humid; she wiped her face on the shoulder of her T-shirt. "Tell me the truth. Did I do the right thing?''

Maria answered without thinking, her answer based on instinct, not textbooks. "He'll be fine. He isn't going to flip out, if that's what you're worried about."

"Are you sure?"

"Yes. Ryan *isn't* unstable. He's angry. He's upset. He's grieving. As long as he gets the help he needs, he'll be fine." She paused for a moment. "He's hurting but—"

"Oh, God," Lena covered her face with her hands then looked up a moment later. "Why is there always a 'but'?"

Maria plunged ahead. She had to, especially after the kiss she and Ryan had shared, the kiss she couldn't get out of her mind. "I do think he should see someone other than me, Lena. This—this isn't going to work out. We've yet to have a real session and I don't think we even can now. Another doctor would be much better—"

Lena's mouth actually dropped open. "Are you nuts? Why on earth would you say that? You're helping him, aren't you? He took Chris out to the camp and they did okay and everything—"

"Yes, but—"

"Then there's nothing to discuss."

Maria was almost desperate now. "You don't understand. It's more complicated than I've explained. I think he'd truly be better off—"

Lena interrupted her with an angry shake of her head. "You're the only therapist in Destin who's qualified for this! It'd take months to find someone else and you just said yourself he might get worse if he ignores his problem. You have to treat him. You're it.''

"Look, Lena…it—it's personal, okay? I can't work with Ryan. I tried to explain this before and you didn't understand, because I was still confused myself. Now…now the problem is a little more defined, if you know what I mean.''

Lena's eyes rounded in surprise as Maria's vague explanation soaked in. "Wait a minute.… Last time we spoke I thought you might be trying to tell me this, but I decided I was crazy. Are you saying you and Ryan…''

Maria's throat went dry. She had a hard time swallowing. "I'm saying Ryan needs to see someone else. I'm sorry to let you down like this, but that's all there is to it. I've developed a problem treating him and—''

"Oh, my God! You *are* falling for him!''

Maria winced. The words reminded her too much of Jackson's admonitions. "I'm not sure I'd put it that way, but—''

With an impatient gesture, Lena held up her hand and stopped Maria's explanation. "Look, Maria, I don't want to sound blunt here, but the bottom line is this—you're going to have to deal with the problem the best way you can. I'm sorry it's clouded the issue, and I certainly pray you can still do the job.'' She met Maria's eyes with a steady stare. "To tell you the truth, it downright scares me…but one way or the other, you've got to handle it. I can't. I've got problems of my own." And with that, she'd left.

Maria stared out the window of the Winnebago. Lena had said she understood, but she didn't. Not really.

How could she when Maria didn't herself?

RYAN HAD BEEN in the house an hour when Lena's voice came over his headset. "We can't wait much longer, Ryan. The sun's starting to come up. I've got the beach barricaded, but you know how that goes…some idiot will ignore it and go around. Any sign of activity?"

Ryan hadn't moved an inch since Chase had left. "I've got nothing."

"Can you confirm he's still on the balcony?"

"Negative." Ryan blinked his eyes and focused on the wooden railing of the house next door. It couldn't have been twenty feet from where he lay. "I've seen nothing here. He could have gone back inside, I can't tell."

"Would a different position be better?"

"I'm sure Chase got the best spot, but I'll look around."

"See what you can do," Lena replied. "If we don't get something going here soon, we're going to have to go in…and to do that, I need more info."

"Ten-four."

Ryan eased backward, away from the window. His muscles were tight and they ached, but he did what he was trained to do; he ignored them. He'd spent a lot of time frozen in spots much less comfortable than this one. Slipping through the silent bedroom, he went back into the hallway. It wasn't always obvious from the outside, but some of the homes in Rosemary extended to a third level. Chase might not have thought of that since he was fairly new to the area. If Ryan could go higher, he might be able to see more.

Sure enough, he found an extra set of stairs at the other end of the hall, behind a closed door. The treads were metal and steep, the whole thing more like a ladder than a staircase.

Anxious to keep the house next door in view, Ryan took the steps two at a time. He came out much sooner than he would have expected, to a small landing. It was a glassed-in widow's walk, a 360 degree view. Unprepared for the sudden openness, he swung around instantly, to face the other side. The shake-lined roof was much closer than he would have thought possible—he could have leaped across the empty gap. A copy of the tower where he stood was on the other side.

Ryan looked across the space and into a pair of terrified eyes.

Startled, he let out a curse as his finger tightened on the trigger of his weapon. He spoke without thinking into his mouthpiece. "Shit! I'm looking right at him, guys... I climbed upstairs and he's right here!"

The man's appearance was strange—he had gray hair and gray eyes and even his skin was gray. He looked ill, Ryan thought, then he amended himself. Not ill—he was past that point. He looked as if he were dying.

The man reacted slowly to Ryan's unexpected presence, shock and fear transforming his face. For one fleeting moment, it seemed as if he wanted to say something, to explain how it had all gone so terribly wrong, but a second later his expression changed radically, almost as if he had no control over his features.

Then he raised his gun and fired.

CHAPTER ELEVEN

HER ARGUMENT with Lena weighing heavily on her mind, Maria was talking with Sarah in the Wagon when she heard a popping sound. All of a sudden the young cop jerked her hand to her ear, her eyes horrified, her mouth falling open. Clearly listening to something one of the other officers was saying over her headset, her expression filled with panic.

With horror, Maria realized what she'd heard.

Gunfire.

RYAN REACTED instantly, his training taking command of his senses and the weapon he held. Through the broken window, he returned fire, but unlike the man across the gap, he hit his target. The shooter fell backward, a glittering red mist painting the walls of the cupola where he'd stood a second before. Clutching his microphone, Ryan clattered down the stairs, half falling, half running. "Subject down," he screamed. "Repeat, subject down. Requesting backup and medics. Right now!"

Lena's voice came into his ear, breathless and jumpy. She was running as she yelled into her microphone. "Talk to me, Ryan! Talk to me...."

He took the second set of stairs at a sprint and careened into the elegant living room. Unable to stop his progress, he crashed into a table and sent two lamps spinning. He didn't look back; he simply kept going...and talking. "I just returned fire. The perp is down. On the third floor. On the widow's walk."

"Ten-four. I'm almost there.... Team assemble on the front porch."

Ryan tumbled out the front door just as a streak of black flew by. It was Lena. He fell in behind her, and by the time they reached the porch next door, the team was collected and ready to breach the house.

Each man had an assigned position, and they took it without delay. The door gave way as the ram was applied and Ryan, usually not this close during an assault, pushed to the front, to Lena's side. He ran with her to the third-story staircase. "He's up here." With his shoulder against the door at the end of the second hallway, he jerked his head upward. "Not on the porch. He was never on the porch. He's on the widow's walk."

They scrambled up the stairs, Lena holding Ryan back as they reached the top. She'd been trained as a front-entry person, one of the most dangerous positions on the team, and she needed to go first. Her weapon out before her, she swung into the open space. Then she cursed.

Ryan pushed his way into the small space as she

dropped to the body and put two fingers against the victim's neck. Half the man's head was gone, but Ryan understood. Lena had to confirm it for herself. After a second, she rocked back and looked up at Ryan, her chest heaving, her breath rasping in the too silent house. "He's dead," she said numbly. Pulling her microphone closer, she spoke again. "EMS, this is L1. Come quiet. Repeat, come quiet."

Ryan listened to her instructions, their meaning soaking in. There was no need now for a wailing ambulance. The man was past help. They looked down at the body together, each lost for a moment in the tragedy.

Finally, Lena spoke. "Maria's back at the wagon. We might as well use her. She'll do a better job than me telling the family."

"You already had her out here?"

"I called her about…something else. Go get her and bring her to the house. I'll take care of the medics."

He started to leave but looking once again at the dead man, Ryan felt his anger rise without warning, a hot, heavy wash of it. How could this guy have treated his life so cavalierly? Didn't he know there were people who would have done anything to have it? A convoluted mix of emotions materialized inside Ryan and all at once he wanted to scream. Ginny and Maria. Life and death. Guilt and love.

Dammit, none of it made any sense any more. None of it at all!

Pivoting on the blood-slicked floor, he cursed, then bolted down the stairs.

"THEY NEED YOU at the house." Ryan's gaze would have been unreadable to anyone else, but Maria easily deciphered his emotions.

It was her own she wasn't so sure about.

When she'd heard the shot, she'd felt as if the bullet had hit her. Her heart had stopped, then dropped to the floor before Sarah had been able to explain what had happened. This wasn't the time or the place to interpret her reaction, but Maria was afraid she already knew what it meant.

She spoke softly. "Are you okay?"

"I'm fine." His voice was terse, his attitude cold. He looked away from her, to the sky where a mixture of pink and purple streaked across the horizon. She waited, expecting more. For a long second he was silent, then he spoke again, his wrath overcoming him as he confessed to what she already knew.

"No, dammit, that's a lie. I'm *not* fine." His expression was full of anger and pain. "I just killed a man who didn't have to die, goddammit! How the hell do you think I feel?"

She put her hand on his arm. "I'm so sorry it ended that way."

"So am I. I ought to feel sympathy for the poor son of a bitch. Instead, I feel…"

His words died off. Maria squeezed his arm and willed him to continue. "You feel..."

"Mad as hell." He looked at her with defiance. "Is that sick? Am I crazy?"

"What do *you* think? Does it feel crazy?"

Her question didn't register—he continued as if she hadn't even spoken. "Suicide by cop," he said resentfully. "He fired that goddamn rifle and I had to shoot back or be killed." He snapped his fingers sharply. "Just like that—and it's over."

Ryan clenched his jaw and then his fists. "It shouldn't have happened. My God, if Ginny had..."

He didn't need to finish his sentence for Maria to understand. He would have given anything—including his own life—to bring Ginny back, and for whatever reason, this man had wanted his taken from him.

"It's not fair, is it?"

He shook his head, dejection outlining every inch of his body.

Maria softened her voice but nothing could soften the truth. "It's over, though, Ryan. That part of your life is gone."

The raw agony in his gaze was almost too painful to bear witness to. The sting went all the way into her heart, the last of her objectivity flowing from the wound his anguish left behind. She'd felt sympathy for him before this, but exposing his rawness so truthfully—so abruptly—suddenly made Ryan seem even more vulnerable. He was a man and he was hurting and she wanted to make him feel better any way she could.

She knew she shouldn't, but she stepped closer and put her hands on his chest, looking at him with all the compassion she possessed.

He stood still for one long beat, then he raised his arms and crushed her against him. His chest was hard, his heart an uneven beat beneath her ear. Two thoughts filled her mind.

She could stay like this forever.

And she'd just made the biggest mistake of her life.

IT WAS AFTER NOON by the time the team finished. Maria walked back to her car, too exhausted to do anything but put one foot in front of the other. The victim's wife had taken the news of her husband's death hard, even though she knew he was unstable. In the end, Maria had had to call the woman's physician and get him to help. He'd sedated her and left a nurse at the house. Walking down the stairs later with Maria, he'd told her a little about the couple. The year before, they'd lost a son in a car accident, he explained. The father had been driving and had reached over to answer his cell phone, then lost control of the vehicle. Their SUV had rammed a bridge abutment then exploded and the son had burned to death. The father had never recovered. He'd spiraled, instead, into a quicksand of recrimination and depression. Hospitalization hadn't helped.

Unlocking the door to her Toyota, Maria climbed

inside, the emotions of the past few hours crushing her with their heaviness. Closing her eyes, she let her head fall against the headrest and cursed. The call-out alone was enough to undo her, but the way she'd thrown herself at Ryan... God, what had she been thinking? If Lena refused to let her take herself off Ryan's case, then Maria only had one choice left, as awkward as it might be. She'd have to discuss the problem with Ryan again. She told herself he'd listen better this time. She could find him another therapist and they'd both be better off.

Lifting her head, Maria pulled her phone from her bag and made a quick call to Mrs. Lowe. The older woman reassured her again that everything had gone fine. Maria had already called once, to talk to Chris before he'd left for school. "Thanks again," she said.

"Not a problem, sweetheart," the older woman replied.

Maria dropped her phone into her purse, then stuck her key into the ignition. The Toyota's motor cranked once...then died. "Oh, no," she moaned. "Not now. Please not now." She'd been nursing the car along for six months. "You can't die now."

The engine paid her no heed. She gave it three more tries, but each time the grinding sound only got louder. Finally she got out of the car and raised the hood to stare down at the twisted wires and parts. She had no idea what she was doing, but she was too tired to realize it.

"Having trouble?"

Ryan's deep voice came from her left. Maria

looked around the edge of the hood. He stood by the back fender. His jaw was stubbled, his eyes exhausted, his uniform filthy. Under the weight of his fatigue, his broad shoulders slumped.

He was the sexiest man she'd ever seen.

Disturbed by her reaction, she pointed shakily to the engine. "I—I think it's dead. It's been making this sound for weeks but I haven't had time to take it into the shop. I guess this is what I get for ignoring warning signs."

"I'll take you home," he said. "Then I can come back and fiddle with it later."

"Oh, no, Ryan. That's not necessary—"

Speaking over his shoulder, he started walking off before she could finish. "I'm parked over here. Let's go."

His shortness was reasonable; the call-out and resulting upheaval had left him with no reserve. She followed him, then stopped when he did, at the tailgate of his truck. "I appreciate the offer, but it isn't necessary," she said firmly. "I can catch a cab to the house and call the tow truck from there."

He threw his gear into the bed where it landed and scattered. "I'll take you home."

The simple way he spoke snatched her breath. She reached up and nervously tucked a strand of hair behind her ear. She told herself this would give them an opportunity to talk. She could tell him that she had to find him another doctor, that she couldn't help him, no matter how badly she wanted to. This was the perfect opportunity for the discussion they needed to have.

Get real. The other side of her brain taunted her sharply. *You want to be with him, too. This has nothing to do with any discussion and you know it.*

With the words ringing in her head, she looked up at Ryan. He'd slipped on his sunglasses, and in their dark lenses, she saw two reflections of herself, two haggard, confused Marias. One was the professional. One was the woman.

"Are you sure?" She asked the question of him, but it was meant for herself.

"I'm not sure of anything anymore." He looked beyond her, to the highway. When she followed his gaze she saw the ambulance pulling out of the subdivision, silent and slow.

A second later, she brushed past him and climbed inside the truck.

THEY PULLED into her driveway thirty minutes later.

"Can you come inside?" she asked as the engine ticked down. "I'd like to talk to you about something."

Talking wasn't what he wanted. As Ryan stared at Maria, he accepted that truth, just as he had the one she'd pointed out to him earlier that morning. Her bluntness had accomplished what even his guilt had been unable to. Ginny *was* gone and life *wasn't* fair.

And there was nothing he could do to change either fact.

Maria hadn't known it, of course, but she'd

reached right inside him and opened up something with those words, something that had been closed since Ginny's death. The consequence of that change was strangely liberating.

"Can you come in?" she repeated.

He nodded his acquiescence, and she started up the sidewalk. He followed her into her entry, a blast of air-conditioning greeting them both. Closing his eyes, Ryan lifted his face to let the coolness wash over him. Mixed in with the chill was the lingering scent of Maria's perfume and of something else, something ephemeral. Something he could only think of as *home*. He never smelled it at his place.

"Can I get you something to drink?"

At her voice, he opened his eyes. She had put her purse down on a table beside the wall, stopping in the middle of the entry to look back at him. In the dim light from the window over the front door, she was impossibly beautiful. His heart did a funny kind of jump.

"A cold soda?" she asked. "Or maybe something stronger? I have some beer—"

He interrupted her. "There's only one thing I want."

She knew exactly what he was going to say; he could read it in her face. He said it anyway.

"I want *you*."

She stood without moving, a frozen shadow in the cool hall.

He came closer and lifted a hand to her hair, picking up a single dark strand.

Her eyes were huge, her breathing a rasp in the silence. "I don't think that would be a good idea."

"Why not?"

"You know why," she said quietly. "I'm your doctor, your therapist. We're not supposed to—"

"You're making excuses," he said roughly. "This is between you and me. It has nothing to do with your profession or my job or any other garbage you can come up with." He dropped his voice. "Admit the truth, Maria."

"That *is* the truth," she protested.

"No." Releasing the strand of hair, he took her shoulders in his hands. She felt fragile in his grip, less substantial than he would have thought. "*This* is the truth."

He bent down and kissed her. Her lips were soft and full, and they tasted so sweet he knew he could lose himself in them forever.

She struggled a second, maybe two, then she seemed to melt against him, her body turning pliant as her mouth opened. Ryan didn't hesitate; he pulled her closer and murmured her name, his tongue caressing hers, his palms dropping to the curve of her back.

She clung to him and knit her hands behind his neck. Tunneling her fingers into his hair, she kissed him back. There was a desperateness to her actions, he realized suddenly, a hunger almost as deep as his own. She obviously tried to keep it within the boundaries of what she allowed herself, but he'd broken through. As if to confirm this, she made a sound in her throat, a sound of desire that only made him want her more.

Without thinking past the moment, he pushed up the back of her blouse and found bare skin. She arched into his touch and he traced the path of her spine with his fingers, each ridge giving way to a silken valley. When he reached the lacy band of her bra, he followed it with his hands to the front of her body, to hold her breasts. They were full and round, the lace that contained them too thin to be a barrier against his fevered caress. He flicked the clasp in the front and the garment fell open. She raised her arms and he pulled off her shirt, the bra going with it as he bent his head to kiss her again.

She tugged at his T-shirt as he continued to press his mouth against her own. They broke apart long enough to rip off his shirt, then a second later she was touching his bare chest, her hands hot and demanding as they danced over his skin. After a moment, she dropped her fingers to the belt buckle at his waist.

She had the buckle almost undone when the back door flew open and Christopher called out.

CHAPTER TWELVE

WITH A HORRIFIED LOOK, Maria froze. Ryan scooped up her clothing and thrust it at her, pushing her into the guest bath, just off the entry, at the very same time. As she slammed the door, she saw him grab his T-shirt and pull it over his head, calling to Christopher at the very same time.

"In here, Chris."

She gripped the edge of the bathroom counter with one hand and closed her eyes, sending up a prayer of thanks. What on earth would she have done if her son had actually walked in on that little scene? If there had been any question before, there wasn't now; she had totally and completely lost her mind.

Ryan's deep voice rumbled in the hallway. "What are you doing home, buddy? School let out early today?"

She heard the clunk of Chris's school bag as it hit the floor. "It's the last week," he answered. "They let us out an hour early every day this week, then on Friday, we just goof off completely." She heard the couch squeak. "What are you doing here, Ryan? Where's my mom? How'd the call-out go?"

"It went fine. She's washing up..." Ryan's voice drifted off as he obviously followed Chris into the den.

Maria stared in the mirror over the lavatory. A wild-eyed woman glared back, a shirt and bra clutched to her bare chest, her lips swollen, her hair completely disheveled. She bore no resemblance to anyone Maria knew. With a groan of disbelief, she dropped her clothing to the floor then twisted the faucets in front of her. Sticking her hands under the gushing stream of water, she splashed it over her face in a useless effort to bring herself under control. Finally, when she couldn't put it off any longer, she donned her bra and shirt, took a deep breath, then opened the door.

Ryan and Christopher both looked up when she entered the den. Maria concentrated on her son; she couldn't bear to meet Ryan's eyes. "Hey, sweetie," she said. To her ears, her voice sounded forced but he didn't seem to notice. "What are you doing home so early?"

He explained one more time, his patient voice making it clear she was an idiot for forgetting his dismissal time.

"And Friday is our last day of school for the year." He looked at her with a pointed expression. "You do remember that, don't you? I'm going to Ricky's house for the weekend. You said I could."

"I remember," she reassured him. "I've already

made chocolate chip cookies for you to take with you. They're in the—''

He was off the sofa before she even finished.

''—freezer.''

Ryan laughed unexpectedly, and Maria found herself doing the same. Hers came easily, but his sounded almost rusty, as if he hadn't laughed in a very long time. As Chris disappeared into the kitchen, they looked at each other and fell silent again, an awkward tenseness coming over them both in the aftermath of what had just occurred.

He stood and came to where she waited. His eyes were dark and hungry, and he spoke with reluctance. ''I guess I should leave now.''

''I think that would be best.''

Unbelievably he reached out and touched her face. Her skin burned under his finger even though he dropped his hand almost immediately. ''I'm sorry,'' he said.

''You have nothing to be sorry for,'' she answered. ''This was all my fault. I don't know what got into me and it can't—''

Shaking his head, he put a finger over her lips and stopped her flow of words. ''No, Maria. You don't understand. I'm sorry we were *interrupted*.... I don't start things I don't intend to finish.''

''Ryan, *you* don't understand.'' She felt her chest go tight, the look in his eyes making her shiver. ''This...this has got to stop, and I told Lena that today. As your therapist I'm bound by certain rules. Those rules don't allow for any kind of—''

He kissed her, hard and fast. She felt dizzy when he pulled away.

''I understand better than you think. In fact, I understand your 'rules' more than you do.'' He paused. ''They don't make sense and you're one foolish woman to hide behind them.''

TAKING A CAB to work, Maria spent all day Tuesday trying to get her nerves back in line and soothe all the clients whose appointments had been canceled because of the call-out. By six o'clock, when she finally got home, all she wanted was a glass of wine and a hot bath. She couldn't focus or concentrate on anything but Ryan. He'd dropped her car at her office that afternoon. He'd repaired it and even washed it, the consideration of his efforts something she couldn't quite believe. Reed had *never* done anything for her like that. *Never*. And she could get used to being treated that way!

She opened the door and called Christopher's name.

Silence answered her.

Maria immediately became uneasy. She dropped her briefcase and purse on the table in the hall then looked around for Christopher's book bag. She'd talked to him twice since he'd come home from school but the blue backpack was nowhere in sight. He was no longer grounded, but he had a 6:00 p.m.

curfew on school nights regardless. She knew even before she went through the house that he wasn't there, though, and neither was a note telling her where he might have gone. She checked the whole place just to make sure, but the empty rooms confirmed her suspicions.

An hour later, he still wasn't home. Maria fell into a pit of self-recrimination. Chris had gotten none of her attention in the past few days. She'd been so busy concentrating on her work, and on Ryan, she'd given the poor kid nothing. She was a rotten mother.

By 8:00 p.m. she'd called all his friends, driven through the neighborhood twice and gone through town once. At eight-thirty she phoned Lena who counseled patience and promised help. Twenty minutes later the phone rang. Ryan spoke the moment she picked up.

"I've got Chris with me. He's fine, nothing's wrong. We'll be there in ten minutes." Without giving her an opportunity to ask questions, he hung up.

Sure enough, the doorbell chimed at nine. With her heart in her throat, Maria threw open the door. Ryan stood on the front porch. Christopher was at his side.

It took every ounce of effort she had not to scream. With relief and then with rage. Obviously sensing her struggle, Ryan put his hand on Chris's shoulder as they stepped inside. "Chris and I've been talking. I told him I'd come home with him so you wouldn't beat him up too badly.''

He spoke in an ordinary voice with just the right amount of nonchalance she always advised upset parents they should use. Swallowing the angry words building inside her throat, she realized with surprise the trick actually worked. Ryan's coolness instantly defused some of her emotion. But not all of it.

''It's a good thing you've come to protect him,'' she said tightly. ''I might be tempted to commit some kind of crime if you weren't a cop.''

Christopher lifted his head and spoke defensively. ''I'm sorry, okay? I shouldn't have been out so late and I know you were worried. I—I know I screwed up.''

The words, if not the sentiment, had been well rehearsed; she could almost hear him practicing.

''Where were you?''

''After I called you, I went over to Ricky's house, just to hang around and talk about next weekend, then we decided to go to the arcade. We played too long, I guess. I didn't know it'd gotten so late and then…then I knew you'd be mad. I headed over to Ryan's.…''

Ryan met her Maria's doubtful expression with a neutral one of his own. ''Lena called and told me he was missing. I found him in the parking lot.''

Still shaking, Maria turned back to her son. ''This is not acceptable, Christopher. You scared me half to death. I have to know where you are. You need to keep better track of time and—"

"Yeah, yeah..."

Ryan still had his hand on Chris's shoulder. As the boy spoke, she saw Ryan tighten his knuckles for just a second then he took away his hand.

"I—I mean, uh, yes ma'am. I'll do better."

"You certainly will," she answered briskly. "Because you'll have plenty of time to practice reading your watch. You are grounded again, Chris. And you can look forward to another month of no equipment. And Mrs. Lowe *will* be staying with you, as well—"

His brown eyes filled with shock then anger. The intensity of it surprised her, especially when he ignored all his punishments but the first. "Mom! You can't ground me. Ricky's party is this weekend. Everybody's going to it—"

"Well, you aren't," she said firmly.

"You can't do that!" he wailed. "We've been planning this for weeks. You—"

"I don't care if you've been planning it all your life. You aren't going, Christopher. We've talked before about taking responsibility for your actions. This has got to stop."

"You don't understand—"

Ryan interrupted the tirade. "Chris, why don't you go on to your room? Let me talk to you mom a bit, okay?"

Any other time, she might have resented Ryan

giving Chris orders, but Maria was too surprised by Chris's reaction to register one of her own.

"But I've gotta explain, Ryan. I've gotta make her understand—"

Ryan didn't say a word. All he did was raise one eyebrow. Maria watched in stunned fascination as Chris fell silent. Shooting her one last look of enraged offense, he ran up the stairs.

"Let's go outside," Ryan said. "I feel like sitting on the patio."

She understood as Ryan tilted his head upward. He didn't want Chris to hear whatever it was he had to say.

She led him through the kitchen to the patio beyond. Ryan pulled out a chair for her, then took the one next to it. As he sat, she spoke.

"Thank you for the help."

"It was no big deal."

"It was to me," she answered. "I knew the minute I came home he wasn't here. I tried to stay calm, but—"

Ryan took her hand in his. "Look, I know this is really none of my business, okay? You can tell me I'm full of it and kick me out whenever you want to, but I've got some advice for you."

She had a hard time concentrating on his words. His touch was too warm; it reminded her of yesterday and of how they'd almost made love. She struggled past the feeling. "Go—go ahead."

"I didn't just find Chris, Maria. He was on his

way to the station when I pulled out of the parking lot. He was looking for me. He wanted to talk."

"He was…looking for you?"

"That's right."

She went quiet. Her son had gone to someone else, a man he barely knew, to talk over a problem. He hadn't come to her. She felt her throat constrict. "I—I don't understand. What am I doing that's so wrong?"

"You're not doing anything wrong," Ryan answered. "You're doing everything you can. Chris came to me because he was feeling guilty over something he's been keeping from you and he needed to unload. That's the part I'm trying to explain to you. The party at his friend's house is a father-son cook-off. They've got all kinds of stuff planned—Chris has already called his dad and asked him. The other boy's mother is helping, but it's mainly a contest for fathers and sons."

Maria stared at Ryan openmouthed. "Chris never told me that!"

"That's why he came to me. He felt bad about keeping the contest a secret, but he didn't think you'd let him go if you knew."

"Oh, my God…why on earth would he think I'd keep him from his father?"

"I don't think he believes you'd do that, but it's complicated, Maria. He's confused. He's doing the best he can."

Stunned and silent, all she could do was nod her

head. A staggering sweep of guilt threatened to smother her.

Witnessing her pangs of remorse, he squeezed her fingers reassuringly. "Look, this isn't the end of the world, okay? You're being too hard on yourself."

"I went to school for too many years to count. I have a Ph.D. in clinical psychology. I ought to understand my own kid better."

"That's the problem. He is your kid." His blue eyes darkened as she looked up at him. "If he belonged to anyone else, you would have solved this by now."

He was right. But if she hadn't been thinking about Ryan, she would have had more time for Christopher. Her son had to come first and she simply hadn't put him there in the past few weeks. She stood slowly.

"Thank you for your help," she said quietly. "I really appreciate you bringing him home."

Ryan left shortly afterward, but before going, he kissed her again. And then once more. By the time he climbed into his truck, Maria's head was spinning. The struggle between what her body wanted and what her mind said was best threatened to pull her apart. She'd never been this confused in her life.

More upset than ever, she went back inside and talked to Christopher. She kept the conversation neutral, but it was one of the hardest things she'd ever done. He looked worried but almost relieved, as if he'd convinced himself Ryan had the power to

make everything okay. His sudden dependence on—
and confidence in—a man she wasn't sure she
wanted in her life was very unsettling. She turned
out her lights and climbed in bed, but sleep didn't
come for a very long time.

RYAN DIDN'T go home after dropping off Chris. He
went back to the station and sat at his desk in the
dark empty office. He couldn't bear to go to the
house on the beach. In the past few days, it'd gotten
even lonelier, even more barren than before. He
knew nothing was actually different inside the
rented dwelling; it only felt that way because *he* was
changing.

Rising from his chair, he went to a nearby window and stared out at the empty parking lot, cursing
Maria. The words held no rancor as they had in the
past, and in fact, they meant nothing. She wasn't the
source of his problems and never had been. All
she'd wanted to do was help him and he'd fought
her every way he could. Despite his very best efforts, she'd managed to not only make him deal with
his grief for Ginny, she'd actually made him feel
alive again. Hell, she'd even made him laugh.

Now it'd gotten worse.

Christopher had wormed his way into Ryan's
heart as well. Until tonight, Ryan had been suc-
cessful in telling himself he didn't care about Maria's son, that he'd only taken him out to the range
to help her. But when Lena had phoned and said

Chris was missing, Ryan had felt the floor go out from under him. He'd jumped in his truck, determined to find the kid or die...then he'd nearly run over him in the damn parking lot.

Ryan shook his head in disbelief. If people had told him two years ago that Ginny would be out of his life, he would have called them idiots. If they'd gone a step further and explained his current situation, he would have knocked them out cold. No way in hell could he ever fall for another woman, he'd thought. And never this soon. And never, ever with a kid, too.

A car drove down the street outside the station and he watched it disappear into the night. Torn and confused, Ryan wished he was somewhere else.

Unfortunately that somewhere else was Maria's arms...

WEDNESDAY MORNING, Maria's strongest inclination was to talk to Christopher, to see if somehow she could get him to open up to her. After thinking about it some more, though, she called Jackson even before she had her coffee. They discussed the situation and he convinced her to keep quiet a little bit longer.

"You're still too angry and too confused to say the right things," Jackson advised. "Give yourself some more time to sort through all this. Give Chris some time, too. I'm sure he has a perfectly legitimate reason—in his mind—for feeling the way he does."

She dropped Christopher off at school, then drove straight to her office and called Reed.

She shouldn't have bothered.

She could hear him rustling papers in the background. "What do you want, Maria? I only have ten minutes."

"And you only have one son," she retorted. "Whom you don't seem to care about at all."

"This is old ground, Maria, and we've covered it more than once. Do you have something new to say about it or did you just call to nag?"

She gritted her teeth. "I thought you might want to know how much he cares about this party, Reed, the one he's invited you to this weekend. It's not just an informal thing—it's a cook-off with the fathers and sons participating in teams. I don't know what your plans are, but I do know you." She paused. "You're going to go, aren't you?"

"I told the boy I'd be there."

"You've told him that before and never shown up."

"I'll give it my best shot."

She struggled to keep her voice level. "Well, your best shot better be better than it was last time." She started to explain the whole affair, Chris's late arrival last night, his desperate attempt to talk to Ryan, then she stopped herself. Reed couldn't have cared less. She settled for simple. "This is important to him, okay? He's been taking some pretty drastic steps lately to draw attention to himself—''

''Are you still harping on that thing with the beer? For God's sake, Maria, give it a rest!''

''That 'thing' with the beer was important, Reed. Chris is way too young to—''

He interrupted rudely. ''I gotta go, Maria. I have a meeting in two minutes and a report I have to look over. I'll do what I can to be there…and in the future, please don't call the office. I don't have time for crap like this.''

He hung up abruptly and Maria let her indignation get the best of her. She slammed down her receiver and screamed a rattling curse, her words destroying the morning quiet of her elegant office. Thank goodness she'd had extra insulation installed. She'd done it for her clients, but conversations like this Reed made her grateful for it herself. Sputtering with anger, she paced back and forth across the carpet and called Reed nasty names.

It made her feel a lot better.

Talking with Katherine Kelso, Ricky's mother, made her feel worse.

The boys *had* been planning it for weeks, she confirmed. A plump, maternal type, Katherine was polite as she refused Maria's last-minute offer to help. ''I know how busy you are,'' she said. ''Don't worry about it. I've got it under control.''

Maria was glad someone felt that way. The rest of the day, in between clients, she concentrated on what she'd say to Christopher. By the time she got home, she'd made herself a nervous wreck. Her anxiety was so obvious, Mrs. Lowe took one look at her and patted her on the back.

"He was a perfect angel, dearie. Don't fret so."

The "perfect angel" looked up as she came into the kitchen. He was working on a sign, something about welcoming fathers, but as she got closer he draped an arm—in an elaborately casual way—over the writing, and she couldn't read it.

Ignoring his action, she went to the refrigerator and opened it up. She studied its packed depths, then looked at him over her shoulder. "How about pizza tonight? I don't have a thing to cook."

His eyes lightened. Pizza was a treat; she always tried to minimize the junk food. "Can I pick?"

"Anything but pepperoni." She tossed him the phone book. "You call, I'm going to change."

She came down fifteen minutes later in shorts and a T-shirt. The sign was gone and Chris was watching television, some kind of nature show. "The pizza will be here in ten minutes," he said. "I got an extra large so I can have the leftovers later."

Maria nodded and sat down on the sofa. Chris stared at the screen, studiously avoiding any hint of a conversation. When the commercial came on, Maria reached over and took the remote from his hand. She turned off the set.

"Mom! I was watching that—"

"Christopher, it was a show about bees. You left the insect world two years ago."

"Yeah, well, I still like them."

"We need to talk," she said quietly. "I want to know why you thought I wouldn't let you go to this party you and the other boys planned. I want to know why you didn't tell me it was a father-son cook-off."

His eyes shot to hers and she read what he was going to say.

She headed him off. "Don't deny it, Chris. Ryan told me all about it and how you felt. He can't tell me *why*, though. Only you can do that and I need to know."

"Are you gonna let me go?"

"Yes," she said slowly. "I'm going to let you go. I understand what this means to you. But I'm not at all happy with the way you went about this…or the way you've been doing a lot of things. You just got your freedom back. I would have thought—" She stopped herself abruptly. This wasn't how she wanted to do it. She leaned closer to her son and touched his arm. "Tell me why you thought I'd wouldn't let you go, Chris. I need to know."

"It's not important." He picked at a loose thread on one of the sofa cushions.

"It *is* important," she countered. "Everything that happens to you is important. If I've done something or said something to make you think I don't want you seeing your father, I want to know what it is. Because that's not the truth.''

''I know how you feel about him.'' The words were so softly spoken, Maria could barely hear them.

''How I feel about your father is not your concern. He and I are adults and we have our differences. That doesn't mean I don't want you to have a good relationship with him. He's still your dad.''

''But you hate him!'' He raised his face and stared accusingly at her.

Dismay filled her at his tone. ''I don't *hate* him. We don't get along and we can't live together, but that doesn't mean I hate him. And even if I did—''

''You *do* hate him. I've heard you guys on the phone, yelling and screaming late at night when you think I'm asleep. I'm not some little kid anymore, Mom. I know what's going on! You might talk about him all nice and everything to me, but I know how you really feel!''

She wanted to crawl under the couch. ''Son, I— I don't know what to say except that this doesn't matter. Your father loves you and I love you and it simply isn't part of the equation if he and I get along or not. We both agree on one thing—the most important thing—that we love you and we want what's best for you.''

He pursed his lips tightly and shook his head. ''You don't understand.''

"Then help me understand…explain how you feel and maybe then I'll get it."

He thought hard for a few minutes—she could almost hear his brain clicking—then all at once he stood up. His hands were two fists at his sides, his whole body tense in a way she'd never seen before. His stance was so different from his childish outbursts of before Maria felt herself grow still and quiet.

"You won't get it," he said quietly. "You'll never understand no matter what I say so I'm not even going to try."

CHAPTER THIRTEEN

MARIA WORRIED herself sick the rest of the week. On Friday, she went to see Jackson to talk about the situation, the needling possibility bothering her more and more that she might be right, that Chris was deliberately acting out. She told Jackson this the minute she got there.

"Did you ask him about it?"

"I did," she said. "He walked away and didn't even answer me."

"Maybe that's not it, then. Maybe it's even more simple. Could he blame you for the divorce?" Jackson said. "Kids do that a lot, you know."

"I know that," she answered. "But right after Reed and I decided to separate, I had 'the discussion' with Christopher. I told him it wasn't his fault and that we still loved him, no matter what…that we would always love him. I thought I covered everything he could have possibly worried about but now I have this awful feeling I missed something important."

"Do you think he's threatened by your relationship with Ryan?"

"I don't have a relationship with Ryan."

"Oh, yes." He put down the watering can he'd been holding over his petunias. They were on the balcony of his home. "He's a client, I forgot. A client that never makes it to his sessions but who takes your kid out for the day, comes to your house for dinner...meets you at bars. Right..."

"C'mon, Jackson, please—"

He folded his arms and stared at her. "Every time we've talked, you've mentioned this guy, okay? And every time you utter his name, you get a goofy look on your face. I may be old, but I remember what that was like. You have feelings for this guy, Maria. Feelings you shouldn't have—"

"That's ridiculous! He's—"

"Save it. Nothing you can say will convince me otherwise. You already admitted you're attracted to him, so it's too late."

"But—"

"Forget it!"

They glared at each other for a few seconds, then Maria sighed. "Christopher adores Ryan, Jackson. He wouldn't feel threatened by Ryan at all."

"Maybe not consciously," Jackson agreed, calming down himself. "But little boys aren't exactly the most self-aware creatures on the planet, are they? Maybe he's jealous. He's had you to himself for a very long time. You have heard of a thing called the Oedipus complex, haven't you? A guy named Freud—"

"But Christopher's personality started to change

right after the divorce. That's the problem, not Ryan."

He came to the swing where she sat and held on to the ropes. "All right, I'll concede that point through logic. But one thing I won't concede is that you are harboring feelings for Ryan Lukas. You like the guy."

"All I care about right now is my son. Nothing else matters."

"You can care about Christopher and a man, too, Maria. They aren't mutually exclusive." The twinkle that usually sparkled in Jackson's eyes was missing. He was more serious than she'd ever seen him. "The problem is that this particular guy happens to be a client, too. I think that line we talked about you drawing has gotten a little blurred. And that means trouble."

"I know that," she said stiffly.

He stared at her a little longer, then spoke quietly. "Do you really?"

"Of course I do."

"Then what are you doing about it? Have you shipped him off to see someone else? Have you severed your professional ties with him? Have you told him you can't be involved with him?"

Maria started to answer angrily, then her shoulders slumped. After a moment, she rose from the swing and walked away from his gaze, to the edge of the balcony. She could smell the ocean. "I've tried to do all of those things, Jackson…and more.

I've told myself he's not the kind of man I could ever be with, client or not. I've told myself he wouldn't be a good role model for Christopher. His job is too violent.'' She filled her lungs with the salty air, and continued. ''I've told myself he's never dealt with his grief over losing his wife, and that I can't compete with a ghost.'' She turned around. ''I've told myself all those things, but I still can't get him out of my head.''

''Why?''

She looked down. ''I don't know why.''

A heavy silence sat between them. It held a tension she'd never felt with Jackson before, a tension that was charged with his obvious disapproval. ''I don't want to be his therapist,'' she said softly.

''That's okay. Maybe he doesn't even need one.'' Jackson's answer shocked her. ''There *are* people who heal themselves, you know. Therapy isn't the answer for everyone.''

Their eyes met in the middle of the tiny balcony, Maria's confused, Jackson's stern.

''But...''

''But you're going to have to make a choice,'' he answered. ''Because you can't be both. It isn't possible.''

Maria nodded, a slow acknowledgment of the truth she didn't want to hear. Her answer was subdued. ''I know that, Jackson. It's just that...I'm scared.''

''I understand, sweetheart.'' Jackson's voice soft-

ened and he patted her on the arm. He was her men-
tor again, the loving one who wanted only to guide
her in the proper direction. "God knows I've been
there myself. When we take away our objections,
we only have one thing left to do. We have to look
in our hearts and accept what's really there." He
patted her once more. "And that's *always* a scary
thing."

RYAN HAD ARGUED with himself since the moment
he'd left Maria's, but when Friday afternoon rolled
around, he lost the fight. Jumping up from the
cursed desk where he'd been sitting all week, he
grabbed his keys, then strode through the lobby and
spoke over his shoulder to the sergeant manning the
front desk. "I'm outta here. You know where to find
me if you need me."

The older man grunted and Ryan swung out the
door. He went straight to Delchamps, the local grocery and got everything he needed then he headed
for the little liquor store down the street. After picking out a nice red wine, he made one last stop. The
woman who ran the florist shop stared in surprise
as when he walked in. A weekly customer before,
he hadn't been in since Ginny had died. He left a
few minutes later.

The roses matched the wine.

When he pulled into the parking lot of Maria's
office, he felt a twinge seeing her Toyota. He
couldn't back out now. Fate had decided for him. If

she hadn't been there, he could have driven off and no one would have known but him. With her still there, it was do or die time.

He threw open his pickup door and marched up to her office. She was standing in the hallway, waiting for the elevator when he came up the stairs. Their gazes came together in the middle of the corridor. Ryan actually felt the collision.

"R-Ryan!" Her hand went up to her hair in a now familiar gesture. For one fleeting moment, she seemed pleased to see him then her expression changed into confusion. "Oh, my god— We—we didn't have a session, did we? I hope I didn't—"

He came toward her, his eyes never leaving hers. "No session," he answered. "You didn't forget."

"Thank God…" She took a breath he could hear. "I've been so rattled lately, I thought—"

He interrupted her. "I've got dinner in the car. Come with me." Her eyes rounded and he added one more word. He *was* a little rusty. "Please…"

"I don't know, Ryan. Christopher's party is this evening, and he's not even coming home until tomorrow afternoon. I want to take him to the sleepover and make sure Reed's actually shown up."

"You're going to stay there until Reed arrives? And embarrass your kid to death in front of his friends?"

"Well…I hadn't thought about it exactly that way."

"Take Chris to the party, Maria, then come out

to my place. Your staying there isn't going to make
Reed be the kind of father he should be. There's
absolutely nothing you can do to make that man
responsible.''

''But if he doesn't show—''

''If he doesn't show up, then Chris will call you
and you can go get him.''

Down the way, somewhere behind Ryan, a door
opened then closed. Maria's eyes flickered over his
shoulder, then they came back to his face.

''Come out to the house.'' He made his voice soft
and convincing. ''There's unfinished business between us. We need to take care of it, once and for
all.''

She wavered, then he held out his hand. After a
long, heart-stopping moment, she reached out and
took his fingers in hers.

MARIA WENT HOME and picked up Christopher, then
she drove to the Kelsos' house. He got mad when
she insisted on walking him to the door, but she paid
him no attention. After a brief conversation with
Katherine Kelso, Maria drove off, anxiety filling her
heart. She was afraid Reed would do what he always
did—screw up—but Ryan had been right. What on
earth could she do about it?

Heading down the old beach road to Ryan's
place, she almost tugged the steering wheel around
right then and there.

This was a mistake. A gigantic, enormous, really big mistake.

But she didn't stop.

Parking behind his big black pickup, Maria climbed out of the Toyota just as Ryan exited the house. In the humid evening air, the noise of her closing car door sounded expectant and final.

As she walked up the stairs, he came down. They met halfway where he handed her a dozen red roses.

Her heart jumped into her throat, making it impossible to speak.

"You can put them on the table," he said casually, leading her up the stairs by the hand. "I thought we might eat on the deck. I'll grill the steaks out there."

They reached the top of the stairs and she buried her face in the cool, sweet petals of the flowers. "They're beautiful." She lifted her eyes to his. "Thank you very much."

"Ginny always liked flowers on the table. I think I've missed seeing them myself."

He said the words with honest regret, nothing more. Surprised by his attitude but inordinately pleased, Maria followed him into the house where Star greeted them at the door. Before she could say something to the animal, Ryan beat her to it.

"Hey, fellow—ready to eat? I got you something special tonight, too."

She watched in amazement as he pulled out a bag of treats, opened it up and handed one to the dog.

"These last for hours," Ryan said. "And he'll work on it till it's done."

The shepherd took the treat daintily then retreated to one corner of the kitchen where his munching filled the silence. This was obviously not the first time Ryan had brought the pet something.

Unsure she wanted to think about what these obvious changes meant, Maria set her purse down on the countertop and pulled out her cell phone. "I need to call my service—have my calls transferred to my mobile just in case."

He tilted his head behind him. "I'll be outside. Take your time."

When she finished her call, Maria stood at the screen door and watched as he prepared the grill, her emotions tumbling inside her at the sight of his lean form. Jackson had been right. She *was* scared, scared to death. She didn't know how to act, how to feel. What would happen if she really fell in love with Ryan Lukas?

What would happen if she already had?

RYAN RAISED his eyes as Maria came out the door. She'd taken off her suit jacket and removed her shoes. She looked younger without her armor, almost scared. He held out a glass of wine as she padded toward him. "I hope you like red."

"I'm sure it's fine."

She made no move to take the glass and he stood perfectly still, an unbidden memory coming to him swiftly. Once he'd been caught in a thunderstorm during a call-out, and lightning had struck nearby. A second before the heart-stopping bolt had hit the earth, he'd sensed its pending arrival. The air had changed; all at once it was animated, full of an electric quality he could taste.

This moment felt the same.

Slowly, his eyes never leaving Maria's, he put the glass down on the railing at his side. He took a single step toward the center of the deck and she mirrored his action. They hesitated, as if trapped by an invisible net, then all at once they came together.

His arms went around her body and Ryan lifted her off the deck, kissing her as he did so. She kissed him back, her tongue seeking his. Throwing her arms around his neck, she murmured his name, over and over.

They stood there locked together, emotions on fire, bodies demanding more. Then, Ryan picked her up and carried her into the house.

WHEN HE SET HER DOWN beside the bed, Maria knew instinctively Ryan wasn't going to be the kind of lover she would have expected.

Despite the explosiveness of their kiss outside, his touch was gentle and slow, and every movement planned and deliberate. He was miles—thousands of miles—away from the angry man who'd first walked into her office all those weeks ago.

He bent down and nibbled lightly on her neck,

his teeth the only sharpness in the moment between them. Maria melted against him. He made his way up and down her throat, his fingers at the buttons of her blouse. In the evening light straying through the blinds, she watched his hands. They were the same hands she'd seen hold a gun, the same hands that were more than capable of delivering death.

And now they were full of love.

With a moan, she undid his shirt, slipping her fingers inside to feel his chest. It was like touching a steel plate, but a warm one, full of the heat she'd been without far too long. Her blouse came off, then she felt Ryan unclasp her bra. Everything fell to the floor between them and a moment later, so did the rest of her clothes. His followed quickly and he lowered her to the bed.

They were moving too fast, she thought, in the back of her mind. Too fast and too far, but once again she couldn't stop Ryan...or herself. Each caress was a jewel, something to treasure, his hands tracing paths she'd forgotten were even there. He shaped his fingers over her breasts, then bent his head to kiss their smoothness, his tongue licking, his mouth pulling. Clutching his back, she gasped as he found her nipples and bit down gently.

After a moment, he rolled her over on the bed, his mouth tracking her spine, his hands following with heated caresses. She'd never had a man devote himself to her. Every place he touched, every inch of skin he stroked was a revelation. Suddenly she felt special, felt...loved.

She struggled for a second, a guilty wash of pleasure coming over her at his unselfishness. She was giving him nothing in return, but he didn't seem to care. In fact, when she tried to twist around and reach for him, he actually held her down and murmured a faint rebuff. This is for you, he seemed to say. My time will come, but for now...this is for you.

She acquiesced, realizing as she did so that he *needed* to give more than to receive. He'd had no one for too long, as well. She relaxed into the soft bed and let him have his way. He turned her over once more and began to kiss the length of her body, her mind filling with the pleasure his touch delivered. When he reached out to part her legs, Maria released the last of her reserve. His fingers were magic as they captured her, then set her free, only to pull her back time and time again. When she finally cried out in earnest, he stopped but only for a moment. Before she could recover, he reached for the nightstand and the foil package he'd already taken out. A second later, when he entered her, Maria lost track of where she was and what she was doing. Her body and mind detached one from another. She floated off and then disappeared....

MARIA PADDED back into the bedroom from the den her phone in her hand. She'd wanted to call the

Kelsos' house—"just to make sure"—she'd told Ryan. He'd kissed her on the neck and said he understood. And he did—he even admired her for her concern. She wasn't the kind of woman who only worried about her kid when she got home at night. Chris meant everything to her.

Putting the phone on the nightstand, she came to the edge of the bed, Ryan's robe wrapped tightly around her.

"The line was busy," she said.

"They're probably on the computer, surfing the Net." He paused. "Chris is fine, Maria," he said softly. "You can relax for a little while longer."

She nodded reluctantly and he pulled her down toward him.

After they made love a second time and he'd regained his senses, Ryan reached out for a strand of Maria's hair. With a lazy slowness, he wrapped it around his finger. It felt like a silk rope as he tugged gently.

She looked at him from the pillow, her brown eyes languid and full. "What are you doing?"

"I'm hanging on to you," he said without thinking. "I have the feeling you might jump up and run out of here again."

She shifted her gaze to the ceiling and seemed to consider his words. "That's exactly what I should do," she said after a minute. "And not just because of Chris. I have no business being with you like this.

I've managed to break every rule in the therapists' handbook.''

He propped himself up on his elbows and stared at her. ''Is that the book that says you can't have a life? The one that says you have to put everyone else ahead of yourself? The one that says you can't fall in love?''

She jerked her gaze to his.

''Yeah,'' he said. ''That's what I said...you heard me right.''

She started so sit up. ''Ryan—''

He put a finger across her lips. ''Don't,'' he said quietly. ''Don't...''

''But—''

''No.'' He spoke more firmly this time. ''Don't spoil it, Maria. We just shared something very special. Don't mess it up by lying to me.''

Her eyes went dark. ''Lying? What makes you think I'd lie about—''

He interrupted her again. ''I know what you were going to say,'' he answered. ''You want to give me the modern woman's speech. 'This was nice, but it doesn't mean anything. You don't have to call me in the morning and I—'''

She mocked his earlier movement; she reached out and covered his mouth with her hand, halting his words. ''You don't have the first idea of what I was going to say.'' She took away her fingers, but he grabbed them and held on. She spoke firmly, ignoring his grip. ''I would *never* tell you this meant nothing. It—'' She stumbled over the words, then took a deep breath and lifted her eyes to his. "It means everything to me…and that's why I'm so scared."

Her answer echoed inside him, and Ryan acknowledged, at least to himself, that he felt the same way. He dropped back against the pillows and thought about what that meant. "Why do *you* feel that way?" he asked.

"For a lot of reasons," she said. "Not the least of which is this—even if our situation wasn't what it is, there are some important issues between us, things I'm not sure we can ever overcome."

"Like what?"

"For one, your career. It's violent, Ryan, and the things you have to do…"

"You mean the fact that I save lives every day? That I put my own on the line for strangers I've never met? That I'm ready to carry the responsibility of someone's death in order to keep others alive?"

She blinked. Then waited a long time before she said anything at all. "Well, no, that's not what I was going to say, but I see what you mean. And I have to admit, I—I never really thought of it that way before. I just saw—"

"—the end result," he stated. "That's all most people see. They don't understand a sniper's job is to save lives, not take them. What else?" he asked quietly.

Her eyes looked sad. "Well, I know you still have feelings for Ginny, Ryan. And that's completely understandable so please don't think you have to say anything, okay? We don't have to complicate things by telling each other what we think we want to hear. That's not what I do—"

He rolled to his back and stared at the ceiling. He wasn't sure he knew how to explain, but he had to try. "I *do* have feelings for Ginny," he confessed, glancing her way. "I always will. We were high school sweethearts, and you always have a special place in your heart for the person you love first. That doesn't mean I can't love someone else, though." He stopped and ran a hand through his hair. "God, I'm screwing this up—"

Beside the bed, the phone sounded suddenly. Reflex had Ryan turning instantly, his hand grabbing up the phone—even though it was Maria's. "Lukas here."

A woman on the other end spoke quickly, her words coming almost too fast for him to understand. "Oh, my! I—I'm sorry, I must have the wrong number. I was trying to reach Dr. Worley, Maria Worley. I guess I dialed the wrong number. I'm so sorry—"

"No, no." Ryan sat up in the bed, all his senses on sudden alert. The woman sounded rattled, upset. "You've got the right number. Dr. Worley is right here. Just a moment."

He covered the receiver and handed it to Maria. "It's for you."

She frowned and reached for the phone. "Who is it?"

"I have no idea but she sure sounds upset."

Ryan watched as Maria said "hello." In less than a second, her expression went from uncertain to worried to something he couldn't even define. "Wh-when did this happen? When did you realize—"

She listened, gripping the phone, for a few more moments as the woman obviously interrupted her to answer. Maria nodded once then again. "I understand," she finally said. "I'm on my way."

She handed him the phone and clutched the sheet to her chest. He'd never seen her eyes so huge.

"That was Katherine Kelso, the mom who was hosting the boys' cook-off," she said in a shaky voice. "Reed never showed up. Chris waited and waited, but the bastard never came. She said Chris seemed okay—he ate dinner with everyone then they started playing games. She didn't realize until just a few minutes ago that he wasn't there anymore." She took a deep breath and held it for a second, then she spoke again, the words coming out in a rush. "He could have been gone for hours and she has no idea where he is."

CHAPTER FOURTEEN

AS THE WORDS left her lips, a swell of panic over-whelmed Maria. Christopher hadn't wandered off to shed a few upset tears. He hadn't left out of em-barrassment. He hadn't gone home to lick his wounds. No, no—she knew, with a mother's certain instinct, something bad had happened. Something really bad.

She jumped from the bed and scrambled for her clothing, the words tumbling out too fast to stop them. "This is all my fault. I should never have let Chris go to that damn party! I *knew* Reed wouldn't show up. I shouldn't have allowed it and I shouldn't have come out here and I shouldn't have—"

Ryan's hand fell on her arm, but she disregarded it, her frantic need for action taking precedent. Only when his voice filled the room, did she look up. The sympathy and understanding in his blue eyes brought her feverish activity to a halt.

"This is not your fault." He spoke slowly and distinctly, just as he had the night he'd brought Chris home. "Your ex-husband's the one to blame here, Maria. Him. Not you. And our being together had nothing to do Chris disappearing. Whether you'd been at home by yourself or here with me, it wouldn't have made any difference.''

The calm way he spoke—and the look in his eyes—was too much. She started to cry with blame and confusion, and he drew her into his arms. ''We'll find him.'' His confident voice was a rumble in her ear where she pressed herself against him, clinging. ''We'll find him.''

The trip back to town felt as if it lasted a lifetime but twenty minutes later, they were on Katherine Kelso's front porch. As she waited for the door to be opened, Maria continued to chastise herself despite Ryan's words. What had she been thinking when she'd gone to his house? The hours they'd spent together had been unlike anything she'd ever experienced, but it was his startling remark that had really sent her reeling.... Had he actually acknowledged they might be falling in love? She wondered suddenly if she had dreamed his remark in all the confusion or if she'd truly heard him speak.

I do have feelings for Ginny...I always will... That doesn't mean I can't love someone else, though.

Maria didn't have time to consider the question more. Katherine Kelso came to the door and let them in, looking almost as upset as Maria.

Maria introduced Ryan to her neighbor. Katherine acknowledged him with distraction, then led them into the immaculate house. Maria had been to the Kelsos' several times in the past. They'd held a block party a year or so ago, and Maria had really liked Katherine and her husband, Zachary.

They reached the living room, and Maria couldn't help herself. She immediately went to the huge picture window behind the couch and stared outside. A generous pool and deck filled the backyard and she could see the party was still going, even though it was almost midnight. Zachary stood guard beside the glimmering water and its occupants. She looked through the crowd of boys but Katherine had told the truth.

Christopher wasn't there.

"Oh, Maria, I don't even know what to say." Katherine spoke from behind her and Maria turned around. "I—I can't believe I didn't see him slip off! I—I don't know what to do...."

"Tell us exactly what happened, Mrs. Kelso. And go slowly."

She nodded at Ryan's words and began to speak in a halting voice. Ten minutes after she started, they knew little more than what she'd told Maria on the phone. A fist began to squeeze Maria's heart, making it hard for her to breathe.

"Did any of the boys see him leave?" Ryan asked.

"I asked every one of them." Katherine twisted her fingers together anxiously. "They all said no. I can ask again, though."

"That might be a good thing to do."

She jumped up from the couch before Ryan could

even finish, then reappeared a few minutes later outside. Standing by Maria's side, Ryan wrapped his hand around hers. "It'll be okay. We'll find him. I promise you."

His words worked their way through the haze of Maria's panic and confusion. Reed had promised her the world and given her nothing but grief. Ryan kept his promises.

She nodded but said nothing.

A few minutes later, Katherine hustled back in, an apprehensive-looking teenager in tow behind her. "This is Matthew Solis," she announced excitedly. "He was in the bathroom changing his clothes when I asked the other boys about Chris the first time. He just told me he did see Chris leave."

Maria's pulse jumped. "What happened, Matthew?"

He was a cute kid with dark spiky hair and bright brown eyes. "I was waiting with Chris for his dad to show up—out front, you know—and he was real upset. He wasn't crying or anything, but I could tell he was mad. Then this guy came up on a motorcycle."

"A motorcycle..." Maria's brow knit.

He nodded quickly. "I didn't know the guy, but I think Chris called him something like Jerry or Kerry. I didn't get his name—"

"Could it have been Terry?"

Matthew got excited. "Yeah! Yeah, that was it. Terry...."

"Terry Maloney." Ryan nodded then turned to Maria. "That's the kid we arrested out at the warehouse. Where I found Chris's drawing."

Emotions too complicated to even name rushed through Maria. Christopher had insisted he didn't know the boy out at the warehouse. He'd obviously been lying all along. She made a tiny sound and put her hand to her mouth.

Ryan gave her a sympathetic look and turned back to Matthew. "What happened next?"

Matthew answered quickly. He recognized authority when he saw it. "They didn't stay. Chris got on the back of the cycle and they took off. Toward the other end of the street."

"What time was this?"

"Right after we ate."

Maria looked at Katherine and she answered the unspoken question. "That was around seven."

Maria groaned. It was almost 1:00 a.m. Six hours. Her son had been gone for six hours and no one had even known. Not even her. She didn't think it could get much worse.

She was wrong.

RYAN TOOK OVER the Kelsos' telephone and began to make his calls. Fifteen minutes later every cop on the street was looking for the two kids. Technically, Chris wasn't a runaway, but everyone knew Maria and wanted to help. After a quick drive around the neighborhood and a check of her own house as well, Maria returned to the Kelsos'. Ryan glanced in her direction as he punched out a new number and waited for an answer. Making calls on her own cell phone, Maria looked drawn and wan and completely different from the woman he'd held in his arm a few hours before. Guilt had replaced her passion; fear had supplanted her joy.

He spoke quietly so she wouldn't overhear him, then nodded with relief. The hospitals were clear. Maria hung up her line at the same time. "Reed hasn't seen him," she said bitterly. "He sounded upset that I woke him." She turned to Ryan. "How about Terry's folks?"

"No answer," he said. "A car's on the way over there right now, though. The boys could be hiding out there and not answering. Who knows what—" He broke off when the pager at his belt suddenly went off.

He glanced down at the flickering number and dismissed it.

"What is it?" Maria asked, tilting her head toward the pager. "It's not—"

"It's the code for shots fired," he said calmly. "Don't get excited—"

"Oh, my God…" Ignoring his admonition, Maria jumped up from the dining room table and ran to where he stood. With her hand on her chest, Katherine Kelso waited on the opposite side of the table.

"Shots fired?" Maria grabbed his arm. "You don't think—"

"I don't know what to think right now but we don't need to panic, okay? I'm sure it's an ordinary call-out." He put his hand on hers and squeezed it in reassurance, then all at once the address registered…1124 Industrial Drive. It was the warehouse where he'd first seen Chris.

MARIA READ HIS FACE. "You're not telling me the truth."

He looked at her quickly. "I *am* telling you the truth. I don't know exactly what's happened, but the code would be different if they'd found him. It'd be the one for a missing child—" His cell phone suddenly chirped, interrupting him.

He flipped it open. "Lukas here."

He nodded as the caller spoke to him. Maria could hear the tinny echo of the other voice but none of the words were distinct. She turned back to Katherine Kelso. The woman started to say something, then Ryan interrupted them both, snapping his phone shut as he spoke.

"I have to go."

His eyes were calm, his air relaxed. Despite his appearance and his earlier words of reassurance, Maria felt her stomach drop. "Wh-what it is?"

"That was Lena. She wants me. I'll call you as soon as I can."

Her voice went up. "Is it Chris? It can't be Chris! The code said—"

He took two steps and looked her straight in the

eye. "Lena said nothing about Chris, okay? It's a call-out and I have to go. That's all I can say." He kissed her once, a fast goodbye. By the time she had recovered, he was gone.

RYAN'S FINGERS gripped his steering wheel, his truck's tires shrieking as they took the corner at the end of the street. A second later he hit the highway going eighty. It was empty of traffic so it hardly mattered, but even if it had been rush hour, he would have been driving the same.

Lena *hadn't* said a word about Christopher, but still, he'd skirted the truth and that left a bitter taste in his mouth. He couldn't have told her where he was headed, though. Maria would have insisted on coming and that was something he simply couldn't allow. Not until he knew what was going on.

The darkened streets went by in a blur and sooner than he would have thought possible, Ryan saw the War Wagon. Slamming on his brakes, he parked the truck and tumbled from the seat. Some other vehicles were scattered around but he paid them little attention. He ran to the front door of the Wagon where Lena met him as he climbed inside.

She was worried. "We've got a unique problem and you're the only one who can really help."

"Okay. Tell me more." Sarah appeared at his side and handed him a vest and uniform. He peeled off his dress shirt and then his pants, changing into the darker clothing. Lena continued her briefing and Sarah went back to her fax machine.

"Looks like the same setup as before, only this time, we've got two complications."

He stepped into the pants and zipped them up. "And they would be?"

"The first is the fact that the shooter has graduated. He's using a .22 now instead of an air rifle."

He reached for the T-shirt and began to pull it over his head. "And the second problem?"

"He's added a twist to go with it. A chemical bomb."

Ryan froze, his head halfway through the neck of the shirt. "A bomb? What in the hell—"

"The guard reported shots fired, just like before. A black and white comes out, a few more potshots are taken, and the guys realize it's not an air rifle. They don't want to get any closer so they call us. Before I can call the team and get out here, dispatch routes a second call. It comes in over a cell phone...sounds like a kid, but they're not sure."

Ryan pulled the shirt down, his eyes on Lena's. "And he says?"

"'We're gonna poison everybody for miles. Come watch.'"

Ryan didn't know what to say. All he could do was stare at her in disbelief.

"You can get the recipes off the Internet. Pipe bombs, timers, poison gas—hell, nuclear designs, too, for all I know. The HazMat guys are here as primary. That's why our code went out as backup only. I ordered an ambulance to bring out special equipment just in case, but I didn't alert Diego. There's no need for a negotiator at this point.''

He nodded numbly, the navy van he'd seen in the parking lot registering now. A few months before, the county had commissioned a Hazardous Materials group. It'd been their vehicle he'd seen on his way in, but he hadn't thought about what that meant.

Lena looked out the window at Ryan's side, then she took a deep breath and faced him once more. ''But that isn't why I need *you*, Ryan.''

He waited.

''He's got some other kids with him. We're not sure how many—at least two or three.''

A cold chill brushed along Ryan's spine, but he stood perfectly still.

''Who are they?'' His voice sounded disembodied, even to his own ears.

''That's where you come in,'' Lena said. ''I can't leave the Wagon, but someone's got to go look.'' Her gray eyes went dark. ''I think he's with them, Ryan. I think Chris is in that warehouse.''

MARIA WASN'T satisfied with Ryan's answer. The minute he left, she ran to the phone and dialed Lena's home number. As she'd known it would, the phone echoed emptily. If the team had gone out, so had Lena. Knowing it was probably useless, Maria tried the station and got the same results. She hesitated only a second then punched in Lena's cell phone. No answer. The minute she hung up, Katherine Kelso's line rang. The other woman grabbed the receiver, and a second later she handed it to Maria.

Her heart froze until she heard who it was. Jackson's voice revealed his concern. "Maria? What's going on? We just got in from a late dinner party and I listened to our messages. What's this about Christopher missing?"

She wanted to cry; she wanted to scream. "He's been gone since seven." Explaining what had happened, she tried to keep her hysteria in check. "I called you because I'm calling everyone. You—you haven't seen him, have you?"

"No, of course not. Do you think—"

"I don't know what to think," she wailed. "All I know is that he's gone...."

"Tell me where you are." In the background, she could hear him rustling paper and saying something about a pencil. "Okay, I'm ready. Give me the address."

She brought herself under control. Almost. "Jackson, you don't need to—"

"Yes, I do," he interrupted. "And I wouldn't be able to sleep anyway. Don't be stubborn, Maria. Let me help you."

"I'm at 5839 Starlight," she managed to say. "It's two streets over from my house."

"I'm on my way."

She didn't realize she'd hung up until Katherine spoke. "I think we need some coffee," she said. "How do you take yours?"

Maria answered in a wooden voice and Katherine bustled from the room. In the empty silence, Maria's earlier recrimination returned full force. This was all her fault and no one would ever be able to convince her otherwise.

What on earth had she been thinking? Sex with Ryan? God, she'd lost her mind.

And now she'd lost her child.

RYAN SPOKE more harshly than he meant to, but he was worried, worried and anxious. "You *think* he's with them or you know?"

"I'm pretty sure it's him." Lena wore a grim expression. "J.L. caught a glance. He saw two or three figures, running from one side of the complex to the other. They were carrying backpacks and wearing caps backward. One of them ran under a security lamp. His cap was black and he had a bright-blue pack." She waited a second, then continued. "He had a SWAT T-shirt, too. One of ours. I know you gave one to Chris when you took him out to the camp. Maria told me he's so proud of it, he never takes it off."

The facts laid out before him, Ryan could do nothing but nod unhappily.

"Besides me, you're the only person out here

who can do a positive ID," she said. "We're backup on this Ops, but I've told the HazMat guys what's going on, and they've agreed to move you in closer to do the recon."

Ryan nodded again, and as he did so, the door to the Wagon opened. On the doorstep a stranger paused, his navy-blue shirt announcing his Hazardous Materials squad status. Ryan didn't know who he was, but he was sure of one thing; if he'd ever seen the guy before he would have remembered. One side of his face bore a horrific scar. It cut his profile from his jaw to just above one eyebrow.

Lena moved toward the door. "George—come in. I was just explaining everything to Ryan."

The other man stepped into the camper, but stayed near the door. Under the harsh lights, his face looked even worse. Lena made the introductions.

"George Rogers is the new head of the HazMat," she explained to Ryan. Turning the other way to the scarred man, she introduced Ryan. "Ryan is our countersniper. He knows the boy."

The two men exchanged nods, and Rogers spoke. His voice was as damaged as his face, harsh and gravelly. "I can get you in there, but I can't guarantee your safety. I have no idea what's going on yet."

"I don't believe in guarantees."

Rogers nodded as if he approved of Ryan's grim pronouncement, then without saying a word, he turned and opened the door. Ryan followed and the humid night swallowed them both.

CHAPTER FIFTEEN

THE AIR FELT liquid as Ryan moved toward the abandoned warehouse. He ignored the sensation and continued forward, dodging quickly from one cover to the next. The parking lot, overgrown and in as much disrepair as the buildings, held a variety of broken-down vehicles and derelict equipment. George Rogers had stopped fifty yards behind the clutter and had pointed out the building where the shots had been fired.

"We got as close as we could with a sniffer." He'd glanced toward the warehouse then back at Ryan. "There are plenty of substances the units can't detect, though. Keep a sharp eye out for anything that looks weird."

Edging closer, now on his own, Ryan trained his gaze on the boxlike building. It was long and low with a metal roof. Broken-out windows dotted the walls every twenty feet. The jagged glass gleamed in the darkness. If Christopher and the other boys were still inside, they had no light and were making no noise.

Ryan slowed his progress as he drew nearer. With his blackened face and dark clothing, he was practically invisible, but movement—even in this kind of obscurity—was always easy to spot. Reaching a clump of tall grass, he dropped to the ground just behind the listing end of a flatbed truck. An open patch of spotty asphalt, all that remained of the parking lot, covered the space between him and the warehouse. Exactly halfway, in the center of the emptiness, a row of overturned barrels cast a deep shadow. He didn't like the setup but there wasn't another option. A fifteen-foot fence, topped with wire, marked the outer limit of the complex. There was no way he could climb it and remain unseen. He had to cross the gap if he was going to get inside.

He waited five minutes, and then five more. Nothing stirred in the damp night air, not even the distant call of a bird. He felt as if the whole world were waiting with him, on hold, anxious and uneasy.

Moving an inch at a time, he pulled his legs beneath him and prepared to run.

He was halfway across the space when the first shot rang out.

"I CAN'T stand this anymore." Maria stood up. Jackson looked at her and so did Katherine. He'd hurried into town as promised and found her at the Kelso house. "I've got to do something. I can't just sit here and wait."

Katherine rose in a fluid movement, her face a wreath of worry. Jackson jumped up, too. "Something has to happen soon, Maria. They're going to find him any minute, I just know they are."

"I hope you're right," Maria replied, "but in the meantime, I'm leaving." She looked at Katherine. "You have my cell phone number. Call me if you hear anything—anything at all and I'll be right back."

She nodded but couldn't hide her concern. "Where are you going?"

"I don't know." Maria grabbed her purse and keys and started to the door, her stomach in knots. "I may just cruise around and look for him. Anything's better than sitting here."

Jackson dug in his pocket and came up with his keys. "I might as well do the same," he said. "Two of us looking doubles the chances."

They walked outside, Maria to her Toyota, Jackson to his Lexus. She went one way and he went the other. Reaching the corner, though, Maria hesitated at the stop sign. She didn't know which way to turn—literally. Finally jerking the steering wheel to the right, she backtracked to her own house and parked at the curb. The windows were as dark and empty as they had been the last time she checked. She knew with one glance Christopher wasn't there.

Easing back into the street, Maria drove slowly through the neighborhood, her eyes adjusting to the gloom. Up one street and down the next. It was a pointless exercise—Destin wasn't that small—the boys could be anywhere and chances were great they hadn't stuck around here. Her desperation grew by the minute, her guilt matching it leap for leap.

Then out of the corner of her eye, a sudden movement caught her attention. She slammed on the brakes and brought the car to a screeching halt. The vehicle rocked in the street as she stared at the house in the middle of the block. There was something there! She saw the movement again. Two seconds later, a black cat tore from the bushes and ran across the road, a sleek gray one racing behind him in hot pursuit.

She felt her eyes fill up with tears, but she didn't let them fall. She put the Toyota back into gear and drove off slowly.

An hour later, she'd done nothing but increase her frustration. She stopped in the parking lot of Delchamps in the center of town and picked up her cell phone. Katherine answered on the first ring.

"Have you heard anything?"

"God, no...when the phone rang, my heart almost cratered. I was hoping..."

Maria lay her head against the steering wheel. "I've been driving all over town. I haven't seen a thing." She turned her head to the side. "This is so pointless I can't believe I'm even doing it but—"

She broke off without warning, a bone-chilling sight coming toward her, breaking the distant darkness. Katherine began to speak, but Maria didn't listen. She swallowed, her mouth going dry all at once as the blue-and-red streaks of light drew closer.

It was an ambulance heading east, traveling away from the hospital. The vehicle went by so fast, it took Maria a moment to realize what was wrong. When she finally understood, her body went cold.

The medics were traveling silent.

RYAN HIT the sandy blacktop and slid. Crashing into one of the barrels, he reached out with one hand and just managed to keep it from tumbling over. He prayed nothing was inside them that might go up in flames. If there was, he'd go up, too.

In between the empty buildings, the shot should have echoed, but it didn't. The clammy night air sucked in the noise and swallowed it whole. All Ryan could hear was the sound of his own heart pounding, his pulse throbbing in his ears. He checked his weapon, running his fingers over the rifle, making sure everything was all right. He couldn't see the mechanics but he didn't need to; he'd memorized the details of the gun long before this night. He knew, by the weight and balance of it, that the rifle was fine.

He couldn't say the same for his night vision goggles. Crashing into the barrels, he'd sent them spinning. Even if he'd been able to reach them, it wouldn't have mattered. He could see from where he crouched the lenses on the left side had shattered. He stared in disbelief; they had to have hit something just right—the goggles were almost indestructible.

He cursed roundly, the words suspended in his mind without being spoken out loud. How in the hell was he going to see without those damned binoculars?

Everything suddenly seemed more complicated.

Lena's voice sounded inside his earpiece, demanding everyone check in. One by one, the team answered. Everyone was fine; the shot had been completely wild.

Ryan spoke softly, pulling the microphone close to his mouth. "I'm okay, but I'm stuck behind a row of barrels and my goggles just broke."

"Can you see anything from your position?"

Ryan angled his head around one of the drums. "Negative. It's like soup out here."

"Can you move in any closer?"

His voice sounded grim, even to his ears. "I have to get closer if I'm going to see inside that building. I'll check in when I can." He pushed the mike back from his lips, gripped his weapon and inched to the end of the barrels. Taking a slow deep breath, he launched himself into the darkness.

MARIA WATCHED the ambulance go by, her heart climbing into her throat with a single leap.

Christopher?

Ryan?

She knew it wasn't rational, but Maria couldn't help herself. She threw the car into gear and tore out of the parking lot, heading in the same direction as the white van. The blue-and-red lights were easy to follow. They painted a trail with long beams of light. She argued with herself as she drove recklessly down the deserted highway.

You don't know where it's going, she said. *The emergency could have nothing to do with you. They might be going to a woman having a baby. They might be on their way to a heart attack victim.*

With every argument she made, two answers came back.

Christopher.

Ryan.

The thought that either one of them might need the help of that vehicle overrode all logic. She drove even faster. Some time in the middle of this catastrophe she'd begun to link the two of them together—Christopher and Ryan. It made no more sense than anything else, but she somehow knew. The call Ryan had taken *did* involve her son and he hadn't wanted to tell her. The fact that Lena hadn't answered her phone only reinforced Maria's suspicions. She'd seen her friend, more than once, look at the ID display on her phone then summarily click it off, especially in the middle of a situation. She'd *known* it was Maria phoning and she hadn't wanted to talk to her.

The ambulance flew down the highway; Maria stayed close behind. On the edge of town, the white van took a right-hand turn, the night going suddenly darker with the abrupt absence of its lights. Unfamiliar with this part of Destin, she slowed the Toyota, taking the turn a moment later. Immediately she spotted the ambulance's taillights up ahead. She sped up, her pulse thumping at the fear she might lose sight.

She shouldn't have worried. A second later, the larger vehicle slowed to a crawl. She did the same, straining her eyes to look ahead in the gloom. As she realized where she was, her stomach turned to water. She'd never been out here, but she knew this was where Chris had been before. Everything fell into place with an awful, heart-stopping click.

She gripped the steering wheel tightly and found herself leaning forward, her body tense, every muscle focused. The lane was full of marked police cars, and at the opposite end, towering over all the other vehicles sat the War Wagon. Ryan's pickup was right beside the Winnebago, parked at a crazy angle. It looked as though he'd slammed on the brakes at the very last minute to miss the camper.

Just beside his truck was another vehicle, a dark van with closed sides and no windows. She squinted to read the letters painted in white on the side, then the ambulance turned and its headlights washed the side of the unknown vehicle with its high beams. HazMat was all it said.

The van belonged to the Hazardous Materials squad. They handled everything from chemical leaks to oil spills. What on earth were they doing here?

She didn't wait for an answer. She pulled the Toyota into the ditch and switched off the engine. A second later she ran from the car toward the Wagon.

Throwing open the door of the camper, Maria jumped inside. Lena looked up, her mouth dropping open while in the back, Sarah gasped. It was the only sound made in the dead silence that followed her arrival. Until Maria spoke.

"I want to know what in the hell's going on." She glared at Lena, her voice shaky, her legs equally unstable. "You tell me right now! Who's the ambulance for? Where's Christopher? Tell me what's going on!"

IN A NORMAL operation, Ryan would have scouted out the area carefully. He would have selected a building or rooftop close to the target and positioned himself in the darkness. He would have waited, staying there in silence and in gloom, his body growing numb, his arms turning to lead, until Lena gave him the green light or until he was relieved.

He didn't have that luxury now.

Someone was shooting and he had to find out who. The threat of a chemical agent added an edge he didn't relish, either. He knew nothing about bombs or their components...his only job was to find a target and fire if necessary.

He didn't let himself think of what it meant if Christopher was involved as well.

He wouldn't have thought it possible, but it

seemed harder than before to see. In the time since he'd come from the parking lot, the fog had grown denser. Thick tendrils of mist wound around the buildings to creep in and out of his vision. He blinked several times, but it didn't help. The murk remained the same. For just a second, the building seemed to disappear then, like magic, it returned, hovering in the air. Ryan waited for the swirling haze to thicken and come toward him. When it did, he glided into its somber depths and vanished as well.

LENA WAS the first to recover. "Calm down, Maria. Calm down and I'll tell you what's going on."

"I *am* calm." Still shaking, Maria looked at her friend and lied, clenching her fists at her sides. "I'm very calm. But I want to know what's happening. Christopher's in there, isn't he?" She tilted her head toward the complex of warehouses.

"We don't know for sure who's in there right now. We haven't gotten close enough yet to see. Ryan is trying to do that as we speak."

"Ryan..."

"I sent him in to look. He'll call in as soon as he can." Lena took a tentative step in Maria's direction. The aisle was narrow and she had to turn sideways, but she moved even more carefully than was necessary, and suddenly Maria understood why. Lena didn't want to upset her anymore than she already was—she didn't want to send her out into the night, screaming Christopher's name. Which is exactly what she felt like doing.

"What's the big blue van?"

"It's the Hazardous Materials vehicle," Lena said quietly. "There's a possibility we might need it. Someone called in a bomb threat, too."

She must have reacted, but Maria wasn't sure. All she could do was stare at Lena in disbelief. "The ambulance...it was quiet...."

"I ordered some special equipment to be on standby just in case. Look, why don't you sit down? Here, on the bench." Lena cleared a spot on a padded ledge that ran along one side of the bus. "Do you want some coffee?" She spoke with calmness, her gray eyes full of care as they looked at Maria.

The sympathy didn't help; without any warning at all, Maria's legs went out from under her. A man she hadn't seen before with a horribly scarred face rushed forward from the back of the camper and caught her at the very last second. He helped her to the seat without saying anything as Sarah handed her the cup of coffee she'd already prepared and Lena patted her on the back.

"Just tell me he's okay...." Maria clutched the plastic foam cup and begged Lena with her eyes. "Tell me Christopher's okay."

"I can't tell you anything right now." Lena pulled at one of the small gold loops she wore in her ears. It was a nervous gesture Maria had seen her make a thousand times before, but this time it took on more significance, an extra meaning.

"But you must think…"

"I don't know yet what to think. There *are* some kids in the building and it's possible one of them might be Chris. They were seen going inside. That's all we know, Maria. I called Ryan so we could make sure. Before we proceed."

Maria had been at enough call-outs to know what that meant. With a trembling hand, she brought the lukewarm coffee to her mouth and sipped. And then she prayed.

THE SOUND OF Ryan's advance was swallowed by the dense night air, just as the noise of the gunshot had been earlier. He was grateful for the cover but worried about it, too. The mist was fluid enough that whoever was inside the warehouse just might catch a glimpse of him. He lowered his silhouette and tried to move quickly. Another few steps and he was up against the building.

Because of his training, his heart beat a steady rhythm inside his chest, slow and measured, but Ryan felt a quickening all the same. This wasn't simply another call-out. The weight of Maria's emotions rested firmly on his shoulders; if Christopher *was* inside this building, what was Ryan going to do? He gripped his weapon closer and decided he'd face that problem when he got to it. Right now, he had to find a spot to see inside.

He made his way down the side of the warehouse.

The windows were at an awkward level. Each time he came to an opening, he had to duck down to avoid being seen. At the same time, he felt the pressure building. He wanted to look, to peer inside, in the worst possible way. He had to find just the right place, though. If they saw him before he saw them... Who knew what would happen?

He rubbed the tin wall with his shoulder as he got too close, a soft sigh of a sound he prayed no one had heard. Inching away from the structure, he made his way to the rear of the building. He'd glanced at blueprints before leaving. There was a door somewhere along the back, but he wasn't sure exactly where.

He stepped carefully, his rubber-soled boots as silent as a whisper in the debris piled up against the walls. Most of the empty cans and scattered papers had blown there, or been tossed, so long ago that they were faded and old. Two cans were new, though. Ryan squinted at them in the darkness. A drop of beer still clung to the edge of one.

He was getting close.

Just as he had that thought, a whisper came to him. Carried on the back of a curling finger of mist, the words and a snatch of music were disjointed and impossible to understand. It was like watching a television deep in the forest, the signal too weak to catch everything. Ryan concentrated and crept nearer.

The voices came again, this time a little stronger.

Ryan strained and crept forward another foot. Despite his best efforts, he still couldn't understand.

The murmurings floated out wetly, too muffled to comprehend.

He understood two things, though. The speaker was young, his voice wavering on the edge between mature and childlike.

And it didn't belong to Christopher.

His chest eased slightly but all at once, the opening to the building appeared at Ryan's left shoulder. He stopped abruptly. He'd expected it to be at least another few yards away; the fog had tampered with his sense of distance.

He tried to do a better job gauging the kids' voices than he had the door's location. The sound of their talking rose and fell, along with music he now heard. After a moment, Ryan was fairly certain they weren't right around the corner. The door led directly to what had been a reception area, he remembered from the blueprints. Beyond the small office, in the back, the rest of the building was one huge storage area. They'd probably settled there.

Slowly, carefully, from one of his pockets Ryan removed a small mirror on the end of a telescoping black rod. Holding it before him, he slipped it around the edge of the door. The room was empty. He replaced the mirror.

With his weapon before him, barrel up but finger ready, he closed his eyes for one long moment. Opening them a second later, he stepped inside. His gaze already adjusted to the pitch-blackness, he quickly glanced around him. A rickety cabinet with one missing door had been pushed against the far

wall, its crooked shelves leaning on each other like
a row of bad teeth. In the dirt, in front of the case,
an empty file cabinet lay on its side. Something
scurried in the opposite corner and Ryan swung
around, a fast fluid movement, his weapon in its
ready position. From the floor a pair of red eyes
gleamed back. A rat.

Raising the weapon once again, Ryan started toward the back, his boots gliding soundlessly on the
concrete floor. As he drew even with the wall that
separated the front office from the storage area, a
darker square caught his eye. In the center of the
plaster, just to the left of the upset cabinet, a window had been cut. Anyone in the office would have
been able to view the storage area, to see who was
moving about. Somewhere along the way, the glass
had been shattered; only jagged shards remained to
gleam in the dark.

The voices he'd heard earlier continued to speak,
but he could tell now, as he moved closer to the cut-
out, that there were more kids than originally seen.
Two or three boys, just as Lena had said, but probably more.

Dropping lower, Ryan edged his way to the window. His T-shirt was glued to his back and moisture
rolled off his forehead. He blinked rapidly trying to
keep the salty sting away from his eyes. Waiting for
his vision to clear, he paused under the casement.
The voices rose, as if in an argument, their accom-
paniment a nearby boom box. Someone was playing
with the volume, cranking it up then lowering it.

When they finally stopped, the volume was much higher. Ryan issued a prayer of thanks. The noise should cover any sounds he might make now. He withdrew his mirror again then straightened and thrust the small device over the broken glass.

A group of kids were huddled in one corner. They'd built a fire in a small container and the glow from the flames illuminated their faces. Not too smart, Ryan thought, but good for him. They wouldn't be able to see past the curtain of light, tiny as it was. He brought the mirror back, tucked it into his pocket, then raised his head and peered over the edge of the sill to get a better look.

Leaning against a nearby pile of tumbled boxes, a .22 rifle rested, its wooden stock reflecting the flicking fire. There was no sign of anything that looked like a bomb, chemical or otherwise. Ryan studied each of the boys carefully, but his first quick glance confirmed what he'd thought earlier.

Christopher wasn't among them.

Ryan let out the breath he hadn't known he was holding. Until this very moment, he'd felt—no, *known*—Christopher was with these boys! So much for a cop's intuition...

He started to kneel, but a movement caught his gaze, a motion in one corner that he couldn't identify, but which he'd definitely seen. It was outside the range of the gleaming fire, something or someone on the periphery of the group. He stared through the cavernous structure at the veiled area, willing himself to see better, but the mental gyrations did no good; he only had one option.

He reached for his weapon.

Bringing the rifle up slowly, inch by inch, he rested the barrel on the edge of the broken window, taking care not to tap the glass barely hanging on to the frame. A slide switch rested on the edge of the scope, a powerful 3-9X variable lens. He pushed it forward silently and placed his eye against the eyepiece. The unit had a duplex reticle, a compli cated aiming guide with thick lines at the outside of the field and thinner crosshairs in the middle. It was a special reticle—designed for low-light usage since the narrower crosshairs were hard to see except in bright light—and it doubled as a range finder.

He bore down on the switch and the reticule glowed gently, powered by two tiny batteries hidden inside the scope, underneath the switch itself.

In the crosshairs, a small figure sprang into focus. He was twirling something in his hands, tossing it up and down then catching it carelessly. At first glance, Ryan thought it was just a small black box, then he recognized the outline of a cell phone. As he watched, the boy moved even farther away from the group, dissolving into the darker shadows of the corner.

But not before Ryan realized who he was.

CHAPTER SIXTEEN

DROPPING SOUNDLESSLY beneath the window, Ryan pondered his next move. Every SWAT call-out was different, but once the location of the principals was known, some kind of action plan generally began to take form. He debated the best possible course, the youth of the offenders and the possibility of the chemicals they'd threatened to use uppermost in his mind.

Overriding everything else, though, was Christopher's presence. If it'd been a bunch of kids Ryan didn't know, he would have still cared, of course, but things would have been different.

This was Christopher.

Maria's Christopher.

In Ryan's earpiece, Lena's voice broke in. She called out his code name and waited for a response.

Ryan had to answer. He counted on the music covering up the sound of his voice. With as few words as possible, he described his location and the scene.

Then he confirmed Christopher's appearance.

"Call Maria," he whispered. "Let her know he's okay."

"She's right here," Lena answered. "I'll tell her. Hang tight."

Once involved in a run, Ryan was never distracted. Just the mention of Maria's name, though, and thoughts of her filled his mind. How had she known where to come? Had something he said tipped her off? As he waited for Lena to return, he let himself be dangerously diverted. What was waiting for him and Maria when this was over? He knew what *he* wanted but would he be able to convince Maria to want the same?

Lena interrupted his speculations. She bit off the words with an unusual tenseness. "Maria wants to talk to you, Ryan. She's insisting..."

"No!" he said. "I can't talk—"

Maria's frantic voice filled his ear. He could almost smell her perfume, almost feel her touch.

"Ryan, is he...is he okay?"

"I can't talk, but Chris is fine. I saw him a second ago. He has a cell phone with him. Get Lena to check out the 911 dispatch and get a trace on that original call." He had more instructions, but he stopped, his hand jerking to his belt in frenzied disbelief.

"What's wrong?" Maria's words held panic. "Ryan? Ryan—talk to me!"

"My phone. It's vibrating," he said in shock. "Someone's calling me."

SHE UNDERSTOOD immediately. Maria ripped off the headset Lena had given her and looked up with stunned surprise. "It's Christopher!" she said excitedly. Jumping up from the bench where she'd been sitting, she grabbed Lena's arm. "He's calling Ryan. It *has* to be him!"

Lena pushed back her microphone and frowned. "What? What are you saying?"

Maria explained, her emotions suddenly electrified. "Ryan gave me his number a while ago. I wrote it down and put it on the refrigerator. Chris must have seen it. Get him back," she cried. "Get Ryan on the radio! I'm sure he'll tell us it's Chris!"

"We'll give him two minutes," Lena said, looking at her watch. "I don't want to interrupt if it is Chris."

"RYAN? It's me...." His voice was scared and young sounding, so young Ryan suddenly remembered Christopher *was* just a kid. "It's Chris. I'm hiding and—"

"I know exactly where you are. I'm watching from the front of the building." Behind the boy, the music had been cranked up again; Ryan doubted the others could hear anything, but he had to be careful all the same. "Don't say anything. Just do what I say, okay? I want you to stay in the shadows by the wall where you are, and I want you to walk toward the front of the building—where the reception area is. Do you hear me?"

"I—I hear you."

"Do it right now, okay? But stay in the dark."

Chris began to walk slowly and Ryan talked.

"Just listen, and when I ask you something, whisper your answers, okay?"

He didn't wait for the boy to respond. "Do the guys you're with actually have a bomb?"

"Nah. They found some yucky green stuff in the warehouse. In a plastic bottle. I don't think it's anything—"

"Do they have more bullets? For the .22?"

"Yeah, there's plenty."

"Is that Terry Maloney back there?" Ryan had seen hardened criminals collapse when they heard their mother's voice through a bullhorn. Surely a teenager would respond if they could find the boy's parents.

"Yeah, it is—" Surprise filled Christopher's voice. "He—he came by when I was waiting for my dad and—"

"I know, Chris. Your dad shouldn't have done that. It was wrong, and he knows it was wrong." Ryan held the phone close and took a deep breath. "But we've got to take care of business...and that means getting you out of there."

Chris took that moment to stop.

"C'mon out," Ryan said softly. "C'mon, Chris..."

"I—I don't know...."

Ryan closed his eyes. "What's not to know, Chris?"

"These guys—they're my friends. You aren't...you aren't gonna hurt them, are you?"

He doubted the friendship, but Ryan wasn't about to say so. These kids were in serious trouble and the consequences were going to be severe—something Chris didn't need to know at this point. "We're not going to hurt them, Chris. But you've got to leave, okay? They're breaking the law and sooner or later, we're gonna have to come in and get them out. It'd be…much better if you weren't there when that happens."

"Why?" Christopher's voice suddenly went tight and Ryan didn't have to imagine the expression that went with it. He'd worn the same look a thousand times when he'd been that age. Angry. Defensive. Scared. The awful memory of his own hard times as a kid suddenly hit him hard.

"What does it matter if I'm there or not? Nobody cares what happens to me."

"That's not true. Your mother cares." Ryan paused, then he spoke fiercely, not caring how it sounded. Nothing meant more to him than this boy and Maria; seeing Chris's silhouette in the crosshairs of his rifle had almost undone him. "And so do I."

Silence filled the phone line.

Ryan softened his voice. "Come on out, Chris. Come out through the door and turn left. I'll be waiting for you."

"You promise?"

"I promise," Ryan said thickly.

MARIA STOOD by the window of the War Wagon with the binoculars to her eyes. Lena dashed from the front to the back, alternating between staring out with her night vision goggles to talking to Sarah in the rear. Sitting at her desk, the young officer was trying to verify the cell phone call to Ryan through the company who handled the service. If it was Chris who'd called him, they'd be able to verify the conversation was still taking place.

There was nothing to see but Maria continued to look anyway. The warehouse drifted in and out of her vision, the ever present fog parting only to give her tantalizing glimpses now and again.

She was just about to put the glasses down when a shadow shifted by the corner of the building. She focused the lenses and tensed. Everything stayed the same and she decided she must have imagined it when she caught the movement again. Staring intently, she spoke over her shoulder. "Lena—get up here. I think I—"

She heard Lena's footsteps, but they stopped. Maria turned to urge Lena forward, then she fell silent as Lena held up her right hand, her left pressed against her earpiece. Clearly she was listening to something over her headset.

A second later, Lena dropped her fingers. "That was Ryan," she said excitedly. "They're coming out. He's got Christopher with him!"

She'd been right! She *had* seen them. Maria whirled back to stare out the windshield, her eyes searching the foggy parking lot for movement. Suddenly halfway between the Winnebago and the warehouse, the haze parted and she saw them both. They were running, low and to the ground, slipping in and out of the darkness like matching ghosts, one tall, one small, one leading, one following. Fear, then relief, came over her in a mind-numbing surge.

Maria ran to the camper door and yanked it open, almost falling down the stairs in her haste to get outside. Christopher and Ryan jogged toward her.

A second later, a loud boom rumbled from the warehouse. The shock wave blew the remaining windows out of the building and sent a cloud of noxious fumes straight into the fog.

CHAPTER SEVENTEEN

RYAN REACTED without thinking. Coughing and sputtering, he grabbed Chris by the back of his shirt and picked him up, halfway dragging him, halfway carrying him. The noise had startled him, but the smell was the worst part. He gagged, the thick, oily odor coating his throat.

Somewhere between the Winnebago and his truck, Maria appeared as well. He tucked her under his other arm and together the three of them stumbled back into the Wagon. Piling inside, they gasped and choked, Lena slamming the doors behind them.

Ryan's eyes were watering so hard he could barely see, but he made his way through the camper, checking the windows to make sure they were tight. They were as secure as they could be, but even still, a stench snaked inside unlike anything he'd ever smelled.

He ripped off his shirt and stuffed it into the nearest air vent. Lena, Sarah and Maria followed his lead, covering the louvers on the sides of the floorboards and securing the rest of the openings with a roll of paper towels. When she finished, Maria came back to where Christopher stood—in a daze—and wrapped her arms around him, her tears flowing. With Sarah and Lena coughing behind them, Ryan reached for Maria and Christopher and enveloped them against him, his heart pounding unnaturally fast.

In two minutes, it was over.

George Rogers appeared beside the Wagon. "It's okay! Come on out!"

Ryan glanced over at Maria, then at the others. "You all stay here. Let Lena and me talk to him first."

Lena took a deep breath, then threw open the door, Ryan coming out right behind her.

"What in the hell—" she said.

"It was nothing," Rogers spoke in a reassuring voice. "A reaction between the heat and some cleaning chemicals the kids had found inside. It looks bad and it smells worse—"

"Mighty damn bad—" Ryan added.

"I know, but it's harmless. The sniffer equipment registered everything." George waved his hand over the soggy air. "It's just a dye, an inert chemical— the worst thing about it is the odor. It reacted with the fire the boys had going. As soon as it hit the fog, though, it dissipated."

Lena nodded quickly, then stepped to one side, her hand at her mouth. Through the headset Ryan still wore, her voice sounded. Each of the team members called in but they all reported nothing more than cuts and bruises. She started to organize an entry but suddenly it wasn't necessary. One by one, the teens wandered out of the building, dazed and scared. The team swarmed over them.

Christopher and Maria came out of the Wagon to stand beside Ryan. The boy watched in silence, then looked up at Ryan. "What's gonna happen to them?"

"They'll go to court," Ryan answered. "The judge will decide."

"What about me?"

Ryan felt Maria's anxious glance; she was even more worried than Christopher.

"You'll have to go with them, Chris," Ryan spoke reluctantly. "You were involved...but I'll talk to the judge and tell him how you helped me."

The boy nodded, his expression relieved. Only then did Ryan realize that Chris had slipped his hand inside Ryan's and was holding on tight. Ryan squeezed his fingers. And he didn't let go.

SHE DIDN'T WANT him to leave, but Maria couldn't say that. Not now. Not with everything that had happened.

Standing on the sidewalk outside her house, Ryan lifted his hand and tucked a curl behind her ear. His touch was soft and gentle and it made her want to cry. He'd driven them home after they'd done what they needed to at the station.

"I'll clean up and come back as soon as possible."

Unable to say anything, Maria stared, her throat tight and achy. Only when he started down the brick walk was she able to call out. He turned and stopped.

"Ryan—I don't even know how to..." She had to pause and start over. "You—you saved Christopher back there. It could have gone so wrong. The kids weren't hurt, but what if—"

Crossing to where she stood, he put his fingers across her lips. "You don't have to worry about 'what-if.' He's okay. That's all that matters right now."

She nodded again. "I know, but I had to say it."

"I understand. We'll talk when I come back." His eyes connected with hers. Deep inside her, a warm sensation started then grew. "There's something I have to say as well."

Somehow she managed to overcome her reaction. It was the hardest battle she'd ever fought...and winning didn't feel like a victory. "I don't think that would be a good idea."

He frowned, a line furrowing across his forehead that she wanted to reach up and ease. But couldn't. "Why is that?"

"I—I have some thinking to do, Ryan. About us. About all the things I was telling you back at your house."

He didn't say anything for a very long moment and all Maria could think of was how badly she wanted to wrap her arms around him. To keep herself still, she made a fist of her hands, hiding them at her sides. A rip developed inside her chest, jagged and cold. Inside her mind, she repeated all her arguments. He wasn't the kind of man she wanted as a role model for Christopher. He wasn't over Ginny. He was supposed to be her patient...not her lover.

"I don't understand." He spoke finally, putting a halt to her silent debate. "What's to think about? We found each other, we've made love, we've got a good thing going between us—"

Maria shook her head, interrupting him. "I have to put my son first, Ryan. I haven't done that and now I'm paying the price. I've been selfish and ignored him and...sleeping with you—I should never have let last night happen."

He stared at her for a measureless moment, then he spoke softly. "You're making a big mistake, Maria. A very big mistake."

"I don't think so," she answered stubbornly. "I *have* to put him first."

"You don't understand." He said the words flatly, but with a confidence that suddenly shook her. It reminded her of how Christopher had spoken the last time they'd fought.

"Wh-what don't I understand?"

"What's good for you is good for Christopher. He wants you to be happy—then he'll be happy, too."

She started to argue, but she couldn't. He was right.

"What about Ginny?" she asked quietly.

His blue eyes widened in surprise. She expected something else to come into his gaze—grief, regret, concern—but none of those things appeared.

"Ginny's gone." His flat answer should have sounded harsh, yet it wasn't. Maria heard the catch behind the words. "You've made me realize that. I have to live now without her." He looked out over the lawn. The morning sun was just coming up. It bathed the street with hot beams of light and he stared at them for a long moment before turning back to her. "It's what she would want." He paused. "It's what she would *do*." He leaned over and kissed her quickly and then he was gone.

Maria stood on the sidewalk, the sun washing over her.

Ryan had countered every one of her arguments without even knowing he'd done so. *He wasn't the kind of man she wanted as a role model for Christopher*—yet he'd saved her son's life. *He wasn't over his first wife*—yet he'd just convinced her he was. Finally *he was supposed to be her patient…not her lover*.

The last thought sent her spinning, and suddenly she remembered all of their times together, the good and the bad. Their conversation at the bar, then later when she'd gone out to his house. His time with Chris. Even the horror of the SWAT incident.

The truth stunned her and stole her breath.

Jackson had gotten close when he'd suggested

Ryan didn't need therapy but he'd missed the biggest piece of the puzzle. Ryan had never needed a doctor; he'd needed a friend. A person who cared. Someone who would listen and understand. Maria had known that instinctively and had responded to him that way, but she hadn't realized exactly what it meant.

Until this very moment.

He'd needed a friend and she'd filled the role.

CONFUSED AND UPSET, Maria closed the door. She'd called Reed from the police station and told him what had happened. He would be there any minute and her life was falling apart—not something she'd like him to witness.

Christopher had made it as far as the tiny guest bathroom off the hall. She could hear him inside. He was sobbing uncontrollably.

Her own already raw emotions spilled out as she listened. With tears in her eyes, she knocked, then opened the door. Chris was huddled on the bathroom floor, his knees pulled up to his chest, his hair standing in spikes around his dirty face. Dropping to the tile, Maria pulled him to her. He was shaking and crying, a delayed reaction to everything that had happened, a reaction he couldn't have let Ryan see.

She murmured against her son's dirty hair and rocked him gently back and forth, her own tears falling. He hadn't let her hold him like this for a long time and her heart swelled at the little boy feel of him.

Maria spoke first. "Christopher...Christopher..."

He wouldn't look at her. She pulled his chin up and stared into his brown eyes. "It's okay, honey. It's okay."

"No—" he hiccuped. "It's not okay. It's not ever going to be okay."

She hugged him a minute longer and rocked him, again, her arms tight. "It will be, I promise."

"No, it won't be. I'm—I'm a goof-up." He pulled away from her and swiped his nose against his T-shirt. "This is all my fault and you're gonna ground me forever!"

She leaned back, her spine against the hard tiled wall. "You are not a goof-up. And I'm not going to ground you *forever*. If I don't believe the punishment the judge metes out is enough, though, I'll add something extra to it, be assured." Her voice dropped with weary exhaustion. "This Terry Maloney boy... Why did you lie to me? You told me you weren't out there the first time he was arrested, but you were."

"I—I *wasn't* there when he shot off the pistol...but I was going to meet him. I went out to the warehouse, but the police had already come."

"I don't believe you," she said sternly. "If that's the case, then how did your drawing get there?"

"Terry had asked me for it. He said he liked it and asked me to do one for him." He dropped his head. "He let me hold his phone out at the warehouse and everything. I thought he kinda liked me...."

He was telling the truth. She could see it in the hang of his head, in the slope of his shoulders. "I'm sure he did like you, Chris. But you have to choose your friends with care." She sighed, guilt coming over her. "Look, this was my fault, too. I should have kept closer tabs on who were hanging out with—"

"Y-you don't understand—"

"You've said that before, but this time you're wrong. I *do* understand. I know I've disappointed you tremendously and that your father has as well. You're a great kid, Christopher. But you've fallen in with the wrong bunch. And it's my job to see that things like that don't happen." She grabbed his arm, her manner suddenly fierce. "I'm going to be a better mother to you. I promise—"

He shook his head miserably. "Don't say that, okay? You're the best mom in the world. And you're the smartest, too. Too smart..." He pulled in his lips as if he wanted to prevent the words from coming out, but they came out anyway.

"You were right, Mom. I I did all this on purpose. All the trouble—the bad grades, the beer, the running off... I —I had a plan and it wasn't a very good one, but I was trying—" he blinked twice and sucked in a deep breath "—I was trying to get you and Dad back together again, just like you said. Like you did that time I got called into the principal's office and the two of you had to come down, because she said she had to talk to both of you. I thought if I could be bad enough you'd get together again and we'd be a family—''

''Whoa, whoa!'' Maria held up her hand and stopped the unrelenting flow of words. They were running together and coming too fast. He couldn't be saying what she thought she'd heard. No way. ''Slow down, Christopher. Slow down and start over. What are you telling me?''

His gaze fell to a spot somewhere between them on the cold bathroom floor. ''I *was* doing everything on purpose,'' he said slowly. ''Just like you guessed that time. I—I couldn't believe it when you cornered me. You'd figured it all out and I—I didn't know what to say so I just walked away.'' He wiped his nose against his sleeve and looked at her. ''I hung out with those guys just to upset you. I don't even like them! Then I hid my report card and forged your name, then I got those kids to come over here with the beer.'' He raised his eyes. ''I did it because I thought you and Dad might get together again. You know,'' he said miserably, ''to... like...discuss how bad I was being. But Dad never came. And you kept defending him even though I knew you hated him. It—It just didn't work right and now I've really messed things up.'' He started to cry again.

Maria looked at the bowed head of her son and

stared in shock. Good God, she'd been right all along, the setup a classic one. As the cerebral terms and technical explanations for what Chris had done ran through her brain, she discarded the words for what they were—a jumble of psychobabble.

"Chris..." She faltered as she spoke his name and he looked up, unfamiliar with his mom being this awkward. "I—I don't know what to say except you haven't screwed up anything. You did what you did because you love me and I realize that. I should have pursued the issue with you when I suspected it." She took a deep breath, the words almost painful as they came out slowly. "But I have to tell you this. Nothing you can do will ever get your father and me back together again, okay? That's not going to happen, no matter what, so you need to remember that." She reached out and lifted his chin. "Do you understand?"

He nodded, his eyes gleaming. "I—I understand...but I—I've still ruined everything!"

"You haven't ruined a thing."

"Y-yes, I have. Dad's on his way over here! It's what I wanted all along and now I know it's the worst thing that could happen!"

She cradled his face with her hands. "Christopher, honey, it's okay—"

"No, it's not. It's not okay," he wailed. "You and Ryan love each other! If Dad gets in the way, you'll never be together! I've ruined everything!"

For the second time in ten minutes, Maria stared

at her son in shock. She dropped her hands. "What on earth makes you think Ryan and I love each other?"

"I can just tell, okay? Don't ask me how! He likes you and you like him!" He sucked in his breath and looked over her shoulder for a second. Then he looked back at her. "I like him, too. He's—he's a really neat guy and he keeps his promises."

Maria didn't know what to say. He was right. Ryan *did* keep his promises and that was only one of the things that made him so special.

They talked a bit more, Maria doing her best to reassure her son, then they struggled to their feet together, each holding on to the other. They parted at the top of the stairs. Ten minutes later, Maria heard the doorbell, but decided Christopher could deal with Reed.

She stepped into her shower and let the hot water sluice over her, thinking of Christopher's words. Out of the mouths of babes was the saying, but she wasn't so sure. There were too many questions. Did she love Ryan? Did he love her? Could they have a life together?

Outside the shower once more, she toweled off. Her eyes were huge in the steamy mirror, full of confusion and fear. She didn't know what to do or how to handle any of this. All her training, all her experience—none of it meant anything in the face of personal anxiety. There was only a single thing she knew for sure. One thing, nothing more.

None of those questions could be answered if she hid from them.

AN HOUR LATER, Ryan rang Maria's doorbell a second time, his left hand resting on Star's forehead as he did so. He'd been nervous when he'd left the house, anxious and not quite sure of how he was going to say what he wanted to express. He'd been halfway to town before he'd realized the dog had hopped inside the truck along with him. Ryan had almost turned around and gone back, then he'd decided to keep going. He hadn't missed Christopher's wild dash inside the house when he'd dropped the Worleys off that morning. The kid had been about to explode. He was probably still upset over everything that had happened; Star might help him.

Maria opened the door. She'd showered and changed clothes, her hair still damp around her face, her white sleeveless dress cool and pristine. A gush of air-conditioning carried the light scent of lilacs out to the porch where Ryan waited. A man stood behind her, an arrogant look on his face as he barked commands into a tiny cellular phone. Something about the option running out at 6:00 p m and they had to make up their minds and now. He was in his midforties, Ryan estimated, dressed in a dark suit with a silver shirt and tie. He barely nodded as he brushed past Ryan and strode quickly to a dark green BMW parked on the street.

"I'd introduce you to my ex," Maria said dryly, "but as you can see, he's in a hurry."

"That's okay." Ryan watched the car roar off down the street. "I don't think I'm missing anything."

Maria smiled her agreement, then held the door open wider.

He took the gesture as a good sign. A very good sign. Ryan's heart jumped inside his chest as if it wanted to go in the house even before the rest of him could. He stepped into the entry and Star padded along with him. Bounding down the staircase, Chris called out with delight. "Wow—what a cool dog! Is he yours? What's his name?"

"His name's Star," Ryan replied. He sent Maria a significant look. "And yes, he's mine."

Christopher and the German shepherd danced around each other in the hallway, threatening a small table. Ryan felt a catch in his throat. He'd never seen either of them—the boy or the dog— look quite as happy.

"Why don't you take the dog outside?" She pointed to a lamp tottering on the table. It settled nearer to the edge than it had been before. "It might be safer for everyone."

Chris grinned at Ryan as if to say *Women? What are you gonna do with them?* "I've got a Frisbee. Can he catch it?"

"I don't know. Take him out and see."

The back door slammed a moment later, the dog

and teenager dashing outside together. Ryan turned to Maria. She looked so cool, so gorgeous, so collected that he had second thoughts. She *was* the doctor, he reminded himself. The woman who'd kept him from working. The woman who had figured out his secrets even before he had.

The woman he could love if she'd let him.

With a deep breath, he took two steps toward her and cradled her face with his hands. She looked surprised but she didn't pull away. In fact, she moved even closer and raised her own hands to link them around his wrists. Her warm touch was incongruous with her cool appearance; where her fingers rested, his skin burned.

He looked into her eyes. "I want to tell you how I feel," he said in a husky voice. "I want to tell you how much you mean to me and how you've helped me and how crazy I am about that teenager in the backyard...but I can't. I don't have the words. They've suddenly run away."

She nodded solemnly. "Maybe it's not the right time. Maybe they aren't ready to be spoken."

"No, that's not it," he countered. "I just can't get them out. You're the doctor...tell me why."

Her face softened as she stared up at him "You said that to me before. You called me 'the expert.' Do you remember?" She shook her head, her hair gleaming in the evening light. "I'm *not* an expert. I'm far from it. I'd think you'd know that by now."

"I don't care," he whispered. "Expert or not. All

I know is that I love you. I love you and I love Christopher and I want to give it all a chance again. I never thought I'd say those words after Ginny died, but I'm saying them now and I mean them, too." His voice turned fierce. "I want you in my life, Maria."

She moved closer, but her words didn't match her action. "Is that the right thing to do? For all of us?"

It seemed as if she were asking herself as much as she was asking him, and she continued before he could answer. "I'm not sure. But I do know this— I won't ever find out if I don't try."

"Of course it's the right thing," he reassured her. "Nothing's ever been so right before. Kiss me and I'll prove it."

She laughed deeply and then she kissed him. When their lips finally parted, each of them was breathless but the question had been answered.

Hand in hand they went to the backyard. To the boy and the dog. And to their future.

INDULGE IN A QUIET MOMENT
WITH HARLEQUIN

Get a FREE
Quiet Moments
Bath Spa

with just two proofs of purchase from
any of our four special collector's editions in May.

Harlequin® is sure to make your time special this Mother's Day
with four special collector's editions featuring a short story
PLUS a complete novel packaged together in one volume!

Collection #1 Intrigue abounds in a collection featuring *New York Times* bestselling author Barbara Delinsky and Kelsey Roberts.

Collection #2 Relationships? Weddings? Children? = *New York Times* bestselling author Debbie Macomber and Tara Taylor Quinn at their best!

Collection #3 Escape to the past with *New York Times* bestselling author Heather Graham and Gayle Wilson.

Collection #4 Go West! With *New York Times* bestselling author Joan Johnston and Vicki Lewis Thompson!

Plus Special Consumer Campaign!

Each of these four collector's editions will feature a
"FREE QUIET MOMENTS BATH SPA" offer.
See inside book in May for details.

Only from

HARLEQUIN®
Makes any time special ®

Don't miss out! Look for this exciting promotion on sale in May 2001,
at your favorite retail outlet.

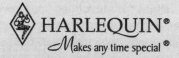

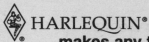

USA Today bestselling author

STELLA CAMERON

and popular American Romance author

MURIEL JENSEN

come together in a special
Harlequin 2-in-1 collection.

Look for

Shadows and *Daddy in Demand*

On sale June 2001

Harlequin invites you to walk down the aisle...

To honor our year long celebration of weddings, we are offering an exciting opportunity for you to own the Harlequin Bride Doll. Handcrafted in fine bisque porcelain, the wedding doll is dressed for her wedding day in a cream satin gown accented by lace trim. She carries an exquisite traditional bridal bouquet and wears a cathedral-length dotted Swiss veil. Embroidered flowers cascade down her lace overskirt to the scalloped hemline; underneath all is a multi-layered crinoline.

Join us in our celebration of weddings by sending away for your own Harlequin Bride Doll. This doll regularly retails for $74.95 U.S./approx. $108.68 CDN. One doll per household. Requests must be received no later than December 31, 2001. Offer good while quantities of gifts last. Please allow 6-8 weeks for delivery. Offer good in the U.S. and Canada only. Become part of this exciting offer!

**Simply complete the order form and mail to:
"A Walk Down the Aisle"**

IN U.S.A
P.O. Box 9057
3010 Walden Ave.
Buffalo, NY 14269-9057

IN CANADA
P.O. Box 622
Fort Erie, Ontario
L2A 5X3

Enclosed are eight (8) proofs of purchase found in the last pages of every specially marked Harlequin series book and $3.75 check or money order (for postage and handling). Please send my Harlequin Bride Doll to:

_____

Name (PLEASE PRINT)

_____

Address   Apt. #

_____

City   State/Prov.   Zip/Postal Code

_____

Account # (if applicable)   **097 KIK DAEW**

Visit us at www.eHarlequin.com

*A Walk Down the Aisle
Free Bride Doll Offer
One Proof-of-Purchase*

PHWDAPOPR2